It rang and rang. The old house echoed with it. And even after it stopped, a fraud of sound like a scream poured through the room.

The master was calling.

But there was no one home to answer. The cook had left immediately after the wake and the housekeeper the next day. Time itself seemed caught in that house, as if the lightning and the thunder had driven it inside to be stilled by the clock.

The master could hear the thunder, too. Out in the backyard. It crackled in the receiver and shook his tomb.

"For God's sake, help me!" he cried in a voice hot with panic.

And the operator answered: "Number, please."

"I need help . . . I'm trapped." This against the thunder.

"I beg your pardon, sir; did you say you were 'trapped'?"

"Yes. Trapped. Yes!"

"Where are you?"

"I'm . . ."—static in the line—"coffin."

"Sir."

"I said I'm in my coffin!"

Midnight

Midnight

Edited by
Charles L. Grant

TOR

A TOM DOHERTY ASSOCIATES BOOK

MIDNIGHT

Copyright © 1985 by Charles L. Grant

First printing: February 1985

A TOR Book

Published by Tom Doherty Associates
8-10 West 36 Street
New York, N.Y. 10018

Cover art by Jill Bauman

ISBN: 0-812-51850-0
CAN. ED.: 0-812-51851-9

Printed in the United States of America

ACKNOWLEDGMENTS

Old Clothes, copyright © 1985 by Ramsey Campbell. By permission of the author.

Road to Granville, copyright © 1985 by Joseph Payne Brennan. By permission of the author.

The Visitor, copyright © 1985 by Leanne Frahm. By permission of the author and the author's agent, Jane Butler.

Sweets to the Sweet, copyright © 1947 by Weird Tales. By permission of the author, and the author's agent, Kirby McCauley.

Masks, copyright © 1985 by Douglas E. Winter. By permission of the author.

The Fly-by-Night, copyright © 1975 by R. Chetwynd-Hayes. By permission of the author, and the author's agent, Kirby McCauley.

The Extension, copyright © 1985 by Thomas Sullivan. By permission of the author.

The Sacrifice, copyright © 1985 by Julie Stevens. By permission of the author.

The Spot, copyright © 1980 by Dennis Etchison and Mark Johnson. First appeared in *New Terrors 1*, edited by Ramsey Campbell. By permission of the authors.

Overnight Guest, copyright © 1985 by Craig Shaw Gardner. By permission of the author.

Intimately, With Rain, copyright © 1978 by Janet Fox. First appeared in *Collage*. By permission of the author.

Spring Fever, copyright © 1985 by Susan Casper. By permission of the author.

Pictures of a Woman Gone, copyright © 1985 by Leslie Alan Horvitz. By permission of the author.

The Green Man, copyright © 1983 by *Fantasy Tales*. First appeared in *Fantasy Tales*. By permission of the author.

Ceremony, copyright © 1985 by William F. Nolan. By permission of the author.

Of Memories Dying, copyright © 1985 by Michael Bracken. By permission of the author.

A Tapestry of Little Murders, copyright © by Mercury Publications. First appeared in *The Magazine of Fantasy & Science Fiction*. By permission of the author.

No Other Gods, copyright © 1985 by R. Bretnor. By permission of the author.

CONTENTS

Introduction by Charles L. Grant   7

Old Clothes by Ramsey Campbell   9

Road to Granville by Joseph Payne Brennan   23

The Visitor by Leanne Frahm   40

Sweets to the Sweet by Robert Bloch   47

Masks by Douglas E. Winter   59

The Fly-by-Night by R. Chetwynd-Hayes   75

The Extension by Thomas Sullivan   99

The Sacrifice by Julie Stevens   108

The Spot by Dennis Etchison and Mark Johnson   116

Overnight Guest by Craig Shaw Gardner   135

Intimately, With Rain by Janet Fox   148

Spring Fever by Susan Casper   157

Pictures of a Woman Gone by Leslie Ann Horvitz   169

The Green Man by Kelvin Jones   201

Ceremony by William F. Nolan   214

Of Memories Dying by Michael Bracken   237

A Tapestry of Little Murders by Michael Bishop   244

No Other Gods by R. Bretnor   261

MIDNIGHT

Introduction
by
Charles L. Grant

Midnight is special.

To be sure, other hours past twilight are quieter, and darker, and more apt to trick the senses into seeing and hearing things that certainly couldn't, or shouldn't, be there; and creatures of the night, real or not, do not always restrict their unpleasant activities to that particular moment, nor is it always their starting point; and a dream does not need the stroke of twelve to shimmer into nightmare.

Yet there is no other time of day, sun- or moonlight, when the air changes so subtly, or the wind shape-changes into something not quite living, or the moon rises above the trees in a less than beneficent manner, or night sounds shift into the dark realm of the unfamiliar.

There is no other time of day when violence seems as obscene, when fear is less a feeling than a garment, and when those things we do not believe in challenge us to disprove them.

Midnight is special.

And since it is, in addition, just as much a feeling we have that the world has altered itself into something we cannot properly recognize, midnight is not necessarily confined to twelve o'clock P.M. The uncanny and the unnatural can slip into noon as well as into dawn, and have on more than one occasion made us double-check the time to be sure that we're not mistaken, that we're really not dreaming.

There are, of course, any number of historical, religious, and cultural reasons, singly and in combination, why midnight and its aura hold such an attraction for us, but none really explain the sensation we get when we look at the clock and see what time it is, as none can pin down that slightly hollow sensation when we hear the bell toll the hour that supposedly belongs to witches and demons.

Midnight is special.

Charles L. Grant
Newton, NJ 1984

Nothing happens to us that isn't real, unless we're affected in some way by drugs or high fever. It's a comforting thought in some ways, and in others a plea that what's happening please be a dream. Sad to say, sometimes it isn't.

Ramsey Campbell, aside from being one of the top short story writers in the field, is also an editor and novelist. His latest book, both here and in his native England, is THE NAMELESS.

OLD CLOTHES

Ramsey Campbell

"Come on, lad, let's be having you," Charlie shouted, and let the back of the van down with a clatter that sent pigeons flying from the cracked roadway. "Anyone'd think it were Fort Knox."

"Don't call me lad," Eric muttered, shoving all his

weight against the door of the house. The July sunlight on his shoulders felt like a weight, too, but the door didn't budge, not until Charlie stumped along the weedy path and threw his weight against the door. It cracked, then stuttered inward, crumpling bills and final reminders and circulars and advertising newspapers, which trailed along the greyish hall toward the ragged staircase. "Go on, lad," Charlie urged. "What are you waiting for?"

"Christmas. Christmas, and the fairy to come off the tree and give me a million pounds." Eric was waiting for his eyes to adjust, that was all. Specks of light, dust that had found sunlight, rose above the stairs, but the house seemed darker than it ought to be.

Charlie gave him a push. "Don't be going to sleep, lad. Time enough for a rest when we've cleared the house."

I'm forty years old, Eric snarled inside himself, and I don't like being pushed. "Try finding someone else who'll put up with you," he muttered as Charlie threw open the first door. "We'll start in here," Charlie said.

The room didn't look as if it had been cleaned for months. Plants with grey fur wilted in pots; cobwebs hung beneath the round table, draped the lopsided chairs. Nevertheless, someone had been in the house since the old lady had died, for the drawers of a bureau had been pulled out, spilling letters. Charlie stuffed the letters into the drawers. "Take the chairs," he said over his shoulder. "You can manage them."

Eric resented being made to feel he'd said he couldn't. By the time he'd finished shifting the chairs, he was wearing grey gloves and a wig. Charlie stared at him as if he'd made a stupid joke. "Give us a hand with the table," he growled.

They had to dance back and forth along the hall and up and down the stairs. As they manhandled the table into the sunlight, Eric thought he glimpsed a pattern round the edge, of pairs of hands or the prints of hands. "Get a move on, lad," Charlie panted, glancing at the darkening sky.

The old lady's relatives must have kicked the papers along the hall, Eric decided as he stooped to a wad of letters that had been wedged behind the bureau. They were thank-you letters, one from a woman who lived a few streets away from Eric: Thank you for putting me in touch with my father; thank you, said another, for my wife, for my son . . . "Never mind prying," Charlie said. "I don't care if she's dead; some things are private."

They were starting on the dining room—spiders fled when Charlie lifted the fat tablecloth—before Eric realized what the letters meant. "What was she, anyway? You never said."

"You never bloody asked, lad. What difference does it make? One of them spiritists, if it's any of your business."

Perhaps it offended him, or maybe he felt that it should, as Eric's father had after Eric's mother died. Eric remembered his father on his knees in church and at bedtime, praying for a sign. They were both dead now, but he'd never felt tempted to contact them, had never been interested in that kind of thing. All the same, he couldn't help peering into each room as he followed Charlie, couldn't help feeling like an intruder as they stripped the beds and unbolted the frames. Venturing into her bedroom, he almost expected to see her or her shape made of dust in the bed. He flinched when something moved, scraping, behind him. It was a raincoat hanging on the door.

The sky was darker when they carried out the bed. By the time they took out the wardrobe, the sky was black. The downpour began as they were about to clear the attic, and so they sat in the cab of the van and ate the sandwiches Charlie's wife had made. She always made half for Eric since she'd taken pity on him, though Charlie gave him less than half. They drank coffee from Charlie's flask, too sweet for Eric's taste, and then Charlie said, ''Can't wait all day. Back to work.''

The grey road looked like a river of tar now, jumping with rain. Charlie shrugged into his plastic raincoat; too bad for Eric if he hadn't brought one. Swallowing the words he would have liked to say, Eric ran out of the cab and into the house. Hall and rooms were squirming with large vague shadows of rain; he thought of the ectoplasm mediums were supposed to ooze, but he grabbed the raincoat from the hook on the bedroom door.

A few shakes and the dust almost blinded him. At least the coat was wearable. He fumbled in the pockets to make sure they were empty. A hint of clamminess in the sleeves made him shiver, but it had gone by the time he'd buttoned the coat on the man's side. Charlie watched him from the bedroom doorway with a kind of dull contempt. ''My God, what do you look like.''

Eric didn't care, or so he told himself. They cleared the attic. Then he slammed the door of the house. For a moment he thought he heard movement inside; it must be the papers flapping. Charlie was already starting the van, and he had to run.

Charlie left him in the drizzle while he drove along the coast to sell the vanload of furniture and ornaments. Eric strolled around town, reading job advertisements that always asked for people younger or more qualified than he was; then he climbed the streets above the factories that nobody wanted to rent, to his flat.

He reached in the right-hand pocket of the raincoat without thinking. Of course his key wasn't in there, but neither was the pocket empty, though the object was only a flower, easy enough to overlook. Nevertheless, he'd never seen a flower like it, especially one looking so fresh when it must have been in the pocket for weeks. He found an old glass and stood the flower in water.

Later he bought chips in the next street and fried himself an egg; then he tried to watch a film about Hawaii through the snow on the television Charlie had given him from one of the houses. Exhausted by the day's work, he was in bed before it was dark. He saw handprints dancing around a table, heard his parents calling to each other, almost saw a shape with arms that could reach around the world. Once he thought he heard metal jingling further down the room he lived and ate and slept in.

The morning was colder. He waited for Charlie to ring the shaky bell and watched newspapers chasing along the back alleys, birds darting out of the steep slate roofs. He changed the water in the glass on the mantelpiece—the flower was already drooping—then he decided to wait downstairs in case the bell had stopped working. He opened the door of his flat, and metal jingled among the coats on the hook.

He'd hung the borrowed raincoat on top. In the left-hand pocket he found two tarnished coins of a kind he'd never seen before. On an impulse he put one in his mouth and bit timidly. The metal was soft to his teeth.

He was gazing at the bite-mark when Charlie rang the bell. He hid the coins under the glass on the mantelpiece and searched the pockets twice to make sure they were empty; then, abruptly, his mind a tangle of half-formed thoughts—Long John Silver, nothing up my sleeve—he buttoned himself into the raincoat. He didn't want to leave it when he could take it with him.

Charlie looked as if he mightn't even let him in the van. "Slept in it, did you?" he said in disgust. "I'm having my doubts about you."

"I thought it'd keep the dust off."

"No dust where we're going." Nor was there, neither

in the house they were clearing nor the one to which the young couple were moving. The wife fussed around them all day, telling them to be careful and not to put that there, and Eric seldom had a chance to feel in the raincoat pockets. There was never anything. Soon he felt more like a stooge than ever, especially when he realized that somehow he'd managed to button the coat on the wrong side, though he remembered buttoning it properly. No wonder the husband avoided looking at him.

Eric half expected the flower and the coins to have vanished: He'd remembered his mother reading him a bedtime story about fairy gold. No, the coins were still there, and the wilting flower. He hung up the coat and tried not to watch it, then made himself go out to the Weights & Scales for a drink. An hour of listening to people decades younger than he complaining about unemployment and immigrants and governments and prophesying the football match up the hill next Saturday, and he went home. The pockets were empty, and so, when he slept, were his dreams.

As soon as he got up, he rummaged in the pockets. Still empty. Much more groping in the old material and he would be finding holes. He put the coat on, out of defiance to Charlie if nothing else, and plunged his hands into the pockets so as to look uncaring as he waited on the doorstep. The right-hand pocket contained a diamond as big as his thumbnail.

He ran upstairs and hid the diamond under his pillow. He ran down, then back up, and hid the coins next to the diamond. The van was just drawing up. Charlie gave him a look that made words superfluous, and took his time in handing over Eric's wages, which were supposed to include Eric's cut from the sale of the contents of the cleared house. The cut seemed smaller than it ought to be. Remembering the diamond, he didn't care. Charlie stared at him when he unbuttoned the raincoat to stow the money in his shirt, but he didn't want to put anything in those pockets in case it might be spirited away.

The diamond made him careless, and so did the old lady whose house they were clearing. "That's not mine," she kept crying as they lifted furniture. "Someone's trying to play a trick on me. Don't bother taking it; I won't have it in my house." They carried on doggedly, hoping her son would arrive soon, and Eric almost dropped a tea chest full of crockery for reaching in his pocket when he thought he felt it move, and kept on reaching in there for something that would make the day worthwhile.

The son, a middle-aged man with pinched eyes and a woeful mouth, arrived as they started on the bedrooms, and calmed his mother down as best he could while they brought down a wardrobe. "Where have you been? I thought you were never coming," she cried as Eric hurried back to the house, missing a step when something rattled in his pocket. It was a pearl necklace. "That's mine. Look at him," the old lady screeched, "you've brought a thief into my house."

"I don't think that's one of yours, Mummy."

"It is, it is. You all want to rob me."

Before Eric could think what to say, Charlie snatched the necklace. "So that's what you've been up to with your bloody silly coat. I ought to give you your cards right now." He handed the necklace to the old lady. "Of course it's yours, ma'am. Please accept my apologies. I've never had anything like this happen before in thirty-eight years of removals."

"Go on then, give me my cards." Eric was sure there must be plenty more where the necklace had come from. "Don't you be making out I'm a thief. You're a thief."

"Watch your tongue, lad, or I'll knock you down."

Charlie nodded fiercely at the son as if to tell him to be angry. "And he will, too."

"Don't call me lad. I'm not a lad; I'm forty, and I'm not a thief—you are. You steal my money you get from selling stuff I carried. And he steals my sandwiches," he told the old lady, thinking that should show her—she was a mother, after all.

"Who said anything about sandwiches? You'll get no sandwiches from me. I wouldn't make you a cup of tea," she screeched, "except to pour it over your head."

Eric had had enough. "See how much you can shift by yourself," he told Charlie. "And when you get tired, Muscles here can help you."

He strode home, feeling as if all he'd said was a burden he'd thrown off, leaving him lighter, almost capable of flying. He didn't need Charlie or his cards, he didn't need anyone. The coat would keep him, however it worked—he didn't need to know how. He restrained himself from searching the pockets until he arrived home, in case it mightn't work in the open. But when he'd closed himself in, he found they were empty.

He hung the coat on the door and went out to the Nosebag Cafe for a pie and chips. When he returned to find the coat empty, he put it on. For a while he watched television so as not to keep reaching in the pockets; then he switched off the set and kept counting one to a hundred with his arms folded. Eventually he dozed and almost saw the face of the shape with arms or hands that could reach around the world, that were reaching into his pockets or out of them. Once he awoke with his hands in his pockets, and snatched them out in a panic.

In the morning he found a stone the size of the palm of his hand, a smooth stone that glittered and looked precious. As soon as he was dressed, he bought the cheapest newspaper to wrap the coins and jewel and stone individually before placing them in a supermarket bag. That left one sheet of newspaper, which he folded around the dead flower.

He clutched the bag to him in both hands all the way to the museum: There were too many thieves about these days. He wouldn't let the girl behind the desk at the museum see what he had; the fewer people who knew, the better. He waited for the top man and occasionally felt in his pockets.

He refused to open the bag until he was in the curator's office. The first item that came to hand was the flower. He didn't expect it to be worth anything; he just wanted to know what it was, while he anticipated learning how wealthy he was. But the curator frowned at the flower, then at Eric. "Where did you get this?"

"An old lady gave it to me. She didn't know what it was."

"And where did she get it? You can't say? I thought not." The curator picked up the phone on his desk. "She ought to know it's a protected species."

Eric gripped the bag and prepared to flee if the curator was calling the police. Instead he called some doctor to find out if any flowers had been taken from a garden, flowers with a long name that included Himalayas. None had, nor apparently had any other garden been robbed, and he put down the receiver. "What else have you in there?"

"Nothing. I've brought the wrong things." Eric tried not to back away too conspicuously. "I'll have to come back," he lied, and managed not to run until he was out of the museum.

He wandered the thirsty streets. Football fans looking for pubs or mischief elbowed him out of the way. He wasn't sure if he wanted to hide the contents of the bag at home or dump them in the nearest bin. He couldn't take them to be valued until he knew where they'd come from, and how was he to find that out? He was beginning to hate

the damned coat; it had made a fool of him, had nearly
gotten him arrested. He'd begun to grow furious, trying to
unbutton it and fumbling helplessly, when he remembered
the address on the letter he'd seen in the medium's house.
At once he made for the hill.

An old lady opened the door of the terraced house and
rubbed her eyes as if she had been asleep or weeping. She
glanced sharply at his raincoat, then shook her head at
herself. "I don't want anything today," she mumbled,
starting to close the door.

"I've lost my parents." He couldn't just ask as if she knew
about the coat. "Someone said you could help me."

"I don't go in for that anymore." Nevertheless, she
stood back for him. "You do look lost. Come in if you
want to talk."

He didn't, not about his parents: Even using them to
trick his way in had made him feel guilty. As soon as he
was seated in the parlor, which smelled of old furniture
and lavender, he said, "Why did you give it up?"

She stared, then understood. "The lady who used to put
me in touch died herself."

"Was she a good medium? Did they bring her things?"

He thought he'd been too direct, for she stiffened. "That's
what killed her, I think."

His hands recoiled from the pockets, where they had
been resting. "What, being brought things?"

"Apports, they're called. Them, aye, and growing old."
She shivered. "One of her guides was evil; that's what she
didn't know."

He gaped at her, out of his depth. "He brought her
flowers and treasures until he got to be her favorite," she
said. "Then he started bringing other things until she was
afraid to hold seances at all, but that didn't stop him. He
started putting them in her bed when she was asleep."

Eric was on his feet before he knew it, and struggling to

unbutton the coat until he realized that he meant to leave it
in her house. She didn't deserve that or the contents of the
supermarket bag. "I've got to go now," he stammered, and
collided with furniture and doors on his way out of the house.

Football fans came crowding up the hill toward the
football ground, singing and shouting and throwing empty
beer cans. He went with them, since he didn't know where
best to go. He couldn't be sure that the old lady's story
had anything to do with the coat, with whatever brought
him presents. Nevertheless, when something in the right-
hand pocket bumped against him, he found he couldn't
swallow.

He wanted desperately to stand still, to prepare himself,
if he could, to find out what was there, but the crowd
crammed into the narrow streets shoved him onward,
wouldn't let him out of its midst. He scarcely had room to
reach down to the pocket; he wished he could use that as
an excuse not to find out, but he couldn't bear not knowing what was scraping against him with every step. Nor
could he simply reach in. His fingers ranged shakily and
timidly over the outside of the pocket to trace the shape
within.

It felt like a cross. It must be; he could trace the chain it
would hang from. He slipped his hand into the pocket and
grabbed the chain before he could flinch, managed to raise
it to eye level. Yes, it was a cross, a silver cross, and he'd
never felt so relieved in his life; the old lady's tale couldn't
have anything to do with him. He dangled the cross into
the supermarket bag and lifted his hand to his mouth, for a
splinter from somewhere had lodged in his finger. As he
pulled out the splinter with his teeth, he noticed that his
hand smelled of earth.

He had just realized that the cross was very like the one
his father had always worn when he realized there was
something in the left-hand pocket, too.

He closed his eyes and plunged his hand in, to get it over with. His fingertips flinched from touching something cold, touched it again and discovered it was round, somewhat crusted or at least not smooth, a bulge on it smoother, less metallic. A stone in a ring, he thought, and took it out, sighing. It was the ring his mother had worn to her grave.

Something else was rolling about in the pocket—something which, he realized, choking, had slipped out of the ring. He snatched it out and flung it away blindly, crying out with horror and fury and grief. Those nearest him in the crowd glanced at him, warning him not to go berserk while he was next to them; otherwise the crowd took no notice of him as it drove him helplessly uphill.

He tore at the buttons and then at the coat. The material wouldn't tear; the buttons might have been sewn through buttonholes too small for them, they were so immovable. He felt as if he were going mad as if the whole indifferent crowd were, too—this nightmare of a crowd that wasn't slowing even now that it had come in sight of the football ground and the rest of itself. His hands were clenched on the supermarket bag at the level of his chest so as not to stray near his pockets, in which he thought he felt objects crawling. He was pleading, almost sobbing, first silently and then aloud, telling his parents he was sorry, he would never have stolen from them, he would pray for them if they wanted, even though he had never believed . . . Then he closed his eyes tight as the crowd struggled with itself, squeezed his eyes shut until they ached, for something was struggling in his pocket, feebly and softly. He couldn't bear it without screaming, and if he screamed in the midst of the crowd, he would know he was mad. He looked down.

It was a hand, a man's hand. A man had his hand in Eric's pocket, a scrawny youth who blinked at Eric as though to say the hand was nothing to do with him. He'd been trying to pick Eric's pocket, which had closed around his wrist just as the holes had closed around the buttons. "My God," Eric cried between screaming and laughter, "if you want it that badly, you can have it," and all at once the buttonholes were loose and the coat slipped off his arms, and he was fighting sideways out of the crowd.

He looked back once, then fought free of the crowd and stumbled uphill beyond the streets, toward the heath. Perhaps up there he would know whether to go to Charlie for his cards or his job. At last he realized he was still holding his mother's ring. He slipped it into his safest pocket and forced himself not to look back. Perhaps someone would notice how wild the pickpocket's eyes were growing; perhaps they might help him. In any case, perhaps it had only been the press of the crowd that had been giving him trouble as he struggled with the coat, one hand in the pocket, the other in the sleeve. Perhaps Eric hadn't really seen the sleeve worming, inching. He knew he'd seen the youth struggling to put on the coat, but he couldn't be sure that he'd seen it helping itself on.

Modern-day cosmopolitan explorers like to get in their cars and drive into the country to see what it's like outside city blocks of stone and glass and steel. When they get lost, they often panic, as if by traveling in the wrong direction they'll fall off the edge of the world. And there are times when that fate is definitely preferable to the alternative they face.

The career of Joseph Payne Brennan spans more decades than some of us have been living, and in that time he has created more than one classic in the field. SHADES OF MIDNIGHT is a superb collection of his shorter work, and CREEP INTO DEATH a disturbing and fine collection of his equally fine poetry.

ROAD TO GRANVILLE

Joseph Payne Brennan

The boulder-strewn Connecticut hills, burned brown by August heat, shimmered in the blue haze of afternoon. Even in these high hills, the heat was oppressive. The only cloud in the brassy-looking sky appeared no bigger than a cotton boll.

He stopped the car in a small parking square just off the highway which the natives referred to as "the mountain road." Far below, in a natural valley, lake waters of the reservoir gleamed in the glaring sun. Small neat islets bearing laurel bushes and evergreens broke the smooth surface of the artificial lake.

Many years before, the valley, known as Hartland Hollow, had held a village: homes, barns, a store, a church, a schoolhouse, a cemetery. For nearly two hundred years people had lived, loved, hated and died down there. The village had been leveled as by a tornado, the cellar holes filled up and the debris carted away. Even the bones in the old cemetery had been dug out and reburied up on the other side of the mountain.

He got out of the car and stood peering down into the valley. Not a sound broke the afternoon stillness. Under that copper-tinted sky the valley seemed to be mesmerized, bewitched, gripped in a strange spell of time. Was it possible, he asked himself, that all those lives were utterly gone, all traces obliterated, all memory blotted away?

In absolute silence, the valley appeared to be etched on

metal. Not a single leaf shook. Not a ripple broke the flat surface of the water. He imagined that he could see many feet down into the lake. Might an ancient wagon track be visible, a forgotten fence line?

An overwhelming eeriness pervaded him, a frightening sense of detachment. In his imagination he could see the waters recede, the forgotten village materialize out of the shimmering layers of August heat. He imagined lost voices trying to cry out, tongues long stilled striving to speak again.

He shook himself, as if the mood which possessed him bore a physical reality. With a disturbing conviction that he was not really himself at all, but an alien being in a borrowed body, he walked back to the car and got in.

As he drove slowly down the winding road, the heat intensified. Although there had been no semblance of a breeze higher up, the motionless air on the mountain top must have been at least a few degrees cooler, he concluded.

As he descended almost to the valley level and turned into the road which skirted the northern edge of the hollow, the heat became stifling, all but unbearable.

He touched the accelerator, with some idea of stirring up a small breeze. The car plunged ahead, bucked, slowed down and stopped. The radiator was boiling over.

He got out and stood watching the steam. After a few minutes, while he waited, perspiring in the sun beside the car, he found a thick rag, gingerly turned the radiator cap and jumped back. Water and steam shot into the air.

Grim-faced, he opened the trunk. Had he put the bucket back in or was it sitting on his garage shelf at home? He spotted it in a corner of the trunk and sighed with relief. Mopping his face with a handkerchief, he closed the trunk and looked about him.

His first impulse was to head off the road to the right, toward the adjacent valley. There was plenty of water there. But the stretch of land between the road and the reservoir was a forbidding tangle of fallen trees, thorn bushes and trailing vines. In addition, he noticed a "No Trespassing" sign.

Hesitating, he glanced up the road ahead, beyond the car. Heat waves were dancing on the blacktop, but he decided to walk along a little distance. Very shortly, he was glad that he had done so. On the left he saw the trace of an old, abandoned and overgrown dirt road. It looked relatively cool under the canopy of interlocking trees. Besides, he reasoned, there must be a few creeks, or springs, along that old road. Perhaps a forgotten watering trough.

After a backward look at the still steaming car, he turned off the blacktop and started along the grass-grown road under the trees.

It remained stifling, but at least he was out of the sun. He pushed ahead resolutely, stepping through grass which at places was shoulder-high. The disconcerting, heat-induced silence persisted. Even the shrill sound of a cicada would have been welcome.

As he advanced, he noticed a faded wooden sign nailed to a blackjack oak along one edge of the overgrown road. He could barely make out the faded letters: "Granville." The town of Granville, he knew, lay across the Connecticut border in Massachusetts. He had heard references to the abandoned road. Strange, he mused, that the woods had been permitted to reclaim it.

He felt as if he were walking through a funnel which led into the open maw of a blast furnace. The heat was like a palpable, cloying substance which might be cut with a knife.

The chuckling whisper of water over stone struck his ear like a benison. Had he only imagined it? He stopped to listen. No. It was a subdued but distinct sound. And it was not far off.

The old road bridged a small creek. The road had dropped here and the creek had to burrow and sluice its way through accumulated mud and silt. On the far side, as if exhausted, it had formed a deep pool, where it rested before wandering off through the woods.

Angling from the road, he slid down the bank through a cluster of cattails. A redwing blackbird flashed away and was gone.

Setting down the bucket, he scooped up water in his cupped hands and sloshed it over his face. It was ice cold. The shock was delightful, but suddenly he felt dizzy and sat down on the bank. For a few seconds his heart thumped and the pool seemed to advance and recede. A touch of heat, he concluded, and sat quietly.

At length, when the pool stayed in one place, he got up, scooped more water and drank. Dangerous, he supposed, but delicious.

He submerged the bucket, drew it up brimming and began to climb the bank. He moved carefully on somewhat unsteady legs.

He started along the road feeling weak but refreshed. He'd rest after reaching the car. Once he got water back in the radiator, he'd drive on. Perhaps, by then, the heat would have begun to break.

He felt tired as he trudged along and he was surprised at his own lack of stamina. He was forty-seven, not overweight, and he had never been seriously ill. Perhaps he should take up jogging. He smiled wryly to himself—scarcely the right time or place to begin!

Walking was not easy on the overgrown road. Once he stumbled on a matted clump of swamp grass and lost water out of the bucket. Although he was beginning to feel light-headed, he doggedly plodded on.

The car seemed infernally far away. He felt as if he had covered the distance to the blacktop road at least three times over. Suddenly a disconcerting thought struck him. Had that dizzy spell at the pool got him mixed up? Was it possible that he was advancing up the road toward Granville, instead of back toward the blacktop?

Carefully lowering the bucket, he sat down near a patch of staghorn sumac and mopped his perspiring face with a handkerchief. Perhaps if he rested a few minutes, he would get his bearings.

He must have dozed off, because the boy driving the flatbed farm wagon sat regarding him for several minutes before he finally looked up.

He regained his feet somewhat unsteadily. "Hello there, son!" He grinned. "I guess this heat's too much for me!"

The lad lifted his wide-brimmed straw hat and set it back on his head. His round blue eyes were speculative. "Thought you'd passed out sure!" he said, adding a bit accusingly, "a-settin' there in the sun!"

The man had a vague idea that he ought to apologize. "Yes, that was foolish," he admitted. "I should have got in the shade."

The boy lifted his hat again. "Goin' to Granville?"

"Granville? Why, no. You see, my car overheated and I came down the road here for water. My car's just back on the blacktop."

The round blue eyes clouded with confusion and then lit up with obvious amusement. For the first time they noticed the bucket of water.

"You carryin' that bucket back for the engine?" the boy asked in mingled glee and astonishment.

The man nodded. "Exactly. Radiator overheated. This weather's bad on a car."

The boy studied him. A faint note of hostility entered

his voice. "Ain't no cars run hereabouts. Nearest tracks over Granby way."

The man frowned. Some of these farm boys, he decided, were not too bright. "I know cars don't run on this road," he explained patiently. "My car's back on the blacktop road."

The round eyes regarded him with utter incomprehension. The heat seemed to press in upon him. He wanted to conclude the aimless conversation and get on his way, but he felt that he had to be polite.

"Where are you heading, son?"

"Headin' fer the Holler."

"The holler? Oh, you mean Hartland Hollow?"

"Hartland Holler," the boy replied stolidly.

Suddenly the man realized that he was indeed walking in the wrong direction. If the boy was heading for Hartland Hollow, then he himself must be advancing up the road toward Granville. That dizzy spell at the pool had mixed him up thoroughly.

He passed a hand over his eyes. "I'm hiking the wrong way. A' bit light-headed, I guess. It's this infernal heat."

The boy picked up the reins. "If you ain't goin' to Granville, git on," he invited without enthusiasm. He waited.

Laboriously, the man climbed over the side of the wagon and sat down. The grey horse lifted its head and the wagon began to creak along the road.

"By the way," the man said, "my name's Finden, Henry Finden."

"How do," the boy replied without turning around. "I'm Jes Orcutt."

After some moments, he added, "Pa's name's Harley."

From his vantage point in the wagon, Henry Finden noticed that the road seemed less overgrown than formerly. Far less. Boneset and oxeye daisies grew along the edge. He hadn't seen any before. Also, the road seemed much less shady. Was it possible, he asked himself, that in addition to walking in the wrong direction, he had also strayed off the first dirt road onto another?

In his mind, he tried to retrace his footsteps in sequence. There was really nothing complicated about it. And yet, that episode at the pool *had* unsettled him a bit. And then he had dozed off . . .

He sat up abruptly. The wagon was turning off the road into a farmhouse dooryard. He must have fallen asleep again there in the wagon, he decided.

A big, unpainted clapboard farmhouse rose up not far from the road. He was sure he had not seen it before. How had he missed it? Surely, he concluded, he must have wandered off onto another road.

The horse plodded halfway up the dooryard drive and stopped in the shade of a big buttonwood tree. The boy jumped down.

"You wait," he instructed Finden. "I'll git Pa."

Carefully, Henry Finden climbed out of the wagon. His legs still felt wobbly. He walked over and sat down under the buttonwood. The farmyard was a hushed harbor of heat. He was grateful for the shade.

A tall, rawboned man wearing a high straw hat and faded blue overalls walked slowly down the dirt driveway, accompanied by Jes Orcutt. He came under the buttonwood and nodded.

"How do. Orcutt. Harley Orcutt."

Finden arose and shook hands, introducing himself.

Orcutt's eyes were blue, like his son's, but not round. They were shrewd, squinty, appraising, set in a wrinkled face of mahogany leather.

"Jes says the heat liked ta gotcha."

Finden nodded, smiling wryly. "Got to me all right, I guess. Left my car on the blacktop, headed the wrong way with a bucket of water and started toward Granville!" As he spoke, he suddenly remembered that he had left the bucket of water sitting in the road.

The shrewd eyes surveyed him with— Was it amusement, curiosity, or a mixture of both? He wasn't sure.

As Jes had done, Orcutt lifted his straw hat and set it back on his head. "Best you set inside awhile. You come on up. Jes, you tell Ma put on the kettle."

Jes loped toward the house.

As Finden followed Harley Orcutt slowly along the driveway, he inspected the farmhouse. It looked decrepit, dilapidated. Squares of heavy cardboard had been substituted for glass in some of the windows. The curling clapboards looked brittle, dried out with blistering heat. Finden could not decide whether their paint had all peeled away or whether they had never been painted at all.

Orcutt led him through a screen door into the kitchen. The room was stifling. A wood fire was burning in the iron stove, where a kettle had already been set.

A chipped deal table, four worn kitchen chairs, the stove, and a standup cupboard painted blue constituted the furniture. Two buckets of water stood on a shelf near the wooden sink. A dipper hung nearby.

Orcutt pulled out a chair. "You set down. Ma's probably primpin' up in there!" He nodded, grinning, toward the adjacent room.

Finden sat down and rested his arms on the table. "I think," he said, glancing toward the buckets, "instead of tea, perhaps just some cold water . . ."

Orcutt looked startled. He grinned rather sheepishly and hurried to get the dipper.

"Heat's gettin' me, too!" he said, immersing the dipper in one of the buckets. "Water's the *first* thing!"

Finden accepted the dipper and drank deeply. Well water, ice-cold, delicious, with no taste of chemical additives.

An enormous fat woman bustled into the room, wiping

her hands on a blue cotton apron. Beneath she wore a dark green dress of some fusty taffeta-like material, trimmed with grease-stained flounces.

Harley Orcutt beamed proudly. "Ma, this is Mr. Finden. Heat give him a mite of a turn."

Mrs. Orcutt curtseyed. The gesture, although grotesque, was somehow touching.

"Tea be right up," she promised, her fat red face creasing into smiles. "Lan' sakes, Mr. Finden! No day fer trampin' the roads!"

Again Finden felt vaguely apologetic; explanation seemed in order. "Well, you see, my car overheated and I walked down the road for a bucket of water."

The Orcutts exchanged glances. There was a brief silence.

"No cars nearer'n Granby," said Jes who had come into the room.

Harley Orcutt glanced out the window and scowled at his son. "Jes, you water that horse and put the wagon in the barn. Now git!"

Jes scampered out.

Orcutt looked toward the sink. "Care to wash up, Mr. Finden?"

"Yes, thank you, I would."

There was a basin and a chunk of homemade yellow soap alongside the sink. Mrs. Orcutt bustled in with a fresh towel.

After he had washed his hands and sloshed cold water on his face, Finden felt better. He followed his hosts into the adjacent dining room.

It was a good-sized room papered with fading pink roses among which chubby cherubs cavorted. The floor was covered with worn yellow linoleum. Calendars and colored prints, obviously clipped from magazines, completed the decor. Four straight-backed walnut chairs were placed around a table covered with a white cloth. The room was less stifling than the kitchen.

The tea, served in chipped china cups, was strong and hot.

Finden was still sipping his first cup when Jes sidled in and took his place.

The boy chuckled. "Old Nell almos' drunk the trough dry!"

Harley nodded. "Hope this heat spell breaks. Six year ago that trough went dry. Lugged well water."

Mrs. Orcutt brushed aside a straggling lock of grey-streaked black hair. "More tea, Mr. Finden?"

Finden accepted another cup. He felt curiously uninclined to converse but made some effort at small talk. The Orcutts appeared at ease, apparently recognizing the fact that he was hot, tired and, probably, somewhat confused.

He retreated to the kitchen with Harley and Jes while Mrs. Orcutt cleared up.

After a decent interval, Finden said that he had better be going. He felt refreshed after the tea, but when he stood up, a wave of dizziness flowed over him. He sat down.

Harley Orcutt regarded him with concern. "You jest set there, Mr. Finden. I'll be right back."

He returned bearing a small flask and a water glass and poured out a potion.

"Sip it slow, Mr. Finden. Throws off that shaky feelin'."

Finden sampled the clear yellowish liquid. A warm inner glow, born not of the brassy skies, soon suffused him. He felt more relaxed and loquacious.

He was chatting away with Harley Orcutt about heat, crops and wells running dry when Mrs. Orcutt came in from the dining room and silently beckoned to her husband.

Excusing himself, Harley left the room. He returned shortly and resumed his seat.

"Ma says why don't you stay for supper. It's no cooler and you ain't feelin' well."

Finden looked up, surprised. "I thank you, but actually I feel fine now!"

Orcutt grinned, glancing at Finden's empty glass.

"That applejack's the best medicine I know. But all the same, you need some vittles. Worst mistake folks make is not eatin' in the heat."

Finden hesitated and Orcutt poured some more applejack.

Supper, served in the dining room, consisted of boiled potatoes, fried steak, whole boiled carrots, bread and tea and apple pie.

Finden was surprised to find that in spite of the heat he was famished.

The Orcutts applied themselves to the meal with diligence. The intake of food was obviously one of their major concerns. Conversation was desultory.

Finden was not sorry. He felt sleepy, listless and dull-witted. As he glanced around the room, he became convinced that his eyes were not focusing properly. For instance, the calendar on the wall opposite him read August 8, 1877. He knew perfectly well, of course, that it was August 8, 1977.

He remained in his chair, exchanging occasional remarks with Harley Orcutt, while Mrs. Orcutt took away the dishes, aided by a reluctant Jes.

Orcutt cleared his throat portentously. "Keeps right hot out there, Mr. Finden. Likely you'd be better off stayin' the night. Sort of a couch in the parlor here. A cool room, too."

Finden protested feebly, but the appeal of a couch in a cool parlor was too great to resist. He literally ached to lie down and fall asleep.

After complimenting Mrs. Orcutt on the meal, he sat chatting with Harley for a few minutes. At length, finding himself unable to keep his eyes open, he followed his host down a short hallway into the adjacent parlor.

The room was small, musty, dim in the gathering twilight. Two overstuffed armchairs, covered with cracked green Turkish leather, squatted in corners. A couch of the same style lay alongside one wall. A round walnut table bearing a kerosene lamp with a rose-colored chimney stood in the center of the room. Several family portraits, too big for the small room, hung on the walls. Heavy-featured farmers, grim and uncomfortable-looking in their store clothes, stared solemnly into the growing gloom.

Mrs. Orcutt hurried in with sheets, a pillow and a light blanket, bid him good night and bustled out.

Harley Orcutt hovered about. "If there's anythin' else . . ."

Finden shook his head. "No, no, I'm fine. Just fine. Nothing at all. And I am grateful!"

Orcutt nodded and went out, closing the door.

Finden draped his clothes on an armchair and crawled between the sheets in his underwear. In spite of the outside heat, the room was relatively cool. He pulled up the blanket.

He had a vague feeling that something was wrong, that something was strangely out of place, but he could not decide what it was.

He was still trying to decide when oblivion overcame him.

His eyes refused to open. They appeared to be fastened shut, stitched together. Light grew; the room was no longer cool. Heat seemed to be covering him, invisible layers of it, blanket after burning blanket.

He stirred, feeling peculiarly disembodied, and managed to sit up. At length his crusted, heavy-lidded eyes opened a slit.

His heart thudded heavily in his chest and he closed his eyes quickly. He must be having nightmares, he thought. He was not yet awake.

He waited a full minute and then very slowly, very carefully, opened his eyes again.

He was lying amid debris on the dirt floor of an open cellar hole. A hot sun, already far up in a brassy-looking sky, beat down on him.

He tried to think, fighting off the panic which threatened to overwhelm him . . . the farmhouse, the Orcutts, the applejack, the meal, his own sleepiness and apathy.

He saw it all suddenly, with a mixture of fury and relief. The drinks had been drugged, of course. They had stolen all his possessions and then dumped him into this abandoned cellar hole, left him for dead.

Well, he wasn't dead, and once he got out of here, he'd teach those murderous hayseeds a lesson.

He started to get up, fell back with a gasp as darkness spun about him. Terribly weak. He'd have to . . . he crouched motionless for a time until the whirling darkness cleared.

He *must* try to think coherently, he told himself. Probably they had knocked him out with a blow to the head. That would explain his weakness and vertigo.

He lifted his arm and gingerly felt his head. His exploring hand did not encounter any contusions, but he pulled it away quickly with a twinge of terror. He tried again, with the same result.

There could be no doubt of it—he had lost all his hair.

Panic crowding him again, he finally managed to sit up. Glancing down, he saw that his clothes were in tatters. They were nothing more than rotted, mouldy rags clinging together.

Somehow he struggled to his feet and leaned against the wall of the cellar hole. One minute the glare of the sun was in his eyes; the next, darkness spun about him again.

After a long interval, the darkness cleared and the sun stayed steady. He stared around the cellar hole.

The floor of the cellar lay deep in mounds of autumn leaves, tangles of burdock, thistle and fireweed. A few scattered sticks of furniture were strewn about. He noticed part of a chair arm covered with a kind of green scurf which once might have been leather. A broken picture frame, half-buried in a drift of leaves, leaned against the opposite wall.

As the sun rose, the place became an inferno. He began scrabbling frantically at the nearest wall in an effort to climb out. The loose stones of the foundation teetered and shook under his thrusting fingers. His feet, after gaining a precarious hold, would slip and lose it.

Looking down, he saw that his shoes were mere crusts of lumpy leather hanging loosely on his feet. He shook them off.

With clawing fingers and bare, questing toes he finally managed to reach the top. He collapsed in the weeds and lay motionless. His heart pounded, shaking his whole body.

Very slowly, he stood up. The dim trace of a road, or path, lay before him and he started along grass-grown tracks. Halfway down, he stopped. The fallen, decayed trunk of a huge buttonwood tree lay across the path.

He stared at it and something stirred in his memory, but renewed panic stirred with it. He refused to think. He could not afford to think too much, he told himself. He was Henry Finden. His car was waiting out on the black-top road. It was terribly hot. It was August. He had been drugged, robbed and dumped in an old cellar hole by the Orcutts. He was going to get in his car and go for the police.

His ordeal had left him confused, that was all. The

shock of it all had caused his hair to fall out. They had stripped off his clothes and dressed him in rags. He was weak, yes, very weak. After all, who *wouldn't* be weak after what . . . what he had been through . . .

Circling the fallen tree, he reached the end of the overgrown drive and entered another abandoned road which the woods were swiftly reclaiming. It was cooler here and he stopped to rest, grateful for the canopy of shade.

He had walked some distance when he saw the faded wooden sign nailed to a blackjack oak: "Granville." Yes, of course. He was on the right road, then. All he had to do was keep walking along this shady road until he reached the blacktop. His car would be waiting. He was Henry Finden. It was August. It was hot . . .

Almost before he realized it, his bare feet had left the cool dirt and grass and were burning on the blacktop. The sun struck him like a sudden heavy hammer. He swayed dizzily and passed a hand over his eyes. His head cleared and he looked down the road.

There was his car, just as he had left it! He hurried along the blacktop on scorching feet until he reached the car.

Panic crowded him once again. His clothes . . . gone . . . stolen . . . rotted away . . . pockets . . . keys . . . car keys.

He fingered the filthy tatters which hung about him, but any vestiges of pockets had long since vanished.

He was still standing there, fumbling aimlessly, when a car approached.

His heart leaped, leaped literally. Here was help! He extended his thumb, grinned apologetically.

The car slowed down, almost stopped. The driver leaned out and looked at him.

The driver's red, sweaty face turned putty-pale. His

mouth dropped open. His head pulled back like a turtle's returning to its shell. The car roared off up the road.

Henry Finden watched until it was out of sight. As he stood regarding the empty road, he became conscious again of his burning feet. And not only his feet. His throat was burning. The top of his head was burning. His entire body seemed to be burning.

Turning, he shuffled off the blacktop back onto the overgrown dirt road.

Possibly, he told himself, the car keys—by some miracle—might be lying in the cellar hole. And then another thought struck him. Perhaps, as he had bent to drink at that roadside pool, the keys had slipped from his pocket.

The pool glimmered in his memory as if it were the final goal of all his life's strivings. El Dorado. The Holy Grail.

Surely, the pool would save him. He would plunge his head into it and drink water as cold as ice. Drink and drink until he could hold no more. He would slip his burning feet into the pool, immerse his whole feverish body in the sweet water . . .

He started along the road. Someone had held hot irons on his feet, poured burning cinders down his throat, buried him in the sun in a cellar hole . . . but the pool would save him.

Before he reached it, he grew so weak that he had to crawl. As he hitched along the grassy trace, he resembled some kind of giant land crab tortuously finding its way back toward the sea.

Now and then he stood up, afraid that he might pass the pool without seeing it. He knew that it lay a little beyond the sign reading ''Granville'' and he watched carefully for the dim wooden board.

He saw it at last and crawled along more slowly. From

time to time he raised his head and listened. And finally he heard it: the chuckling whisper of water over stone.

He found the place easily enough because the creek, working under the old road, had caused it to sink.

Turning off, he crawled through a cluster of cattails.

He squirmed frantically toward the pool as if it might recede before he reached it. On the edge, he stopped and looked down into the clear depths.

A demon thing, a death's head, hidden in the deep recesses of the pool, stared up at him. Its filmy eyes bulged and it opened its sunken mouth in mock horror, mimicking him. The yellowish, tightly stretched skin of its hideous face was beginning to flake off. It was hairless. It resembled nothing so much as a disinterred mummy.

Finden screamed, and the thing screamed soundlessly back at him.

The brassy sky pressed down intolerably. A searing wave of fire seemed to flash through every fiber of his body.

He toppled into the pool and sank out of sight.

Midnight has a reputation of dealing almost exclusively with the violent, the unspeakable, and the stomach-churning. That isn't true. Gentleness can also be terrifying—the difference between the razor and the club.

Leanne Frahm lives and works in Australia and has appeared in such diverse anthologies as FEARS and UNIVERSE.

THE VISITOR

Leanne Frahm

The doorbell chimes, a faintly cracked melody, off-key.

I am in the shadowy sitting room when I hear it. I'm startled by the unexpected sound. I glance up, and jump again, for the muted tones have brought Aunt Florrie out. She enters from the direction of the kitchen. Lord knows what she does there—restlessly checking the gleam of the old copper-bottomed pans, perhaps, or scrutinizing the stove top for careless grease spots.

I smile at her as I rise from the faded flowered settee, but she stares straight ahead, unwilling to acknowledge me. With a rueful shrug, I join her, and we go to greet our caller. It should be a tight fit, with both of us crowding the narrow, darkly patterned hallway, but I'm amazed again at her frail insubstantiality. I yearn briefly to touch her; a whiff of lavender reaches me, and I must be content with that intangible contact.

The door opens upon Mrs. Ivors. She's old, as old as Aunt Florrie is. She smiles, her seamed face taking on a hundred wrinkles, but her eyes are still sharp and bright. I'm pleased to see her, happy that she still comes to visit, despite the difference in our ages.

I was, in the old-fashioned vernacular, "reared" by Aunt Florrie after my parents died so long ago. She took me into her house, with its multitude of crowded, dim rooms, its faded antimacassars and crocheted runners, its air of musty timelessness. Her friends became my friends, and I'm comfortable with old women, with their ancient gossip and time-honed wisdom. Aunt Florrie has left me a great legacy.

I look worriedly at her now, wondering whether she's glad to see her old friend or whether the reminder is too painful. A prim, shy smile lights up her face, removing the expression of grim sadness she's worn lately, and I relax.

We troop down the corridor to the sitting room. Mrs. Ivors perches on the firmly stuffed Genoa lounge like a dully plumaged parrot, chatting inconsequentially and engagingly. I simply smile, and let the one-sided conversation wash over me. I glance at Aunt Florrie, who is also sitting now, nothing of the parrot about her, erect and motionless, nodding occasionally with a tiny dip of her head.

She and Mrs. Ivors had been school friends, and their friendship had endured for sixty years. It's hard to imagine these two bent, wiry, white-haired women with skin hanging slack and creased as plump and smooth-skinned adolescents, but the age-blurred sepia photographs in the old album that Aunt Florrie would display with such delight shows them thus, peering up at the lens through thick brown lashes, with nervous giggles trembling on their lips.

There's a sudden pang of pity stabbing through me as I think of that lost girlhood, and I bend my head quickly so Mrs. Ivors won't see my watery eyes.

But Mrs. Ivors talks on, oblivious. It takes very little encouragement for her to spend a whole afternoon talking. I find myself almost half-asleep, listening to her. Gradually her voice lowers and slows. I stiffen, suddenly aware of what she's saying. ". . . the accident, dreadful, so dreadful . . ."

Aunt Florrie's face is expressionless. I can't bear for people to mention the accident in front of her, but then, how can they know? It's part of Mrs. Ivors' own coming to terms with death that makes her dwell on it. Her soft sympathy overwhelms the room in a treacly flood while I gaze at the rug beneath my feet, abstractedly tracing the pattern of ornamental scrolls and volutions that I know by heart.

Somehow she leaves that particular subject, and I can breathe again without difficulty. I can see that Aunt Florrie relaxes too, and even smiles occasionally as Mrs. Ivors talks on.

The blinds are slightly raised, and gradually a single shaft of sunlight penetrates the dimness. It strikes Aunt

Florrie's face, and her skin takes on a grey transparency behind the whirling dust motes. The sitting room is dusty, of course. The whole house is dusty, with the peculiarly fragrant dust that comes with age.

I remember once when Aunt Florrie was having the trims repainted; the architraves were to be a glossy cream. When the painter had finished, Aunt Florrie called him back. "Look at this," she accused. "Your paint is lumpy."

The painter, an imperious Dutchman, drew himself up and looked down at her through half-closed lids. "My paint is never lumpy," he said.

"But look," Aunt Florrie insisted. She drew her finger over the offending woodwork. "Tiny lumps."

The painter strode to the window. The venetian blinds clattered dramatically as he yanked them up and light poured into the room. "Look at *this*," he said.

Sure enough, the air was alive with the drifting motes. "It is impossible to get a smooth finish; they touch and cling. It is your fault, not mine."

Aunt Florrie acknowledged tight-lipped that it was, paid him his money, and drew the blinds on the dust. She never mentioned the subject again.

And here she sits now, screened by the particles, obscured by the sunlight. I want very much to go over and close the blinds completely.

The afternoon wears on. Tea is brought in. Mrs. Ivors relates a series of sketches of old friends, what they are doing, how they are coping. Most of the information seems to revolve around their health, and much of that is poor. She manages to speak quite clearly around her mouthfuls of tea and biscuits.

I hear Aunt Florrie ask in a small voice for a biscuit to be passed. Automatically I reach for the plate, then withdraw my hand quickly, embarrassed. I hope Mrs. Ivors hasn't noticed. I give a tiny frown and shake my head slightly at Aunt Florrie as Mrs. Ivors delves into her purse for a moment, searching for a photograph of grandchildren she's suddenly remembered, but of course Aunt Florrie ignores me.

She's looking tired now, I notice. I'm not surprised. This is the longest she's sat for some time, but I don't expect she'll go while Mrs. Ivors is here. I know her stubbornness too well.

Finally, with the darkness of evening approaching, Mrs. Ivors rises. She's had, she says, such a wonderful time, and will come again, soon. She dons her faded black coat. Company, she continues, nodding wisely, is what's needed after an event such as the . . . accident. Aunt Florrie is on her feet and begins to smooth her skirt with nervous little sweeps of her hand. I smile thinly at Mrs. Ivors, hoping to dismiss the topic by standing also.

Despite the deepening lines of fatigue in her face, Aunt Florrie joins me as we see Mrs. Ivors to the door and into the twilit street. A final wave, and she is gone.

I'm surprised at my own sense of relief. The afternoon has been a strain even for me. I'm about to return to the sitting room when I notice Aunt Florrie still standing in the hallway, her hand resting lightly on the age-darkened mahogany dresser. I stop and turn back to her. The dresser is crowded with china bric-a-brac collected over many decades. I know all the pieces so well. It was always a treat, when I was young, to be allowed to touch them under Aunt Florrie's supervision—the Dresden girl and swan, the Wedgewood bonbon dish and lid, the china fan (Souvenir de France), the floral painted cups and saucers, crazed in places, but still elegant.

Aunt Florrie raises a thin ghost of a finger to gently stroke the Imrami vase I have always loved most, with its

swirling complexity of colors and golden outlines. Her
expression is again one of infinite sadness, and I long to
touch her, to hug her as I used to. But that's impossible.
I've tried before, and there is just nothing there.

I know why she is upset—Mrs. Ivors has mentioned the
accident. I feel a sudden rush of anger at her unthinking
garrulity, but it expends itself immediately. She could
hardly be expected to realize what has happened.

It *was* a terrible thing, the accident. I try not to think of
it very often, which isn't too hard as so many bits of it are
still blank or blurred in my memory. Aunt Florrie and I,
taking a taxi to a matinee—such a simple thing. But that
day . . . a child running onto the road; the driver swerving
reflexively and into an electricity pole; Aunt Florrie badly
injured . . .

Aunt Florrie leaves the dresser and wafts slowly down
the corridor, eyes glistening in the dimming light. Usually
I would go to the sitting room for the evening, but tonight
I can feel the bond between us is strengthened by the
intensity of the emotion radiating from her, and I follow
her instead. I've never done this before, I realize. Usually
I let her come and go as she pleases, respecting even more
so now her privacy. Suddenly I'm intensely curious.

She glides up the stairs, hardly visible, grey upon grey,
and enters her bedroom. I stand in the doorway, unwilling
to disturb her further.

I'm amazed to see her form divest itself of the printed
frock and put on the cotton nightgown that lies on her bed.
So much is as it was I have to fight the tears from my own
eyes. She pulls down the coverlet—if I touched it, would I
find it had really moved, or do material things join her in
her illusion?

She slides beneath the blanket, and I can see by a faint
motion that she is sobbing, silently. A fierce desire to
protect her in her grief comes over me. I will sit by her

tonight, even though she won't realize it. I never seem to need sleep lately.

I sit in the rocking chair beside her bed as she sleeps restlessly. It's comfortable, but there must be something wrong with the runner. I must get it looked at. No matter how hard I try, I can't seem to make it rock anymore.

W.C. Fields had special feelings about children and how they can control our lives. Mr. Fields, along with Jonathan Swift, had definite answers to the problem. What neither considered is the fact that children are usually anything but passive, especially those children born of continual midnight.

Robert Bloch is the master of psychological terror as well as the sort of wry humor (not to mention horridly delightful puns) whose laughter is often the prelude to a scream.

SWEETS TO THE SWEET

Robert Bloch

Irma didn't look like a witch.

She had small, regular features, a peaches-and-cream complexion, blue eyes, and fair, almost ash-blonde hair. Besides, she was only eight years old.

"Why does he tease her so?" sobbed Miss Pall. "That's where she got the idea in the first place—because he calls her a little witch."

Sam Steever bulked his paunch back into the squeaky swivel chair and folded his heavy hands in his lap. His fat lawyer's mask was immobile, but he was really quite distressed.

Women like Miss Pall should never sob. Their glasses wiggle, their thin noses twitch, their creasy eyelids redden, and their stringy hair becomes disarrayed.

"Please, control yourself," coaxed Sam Steever. "Perhaps if we could just talk this whole thing over sensibly—"

"I don't care!" Miss Pall sniffled. "I'm not going back there again. I can't stand it. There's nothing I can do, anyway. The man is your brother and she's your brother's child. It's not my responsibility. I've tried—"

"Of course you've tried." Sam Steever smiled benignly, as if Miss Pall were foreman of a jury. "I quite understand. But I still don't see why you are so upset, dear lady."

Miss Pall removed her spectacles and dabbed at her eyes with a floral-print handkerchief. Then she deposited the soggy ball in her purse, snapped the catch, replaced her spectacles, and sat up straight.

"Very well, Mr. Steever," she said, "I shall do my best to acquaint you with my reasons for quitting your brother's employ."

She suppressed a tardy sniff.

"I came to John Steever two years ago in response to an advertisement for a housekeeper, as you know. When I found that I was to be governess to a motherless six-year-old child, I was at first distressed. I know nothing of the care of children."

"John had a nurse the first six years," Sam Steever nodded. "You know Irma's mother died in childbirth."

"I am aware of that," said Miss Pall, primly. "Naturally,

one's heart goes out to a lonely, neglected little girl. And she was so terribly lonely, Mr. Steever—if you could have seen her, moping around in the corners of that big, ugly old house—"

"I have seen her," said Sam Steever, hastily, hoping to forestall another outburst. "And I know what you've done for Irma. My brother is inclined to be thoughtless, even a bit selfish at times. He doesn't understand."

"He's cruel," declared Miss Pall, suddenly vehement. "Cruel and wicked. Even if he is your brother, I say he's no fit father for any child. When I came there, her little arms were black and blue from beatings. He used to take a belt—"

"I know. Sometimes I think John never recovered from the shock of Mrs. Steever's death. That's why I was so pleased when you came, dear lady. I thought you might help the situation."

"I tried," Miss Pall whimpered. "You know I tried. I never raised a hand to that child in two years, though many's the time your brother has told me to punish her. 'Give the little witch a beating,' he used to say. 'That's all she needs—a good thrashing.' And then she'd hide behind my back and whisper to me to protect her. But she wouldn't cry, Mr. Steever. Do you know, I've never seen her cry."

Sam Steever felt vaguely irritated and a bit bored. He wished the old hen would get on with it. So he smiled and oozed treacle. "But just what is your problem, dear lady?"

"Everything was all right when I came there. We got along just splendidly. I started to teach Irma to read—and was surprised to find that she had already mastered reading. Your brother disclaimed having taught her, but she spent hours curled up on the sofa with a book. 'Just like her,' he used to say. 'Unnatural little witch. Doesn't play with the other children. Little witch.' That's the way he kept talking,

Mr. Steever. As if she were some sort of—I don't know what. And she so sweet and quiet and pretty!

"Is it any wonder she read? I used to be that way myself when I was a girl, because—but never mind.

"Still, it was a shock that day I found her looking through the Encyclopaedia Britannica. 'What are you reading, Irma?' I asked. She showed me. It was the article on Witchcraft.

"You see what morbid thoughts your brother has inculcated in her poor little head?

"I did my best. I went out and bought her some toys— she had absolutely nothing, you know, not even a doll. She didn't even know how to *play!* I tried to get her interested in some of the other little girls in the neighborhood, but it was no use. They didn't understand her and she didn't understand them. There were scenes. Children can be cruel, thoughtless. And her father wouldn't let her go to public school. I was to teach her—

"Then I brought her the modeling clay. She liked that. She would spend hours just making faces with clay. For a child of six, Irma displayed real talent.

"We made little dolls together, and I sewed clothes for them. That first year was a happy one, Mr. Steever. Particularly during those months when your brother was away in South America. But this year, when he came back—oh, I can't bear to talk about it!"

"Please," said Sam Steever. "You must understand. John is not a happy man. The loss of his wife, the decline of his import trade, and his drinking—but you know all that."

"All I know is that he hates Irma," snapped Miss Pall, suddenly. "He hates her. He wants her to be bad so he can whip her. 'If you don't discipline the little witch, I shall,' he always says. And then he takes her upstairs and thrashes her with his belt—you must do something, Mr. Steever, or I'll go to the authorities myself.''

The crazy old biddy would at that, Sam Steever thought. Remedy—more treacle. "But about Irma," he persisted.

"She's changed, too. Ever since her father returned this year. She won't play with me anymore, hardly looks at me. It is as though I failed her, Mr. Steever, in not protecting her from that man. Besides—she thinks she's a witch.''

Crazy. Stark, staring crazy. Sam Steever creaked upright in his chair.

"Oh you needn't look at me like that, Mr. Steever. She'll tell you so herself—if you ever visited the house!''

He caught the reproach in her voice and assuaged it with a deprecating nod.

"She told me all right, if her father wants her to be a witch, she'll be a witch. And she won't play with me, or anyone else, because witches don't play. Last Halloween she wanted me to give her a broomstick. Oh, it would be funny if it weren't so tragic. That child is losing her sanity.

"Just a few weeks ago I thought she'd changed. That's when she asked me to take her to church one Sunday. 'I want to see the baptism,' she said. Imagine that—an eight-year-old interested in baptism! Reading too much, that's what does it.

"Well, we went to church and she was as sweet as can be, wearing her new blue dress and holding my hand. I was proud of her, Mr. Steever, really proud.

"But after that, she went right back into her shell. Reading around the house, running through the yard at twilight and talking to herself.

"Perhaps it's because your brother wouldn't bring her a kitten. She was pestering him for a black cat, and he asked why, and she said, 'Because witches always have black cats.' Then he took her upstairs.

"I can't stop him, you know. He beat her again the night the power failed and we couldn't find the candles. He said she'd stolen them. Imagine that—accusing an eight-year-old child of stealing candles!

"That was the beginning of the end. Then today, when he found his hairbrush missing—"

"You say he beat her with his hairbrush?"

"Yes. She admitted having stolen it. Said she wanted it for her doll."

"But didn't you say she has no dolls?"

"She made one. At least I think she did. I've never seen it—she won't show us anything anymore; won't talk to us at table, just impossible to handle her.

"But this doll she made—it's a small one, I know, because at times she carries it tucked under her arm. She talks to it and pets it, but she won't show it to me or to him. He asked her about the hairbursh and she said she took it for the doll.

"Your brother flew into a terrible rage—he'd been drinking in his room again all morning; oh, don't think I don't know it!—and she just smiled and said he could have it now. She went over to her bureau and handed it to him. She hadn't harmed it in the least; his hair was still in it, I noticed.

"But he snatched it up, and then he started to strike her about the shoulders with it, and he twisted her arm and then he—"

Miss Pall huddled in her chair and summoned great racking sobs from her thin chest.

Sam Steever patted her shoulder, fussing about her like an elephant over a wounded canary.

"That's all, Mr. Steever. I came right to you. I'm not even going back to that house to get my things; I can't stand any more—the way he beat her—and the way she didn't cry, just giggled and giggled and giggled—sometimes I think she *is* a witch—that he made her into a witch—''

Sam Steever picked up the phone. The ringing had broken the relief of silence after Miss Pall's hasty departure.

''Hello—that you, Sam?''

He recognized his brother's voice, somewhat the worse for drink.

''Yes, John.''

''I suppose the old bat came running straight to you to shoot her mouth off.''

''If you mean Miss Pall, I've seen her, yes.''

''Pay no attention. I can explain everything.''

''Do you want me to stop in? I haven't paid you a visit in months.''

''Well—not right now. Got an appointment with the doctor this evening.''

''Something wrong?''

''Pain in my arm. Rheumatism or something. Getting a little diathermy. But I'll call you tomorrow and we'll straighten this whole mess out.''

''Right.''

But John Steever did not call the next day. Along about supper time, Sam called him.

Surprisingly enough, Irma answered the phone. Her thin, squeaky little voice sounded faintly in Sam's ears.

''Daddy's upstairs sleeping. He's been sick.''

''Well, don't disturb him. What is it—his arm?''

''His back, now. He has to go to the doctor again in a little while.''

''Tell him I'll call tomorrow, then. Uh—everything all right, Irma? I mean, don't you miss Miss Pall?''

''No. I'm glad she went away. She's stupid.''

"Oh. Yes. I see. But you phone me if you want anything. And I hope your Daddy's better."

"Yes. So do I," said Irma, and then she began to giggle, and then she hung up.

There was no giggling the following afternoon when John Steever called Sam at the office. His voice was sober—with the sharp sobriety of pain.

"Sam—for God's sake, get over here. Something's happening to me!"

"What's the trouble?"

"The pain—it's killing me! I've got to see you, quickly."

"There's a client in the office, but I'll get rid of him. Say, wait a minute. Why don't you call the doctor?"

"That quack can't help me. He gave me diathermy for my arm and yesterday he did the same thing for my back."

"Didn't help?"

"The pain went away, yes. But it's back now. I feel— like I was being crushed. Squeezed, here in the chest. I can't breathe."

"Sounds like pleurisy. Why don't you call him?"

"It isn't pleurisy. He examined me. Said I was sound as a dollar. No, there's nothing organically wrong. And I couldn't tell him the real cause."

"Real cause?"

"Yes. The pins. The pin that little fiend is sticking into the doll she made. Into the arm, the back. And now heaven only knows how she's causing *this*."

"John, you mustn't—"

"Oh what's the use of talking? I can't move off the bed here. She has me now. I can't go down and stop her, get hold of the doll. And nobody else would believe it. But it's the doll all right, the one she made with the candlewax and the hair from my brush. Oh—it hurts to talk—that cursed little witch! Hurry, Sam. Promise me you'll do something—anything—get that doll from her—get that doll—''

Half an hour later, at four-thirty, Sam Steever entered his brother's house.

Irma opened the door.

It gave Sam a shock to see her standing there, smiling and unperturbed, pale blonde hair brushed immaculately back from the rosy oval of her face. She looked just like a little doll. A little doll—

''Hello, Uncle Sam.''

''Hello, Irma. Your daddy called me; did he tell you? He said he wasn't feeling well—''

''I know. But he's all right now. He's sleeping.''

Something happened to Sam Steever; a drop of ice water trickled down his spine.

''Sleeping?'' he croaked. ''Upstairs?''

Before she opened her mouth to answer, he was bounding up the steps to the second floor, striding down the hall to John's bedroom.

John lay on the bed. He was asleep, and only asleep. Sam Steever noted the regular rise and fall of his chest as he breathed. His face was calm, relaxed.

Then the drop of ice water evaporated, and Sam could afford to smile and murmur ''Nonsense'' under his breath as he turned away.

As he went downstairs, he hastily improvised plans. A six-month vacation for his brother; avoid calling it a ''cure.'' An orphanage for Irma; give her a chance to get away from this morbid old house, all those books . . .

He paused halfway down the stairs. Peering over the banister through the twilight, he saw Irma on the sofa, cuddled up like a little white ball. She was talking to something she cradled in her arms, rocking it to and fro.

Then there was a doll, after all.

Sam Steever tiptoed very quietly down the stairs and walked over to Irma.

"Hello," he said.

She jumped. Both arms rose to cover completely whatever it was she had been fondling. She squeezed it tightly.

Sam Steever thought of a doll being squeezed across the chest—

Irma stared up at him, her face a mask of innocence. In the half-light her face did resemble a mask. The mask of a little girl, covering—what?

"Daddy's better now, isn't he?" lisped Irma.

"Yes, much better."

"I knew he would be."

"But I'm afraid he's going to have to go away for a rest. A long rest."

A smile filtered through the mask. "Good," said Irma.

"Of course," Sam went on, "you couldn't stay here all alone. I was wondering—maybe we could send you off to school, or to some kind of a home—"

Irma giggled. "Oh, you needn't worry about me," she said. She shifted about on the sofa as Sam sat down, then sprang up quickly as he came close to her.

Her arms shifted with the movement, and Sam Steever saw a pair of tiny legs dangling down below her elbow. There were trousers on the legs, and little bits of leather for shoes.

"What's that you have, Irma?" he asked. "Is it a doll?" Slowly, he extended his pudgy hand.

She pulled back.

"You can't see it," she said.

"But I want to. Miss Pall said you made such lovely ones."

"Miss Pall is stupid. So are you. Go away."

"Please, Irma. Let me see it."

But even as she spoke, Sam Steever was staring at the

top of the doll, momentarily revealed when she backed away. It was a head all right, with wisps of hair over a white face. Dusk dimmed the features, but Sam recognized the eyes, the nose, the chin—

He could keep up the pretense no longer.

"Give me that doll, Irma!" he snapped. "I know what it is. I know *who* it is—"

For an instant, the mask slipped from Irma's face, and Sam Steever stared into naked fear.

She knew. She knew he knew.

Then, just as quickly, the mask was replaced.

Irma was only a sweet, spoiled, stubborn little girl as she shook her head merrily and smiled with impish mischief in her eyes.

"Oh, Uncle Sam," she giggled. "You're so silly! Why, this isn't a *real* doll."

"What is it, then?" he muttered.

Irma giggled once more, raising the figure as she spoke. "Why, it's only—candy!" Irma said.

"Candy?"

Irma nodded. Then, very swiftly, she slipped the tiny head of the image into her mouth.

And bit it off.

There was a single piercing scream from upstairs.

As Sam Steever turned and ran up the steps, little Irma, still gravely munching, skipped out of the front door and into the night beyond.

For parents, it is difficult to imagine a monster more horrid in mien and destructive in power than a child on a rampage. It's a terror that fills us with guilt because kids are supposedly innocent and sweet, and we are their protectors until they can protect themselves. Like midnight, that belief is more a state of mind than an actual fact.

Douglas E. Winter is unquestionably the field's premier critic (in the truest sense), and is currently preparing for publication a study of Stephen King (THE ART OF DARKNESS, for NAL) and a collection of interviews with the field's best and best-known writers (for Berkley).

MASKS

Douglas E. Winter

For the past two hours, Danny had waited. He had
waited in his bedroom, hoping that Daddy would come
home, hoping that the knocking at the front door would
stop, hoping that she would leave for groceries—and that
maybe, just maybe, she would leave forever. But he knew
that none of these things would happen—that downstairs,
curled up on the embroidered couch, the woman who
called herself Mommy was waiting too. She was waiting
for the creatures to come, for the knocking to begin again.
She would reluctantly part from the television set and
answer the door, and those stupid kids would stand out
there on the porch, whining through their cheap plastic
masks. They would pretend to frighten her, and she would
pretend to be frightened, but everybody knew they were
just begging for candy. It made him sick—and in a way, it
made him scared.

Danny had waited in his bed, looking at the wall.
Indiana Jones stared back at him, eyes glazed but amused:
''What are we doin' *here*, kid?'' On the poster, Indiana
looked just like Danny's father, and everybody said that
Danny and his father, looked so much alike. Danny had
put on his checked flannel pajamas and, over them, his
father's old Army fatigue shirt. The shirt tented around
him, reaching almost to his knees; he tried to imagine
himself camouflaged, Indiana Jones lying in ambush for
the next band of masked invaders. But when he pulled on

his mask, he felt no different—he was still Danny Martin, not some make-believe character ready to prowl the neighborhood in search of treats. The woman downstairs didn't understand; she didn't even listen when he tried to explain. So he had waited for his father, waited for the knocking to end, waited for Halloween to be over.

Danny had waited, watching the poster on his wall bleakly as Indiana's face seemed to wrinkle with age, shadows shifting as the night breeze tickled the trees outside his window.

He had waited, but he couldn't stop feeling like a baby. Just what she had called him. A baby. Ten years old and can't even go out trick-or-treating with his little brother on Halloween.

"But I don't feel like it."

Her eyes, those freezing blue eyes, had widened, and he knew that he had broken the final strand of her thin-corded patience.

"Don't *feel* like it? I'll tell you something *I* don't feel like, young man. I don't feel like listening to back talk. I don't feel like listening to you at all. Just five days ago I spent a good ten dollars of my money . . .

Daddy's money.

". . . on this mask that you just *had* to have, and now what do I get for it? 'I don't feel like it.' And your brother's got to go with somebody . . .

Tommy Niebur's mother is taking him.

". . . but you don't *feel* like it. Well, I don't feel like *you*. So go to your room—no dinner, no television, no nothing. I don't want to see you till morning. Have you got that?"

"Yeah."

"What?"

"Yes."

"Yes, what?"

He couldn't say that word—he wouldn't say that word, that hated word. But he had to, didn't he?

"Yes, Mommy."

He walked past her, heading for the stairs. "Can I say something?"

"One thing, and you'd better not . . ."

"Is Daddy coming home tonight?"

"I told you, and if you'd been paying any attention you would know, that Daddy has to work very late. He has a court appearance in Philadelphia tomorrow, and he may not even come home tonight. Now get to your room."

He turned away. Deron was standing at the top of the stairs, eavesdropping as usual. And wearing that stupid Darth Vader outfit, like it was a brand new idea or something.

Danny stomped up the stairs, whispering to his brother as he passed: "Bring me some candy."

"Why should I?" Deron's shrill voice seemed to whistle through the black plastic face; it sounded like Michael Jackson's impression of James Earl Jones. "You're too old . . . remember?"

Danny went straight to his bedroom and slammed the door, hard. And that was when he began to wait, at first half hoping that she would storm after him, then settling in, listening patiently for the opening garage door that would signal the arrival of his father, back from another endless day at work. But he heard only the knocking at the front door, the giggling voices, the stupid shouts of "trick or treat," the rustling of paper sacks. He could imagine the greedy, grabbing hands, hungrily taking the packages given away by the woman downstairs.

The woman who pretended to be his mother.

His father had promised to be home on Halloween. He had promised. Danny remembered what had happened when he had missed Deron's birthday party—he was late, at work, as usual. The next morning, Deron was still pouting; his bottom lip seemed to have turned inside out. He was slowly spooning his bowl of Rice Krispies into a thick mush.

"Tell you what," Dad had said. "Halloween's just about three weeks away. We'll have ourselves another party then—and there's no way I'm going to miss that."

Deron's eyes seemed to light up a little.

"No way," Dad had repeated. "Is that a deal?"

Then Deron seemed to think real hard. "Can . . . can I be Darth Vader?"

"Again?" Dad had groaned. He reached over the newspaper and stuck his finger into Deron's soupy Rice Krispies, took a taste and yelled, "Yuck!"

Deron smiled and began to shovel the Rice Krispies into his mouth. "But it's really good yuck," he said, and began to laugh. Soon everyone was laughing—even Janice. Danny could tell that everything was going to be okay.

"We're gonna party," Dad had said. "And wait till you see the mask that *I've* got for Halloween. Real booga-booga stuff."

Danny saw Janice roll her eyes, reaching for a cigarette. Her smile seemed suddenly false. *Grow up,* he imagined her thinking. *Next thing you know, he'll want to go trick-or-treating. . . .*

Dad was a real nut for masks. He had lined one book-shelf of his study with them. His favorite was probably a tiny plastic mask of some superhero called the Phantom, which he claimed was part of the first Halloween costume he had ever worn when he was a kid. "I was cool as a moose," he would say, "back in the bad old, sad old fifties." But he also had an expensive glow-in-the-dark latex mask that fit over his whole head, not just the face; Daddy said it had been designed by some guy named Don

Post especially for that movie *Halloween III*. Danny didn't know whether that was true or not, seeing how Daddy never let him see those kinds of movies when they came on HBO, but if Daddy said it was true, it had to be true.

Just like when Daddy said he would be home for Halloween.

The woman downstairs had lied; she knew that Daddy was coming home tonight. Just thinking about her made him angry. If he had to call that woman "Mommy" one more time, he knew he would puke. Her name was Janice something-or-other, Janice Martin now, and she had moved in here—right into Mom's house—just six months after his mother had gone away.

His real mother was named Melanie, and his father, when he talked of her at all, would say that she had "gone away." But dead was what he meant. His real Mommy was dead.

The first time that Danny had seen an actual funeral was on television, when that Princess Grace lady had died. He remembered sitting with his mother—his real mother—and watching these handsome people filing into a gigantic cathedral. It seemed like they had come to worship that big coffin. His mother had laughed a little when he told her that, but mostly she had cried; he remembered that quite clearly. And one other thing: They had had fried chicken that night for dinner.

He had wanted fried chicken on the day of his mother's funeral, but his father had taken him and Deron to Burger King instead. He should have known that this funeral would be different; she wasn't a princess, just his mommy. There was no television, no church, no people in fancy clothes. Reverend Lowe, some chubby, smiling guy that his father knew, gave the service in some place called Iwry's Funeral Home. Until Johnny Sheldon showed up with his mother, Danny didn't know anybody—there were just these men in grey suits from Daddy's office and ladies who looked like they wanted to cry but couldn't quite understand why. Through it all, his father had sat next to him, in the front row of seats. Deron sat with a Spiderman coloring book at his other side. His father's eyes were wet, unfocused, looking at the people, the flowers, the floor, the ceiling, the walls—everywhere except that long box standing just a few feet away. Once Danny thought he heard him say something, but it wasn't meant for Danny. Maybe it wasn't meant for anyone. Only after Reverend Lowe had talked a long, long time about love and shepherds and dust and taking away, did Daddy finally lean over to Danny and whisper: "Come on. It's time to say good-bye to your mother."

It was too late. Danny had said his good-byes two nights before, while lying in bed, staring into a night without stars. He had wanted a star to wish upon—to wish he may, to wish he might, to wish there were no hospitals, no emergency rooms, no ambulances that screamed through the night with their payload of sick mothers, taking them away to die. But there was only darkness out there.

So when his father pulled him forward and boosted him up to peek inside the coffin, he really had nothing to say, nothing to do but cry for the wish that could never come true. And then he saw, to his horror, that the thing inside the box was not his mother.

It had her hands folded against her chest; it was wearing her clothes. But it was not her face, not really. She had never worn her hair that way; she had never smiled that way. Her face had been painted, pushed, twisted . . . into a mask.

"It's not my mommy!" he had screamed. And he had lunged away from that horrible face, his father stumbling beneath the sudden shift of weight, nearly dropping him.

Deron, cowering behind his father, started to cry, and Danny could hear the sudden rush of voices in the room, the coughs, the whispers, the words, repeated over and over . . . *not my Mommy* . . . until Reverend Lowe lurched forward, stiff-necked in his white collar, grasping at Danny's flailing hands. He screamed again, and his father staggered backward several steps; when he looked into his father's eyes, so close and yet so distant, he saw tears pooling, then falling down his cheeks even as he glanced back into the wooden box with the crazy hope that his son's words were true.

His father seemed to crumple into Aunt Rita, who had appeared out of nowhere to gather Danny into her arms, rushing him from the room, away from the voices, away from the box. In the hallway outside, she made him drink a cup of Seven-Up. It was warm and made him belch. Then she led him to a small room; there was a picture of Jesus on the wall, a water cooler, and a cot. And Aunt Rita gently spread him along the coat, kissed his forehead and held his hand. She told him the story about the cat in the hat. She told him the story about green eggs and ham. She started to sing something, and Danny fell asleep.

It was six months later—Danny was sure of that, because he had worked it out after overhearing one of Daddy's lawyer friends at the wedding reception—that Daddy brought that woman home for dinner. This was Janice, Daddy said. She was a secretary at the law firm where he worked. She had been oh-so-helpful when things had gone wrong, when the ambulance had come, when Mommy had . . . gone away. After a while, Daddy had said, "Janice is going to be your new mommy."

That was the one time—the only one time that Danny knew of—that his father had lied.

Janice looked like one of those girls on the Clairol commercials—always smiling and tossing her hair from

side to side. She was younger than Daddy—a lot younger—
and she would call Danny and Deron her "little brothers"
when people came over to visit.

She put mayonnaise on Danny's ham sandwiches, even
though he told her that he didn't like mayonnaise.

"It's good for you," she said.

She made Danny sit far away from the television set,
where he couldn't see and hear as well as he could close
up.

"You'll hurt your eyes," she said.

She made him go to bed at the same time as Deron,
even though he was four years older.

"You need a good night's sleep," she said.

And she made him call her "Mommy," when she wasn't
his mother—when she knew she wasn't his mother.

"You've got a new mommy now," she said.

Daddy didn't seem to notice. Danny had tried to tell him
once, but his father didn't understand. Maybe it was because he didn't have much time.

Danny usually saw his father about forty-five minutes a
day—fifteen minutes in the morning, over a hectic breakfast where everyone battled for the newspaper, and then
just before bedtime, when his father, who ate dinner at the
office, would straggle in, looking very tired. He would
pour himself a drink, then hunker down in front of the
television set. And Janice would hover over him, shooing
Danny and Deron off to bed.

Daniel Michael Martin, Sr., worked in one of those
Washington, D.C., law firms with a bunch of names
("Dewey, Cheetham & Howe," Daddy would joke); he
was something called a litigator, which a younger Danny
had thought might have something to do with crocodiles
until his father explained that not all lawyers went to court
and that those who did tended to call themselves litigators.
But whatever it was that Daddy really did, he seemed to

do it all of the time—every night, Saturdays, even Sundays. He wanted to "make partner," he had told Danny, "which means I have to dig my own grave before I can sleep in it."

Daddy had laughed. Danny wasn't sure if he was really trying to be funny. Things had gotten worse lately; his father worked longer and harder—and he drank more when he came home at night. If he came home.

Why didn't she answer the door?

Danny seemed to awaken with the sudden sound of knocking. It had been quiet for so long; he had waited for two hours that seemed longer than any movie he had ever seen. There were so many memories that they seemed to run together like a dream. Had he fallen asleep?

He shook his head, rubbed at his eyes. The knocking downstairs sounded like the shots of a distant cannon. He imagined the front door caving in, ten-foot-tall gorillas pawing into the living room, dragging Hefty Bags stuffed to the brim with helpless trick-or-treaters.

"Hey!" he called. "Janice?"

But she wasn't in the living room; peeking from his doorway, he could see the sofa, the rocking chair, the right half of the television. He could just make out the curly hair that crowned the head of Magnum, P.I. And Magnum was smooching with some blond girl who looked like she really liked having her face scrubbed down with that Brillo-pad moustache. The music was mushy—and loud. Maybe Janice hadn't heard him calling. Maybe she hadn't even heard the knocking.

Danny started down the stairs, slowly at first, but nearly running as the knocking began again.

"Hello?" He knew he was in trouble; she was in the kitchen or the bathroom or somewhere, and when she found him scouting around outside of his room, she would whale him good—like that time she took a belt to him when he broke the china teapot.

But somebody had to answer the door. What if it was Jamie and Rick out there, standing in the cold, knowing that Danny was inside and not answering? They'd soap the windows or dump over the trash cans—or, knowing Jamie, maybe even slash the tires on the station wagon.

So Danny quickly went to the door, steeling himself for the whiny cries of "trick or treat" and a sea of E.T. masks.

But when he opened the door, no one was there.

"Janice?"

On the low table between the front door and the adjacent hall closet sat a straw basket filled with Janice's gift-wrapped goodies, ready for the next wave of costumed creeps. As Danny closed and locked the front door, he thought about swiping one of the packages. He wondered what was inside.

Mom used to have the neatest things for Halloween treats—candy apples and taffy strings and popcorn balls that she made with a little help from Danny and Deron . . . and Daddy. He giggled, remembering Daddy, hands all brown and gooey with molasses, chasing Mom around the kitchen, walking out of kilter like a drunken Franken-stein's monster.

And Mom would buy other stuff, too—especially Danny's favorite candy, Mars Bars.

That alone was enough to prove that Janice wasn't his mother. She didn't buy him Mars Bars; she didn't believe in candy.

"It's bad for your teeth," she said.

So she made something up, all by herself, while Danny and Deron were at school. She had wrapped her stuff in little packages, strangled with orange and black ribbons, like spooky Christmas presents. She gave them to the trick-or-treaters, but didn't offer any to Danny or Deron. She didn't even tell them what it was.

Looking at the basket now, Danny wasn't sure that he wanted one. The packages he had seen earlier in the evening were precise little rectangles—brownies or fudge, he guessed. But these were odd lumps; he thought, for no reason, that they might be bags of mud. Or maybe half-chewed apples. When he prodded one with his finger, he felt warmth; the paper, and whatever was beneath the paper, seemed to give with a wet sigh. He pulled his finger back as if he had touched a white-hot burner, then wiped it along the leg of his pajamas.

He would wait for Deron to come home, and if the little brat didn't give him some candy—hopefully a Mars Bar—well, he'd sneak into his room later and lift something.

He noticed the little clock beside the basket; the red digits blinked 10:24.

He had waited longer than he thought—a lot longer. He must have fallen asleep. Deron ought to be home by now . . .

Daddy ought to be home by now.

He went back upstairs.

Deron's room was a shambles, as usual. In the dark, the floor was like an obstacle course; Danny stumbled over schoolbooks, side-stepped a knapsack, jumped over a pile of clothes. He kicked shoes aside, almost stepped squarely on top of a G.I. Joe assault vehicle. Didn't Deron know about drawers? Trying to get that kid to clean up after himself was like trying to get him to brush his teeth. "Old Yeller" was what Daddy called him. Gross was a better word.

"Deron?"

For a moment, Danny thought that his brother was

curled in bed, asleep; then he saw that it was only a trick of shadows on the rumpled sheets.

Satisfied that no one was there, Danny started back toward the hall. That was when he saw, in the faint swathe of light angling through the doorway, Darth Vader's face peering out from a pile of dirty T-shirts.

So Deron was back from spooking the neighbors and begging for candy. Funny, though, that he should leave his precious mask in the middle of the floor. What a slob.

"Deron?"

No answer. Nothing. Not a word.

"Deron? Come on, Deron." *You little shit,* he wanted to add. But that was when the knocking began again.

Danny sprinted into the hall, toward the stairs, glancing into the study and the guest bathroom as he ran. Nobody there. Then he was down the stairs, two and three at a time.

When he slid to a stocking-footed stop on the landing, the knocking had stopped. He pulled the security chain aside; it swung, jangling, away from its mounting.

"Boo!" he screamed, yanking the door open.

There was no one there.

He eased out onto the doorstep. It was cold, and his toes curled on the icy concrete. The wind was rising, whistling in the night and scattering twisted leaves across the lawn.

"Jamie!" he called. "Jamie and Rick! I know it's you! It's gettin' late, you punks! You better get on home or your momma's gonna get you!"

He stalked back into the house, slamming the door, fumbling the chain lock back into place with his cold, stiff hands. Then for good measure, he slipped the dead bolt into place. Home for the night, locked up tight. He grinned with relief. His father's Toyota had been parked in the driveway, right next to the station wagon. Maybe Deron was too little to remember, but Danny remembered. His father had promised, and he hadn't forgotten his promise. He hadn't lied. He was home, and we were "gonna party."

Danny tried the living room first; he switched off the television set just before Magnum closed down another case. Then he checked the kitchen. Nothing seemed to have changed. The light above the oven glowed. A folded magazine and three place mats decked the table. The door to the basement was open slightly, just as he remembered it from hours before. The thin gap showed only darkness—no one in the basement.

"Dad?" He moved on down the hall, toward the study, flipping light switches as he went. The study was dark; Danny fingered the goose-necked lamp on his father's desk.

"Dad?" A briefcase lay open on the desk chair. Paper, pens, thick file folders. On the desk was a suitcoat. But Danny couldn't remember what his father had been wearing that morning when he left for work.

"Dad?" Danny thought he heard something. A leak. The drip of a faucet. Something wet.

He looked up, saw the row of masks smiling down on him from the middle bookshelf. But something was wrong; something was missing, or changed. There was the impish plastic Phantom mask on the far left, its black and purple paint scratched and scarred. At the far right sat the Don Post skull, literally grinning its teeth out. In between were ghoulies and ghosties and gremlins and . . . something different, something he didn't really like to look at for very long, something that looked like the twisted face of a pig that had been stuffed with the head of a boy. A human ear seemed to squeeze out from the left pink ear of the pig, and the left eye dangled on a red, bulbous stalk. Yellowish teeth protruded donkey-like from the mouth, dripping ropes of blood and saliva.

For a moment Danny's stomach cramped; his mouth tasted like bad cider. The pig-boy mask made him feel awful; it was "real bogga-booga stuff," and he didn't want to touch it. He didn't want to be near it. He didn't want to be in the same room with it.

Then he thought he heard the mask drip—thought that it was really leaking blood and spit. When the knocking came again, he jumped; it was as if a cold hand had slid across his neck and pinched his ear.

The knocking came once. Twice. Three times.

Daddy was home. His car was here; his briefcase was here; his coat was here. His mask was here.

So where was Daddy—and Deron? Were they out trick-or-treating? Then why didn't they have their masks?

The knocking stopped.

And started again.

Once. Twice. Three times.

He didn't move, hoping that someone else would answer the door. But the house was silent . . . except for the dripping. And the knocking.

They're outside, he suddenly realized. They went outside with a key. They're outside on the porch, knocking for me to let them in.

Once. Twice. Three times.

"I'm coming, Dad!" he yelled. He was nearly laughing, nearly crying, and his voice cracked as he ran down the hallway. "Hold your horses! I'm coming!"

But when he opened the front door, no one was there.

He shut the door gently, backing away from it, fighting the tears that poured freely down his cheeks. And he called for her then. She was home. She had to be home. She wouldn't leave him; she hadn't gone away.

He called for her. The word tore at his throat, but he called for her.

"Mommy?"

He hung the chain, homed the dead bolt.

"Mommy?"

The knocking came again.

Danny stared at the front door; the sound didn't seem right—it didn't seem to be coming from outside. He took a deep breath. He wiped his forearm across his eyes and nose, dabbing away the tears. Then he yanked the chain lock away, for the final time.

"All right," he said. "All right. You want to come in? Well, come on. Come on in." And he twisted the dead bolt—it gave with the crackle of a splintering branch—and stepped back.

He heard a metallic gasp as a doorknob turned; his eyes widened as he saw that the brass knob of the front door had not moved. It was the sharp click that drew his eyes from the front door, across the basket of secret Halloween treats, to the adjacent hall closet; its doorknob was rotating ever so slowly, a crack of darkness appearing to its left, expanding, yawning outward as the closet door opened, offering up the enticing darkness within. Danny faced the closet, and he started to speak, but then she came out of the shadows, out of the closet and into his world. In her hand, she was holding something that looked like his Indiana Jones mask, but it had hair, real hair—she was holding it by its hair.

At first, he didn't know her. But when the bright lights met her upturned face, he recognized her eyes.

At least he recognized her eyes.

She had taken off her Mommy mask.

Creatures of the night have been categorized into vampire types, werewolf types, and other types. They have also been pushed into the drawer marked "fantasy." When the drawer is opened, what you have are clichés, for the most part. Except for those who never had a home there in the first place—the creatures who spend most of their lives with us.

R. Chetwynd-Hayes is the author of a number of fine fantasies, many of them marked by humor blended into the dark. "The Fly-by-Night" is but one story in a connected series collected in THE MONSTER CLUB.

THE FLY-BY-NIGHT

R. Chetwynd-Hayes

*Let it be known that there is the earth and all
things that do breathe, eat and walk thereon.*

*Then there is the underearth and all things that
do not breathe, eat or walk, but most certainly
exist. They have no flesh, but have substance;
they neither spin nor toil, but find much to do;
they speak not, but communicate. Their natural
habitat is the lower regions of that uncharted
country men call Hades, and since time began,
they have crawled, slithered or flown between the
dark, fire-tipped mountains that border mist-filled
valleys.*

*But there are those which over countless ages
have evolved and become aware. With knowledge
comes desire, and after desire comes determination,
and after determination comes action. They wormed
their way up through the dark tunnels which
spiral around the place where lost souls mourn
the passing of life, and came at last to the plane of
the air-breathers. To some the light was not good
and they either perished, or took to haunting the
dwelling places of shadows, or ventured forth
only when the sky was masked by night clouds.
But some adapted, merged into their surroundings and learned to imitate the appetites of man.
Such a one was named by the wise men of old as*

The Flucht-Daemon, but the common people drew
upon their own limited vocabulary and called it:
The Fly-by-Night.

The cottage stood on the edge of a great forest and to a person of vivid imagination it appeared to have crawled out from the shelter of giant trees and was now tentatively tasting the sunlight. A small garden was bordered by a white picket fence, and within its confines neat rows of cabbages, feathery carrots and sturdy potato plants presented a green, patchwork carpet that trembled under the caress of the morning breeze.

Long ago the cottage had been the dwelling place of a woodcutter, and before that a charcoal burner, but now it was occupied by Newton C. Hatfield and his daughter Celia. Newton was a novelist of some repute; Celia was a would-be actress, who, when resting, tried to follow in her father's literary footsteps. The third occupant was a black cat who answered to the name of Tobias; a mighty hunter before the Lord, who brought live field mice home, then watched with an expression of profound surprise when Celia jumped up on to a chair and gave a pretty performance of feminine alarm. On such occasions Newton would corner the mouse, take it out to the edge of the forest and there release it.

"Damn nonsense," he growled. "Frightened of a creature that will fit into the palm of your hand."

"But it might run up my legs," Celia protested.

"What the hell would it want to run up your legs for?" her father enquired. "It hasn't got the morals of some of those types you go about with."

"You are a disgusting old man."

"Disgusting I may be; old never."

One day Tobias brought home a bird.

It was a fine healthy starling that was in no way hurt, for Tobias treated his victims gently, being content to take joy in the hunt, then sit back and wait for the applause. The bird, once released, flew round the room and made a futile attempt to force its way through the windowpanes. Celia was full of concern and hampered her father's efforts to capture it by clutching his arm and exhorting him to be careful—don't hurt it—poor little thing, and other compassionate ejaculations. Newton finally netted it with a looped bath towel, then released it out the front door and watched the black streak as it sped for the nearest tree.

"Women!" he shook his head with deep concern. "I will never understand you. You go up the wall when a tiny mouse stirs a paw in your direction, but go all ga-ga when a bloody great bird goes flapping round the place. Do you realize if that had got entangled in your hair, you would have had something to scream about?"

"But . . . but it was only a poor little bird."

"And what about that ferocious tiger we've got sitting under the table?"

Celia bent down and tickled Tobias's ears, an action which earned his full approval.

"He was only acting according to his nature."

Newton made straight for his typewriter.

"I give up."

Two days later Tobias brought home something that was not a bird or a mouse.

They found it when they came home one evening after a visit to town. It was crawling over the carpet and made a strange twittering sound when they entered the room. Newton swore and glared at Tobias, who was crouched in one corner and watching his capture with intense interest. Celia ran forward with a cry of concern.

"Oh, poor little thing."

Newton grabbed his daughter's arm and pulled her back.

"Hold it. Before you go into raptures, I should first of all find out what it is."

"It's some kind of bird."

"Is it?" Newton bent forward and examined the creature carefully. "Well, I've never seen a bird that looked like that. Look for yourself."

The creature—before it unleashed its tail—was about six inches long and had a pair of black leathery wings that assisted it to crawl over the carpet. But when the tail suddenly uncoiled, and it appeared to have been tucked away between the minute hind legs, another three inches was added to its length. Newton went out into the hall and returned with a thick walking stick.

"You're not going to hurt it?" Celia exclaimed.

"Oh, for heaven's sake." He brushed her to one side, then inserting the point of the stick under one wing, flipped the creature over on to its back. "Now, have you ever seen anything like that?"

A tiny, black fur-covered body, which terminated in bent hind legs; a narrow little white and completely hairless face that was lit by a pair of exquisite blue eyes and surmounted with a mop of shining black hair. The tiny teeth were white, and pointed, the ears tapered, the red lips full and parted. Newton had the impression it was grinning at him.

"Isn't it sweet?" Celia said.

"Sweet!" Newton's bellow of rage made the creature look up, and its lips slowly closed. "Sweet! That is the most horrible thing I've ever seen."

"Oh, it's not. I should think it's some kind of bat."

"Ah!" Newton nodded grimly. "A mouse. A flying mouse."

"Yes, I know, but it's not the same. Oh, look at his eyes!" Celia bent forward and assumed a winsome smile. "He's not a nasty old mouse, is he then? He's a little dinkom-diddens. Yes, he is . . . he's a little dinkom-diddens . . ."

"For heaven's sake, stop it. How the hell you can make noises at a . . . a monstrosity like that is beyond me. Let me get a shovel and I'll put it outside somewhere. Preferably as far from the house as possible."

Celia made a cry of protest and the creature blinked its blue eyes and seemed to look upon her with approval.

"How can you be so heartless? It's probably hurt; otherwise it would be flying about. We must look after it until it's well. As it was our cat that injured it, that's the least we can do."

"Then let the cat look after it," Newton suggested.

Celia ignored this trite remark and busied herself in lining a plastic clothes-basket with one of Newton's woolen vests, an act of vandalism that roused his freely expressed wrath. Then she gingerly picked the creature up and laid it in this homemade nest. A second later and she was wringing her hands.

"Gosh, but it's cold. It's like ice. Do you think we ought to put a hot water bottle . . . ?"

"No, I don't," Newton roared. "I can't understand how you were able to touch it. Do you realize, it might have bitten you?"

"Nonsense. It looks so happy and content. I wouldn't mind betting it was someone's pet."

Newton shut himself in the back room he used as a study, and Celia, still consoling the creature with comforting words, carried the basket into the kitchen and deposited it near the fire. But what disturbed her was the fact it refused to accept any form of nourishment. She tried bread and milk, some of Tobias' cat food, a plate of cold lamb, some rice pudding left over from yesterday, and finally a quarter of a pound of smoked ham that had been purchased for Newton's tea—all to no avail. The creature ignored all offerings, but continued to stare up at Celia with possibly greater approval than before. Neither did it appear to want to sleep, but lay on Newton's woolen vest and watched its protector as she moved round the kitchen, and even sometimes peered over the basket when she moved out of sight.

"I'm awfully worried," she informed Newton at bedtime. "It hasn't eaten a thing and is wide awake. Do you think I ought to take it to a vet?"

"Wouldn't be a bad idea." Newton nodded. "A vet could put it to sleep in no time at all."

"You are a cruel, unfeeling beast."

"Perhaps I am. But that thing gives me the willies."

It was three o'clock in the morning when she entered his room. "Dad, wake up. It's gone."

He sat up, turned on the bedside light, then blinked.

"What! Who's gone?"

"It has. I went downstairs to see if it was all right, and the back door was open and it's gone."

"Good."

"But, Dad, listen. Don't go back to sleep. Who unlocked the back door?"

"That's a point." He sat up and scratched his head. "You can't have locked it."

"But I did, and I remember the little thing sat up and watched me. Honestly, would I go to bed and leave the back door wide open?"

Newton yawned. "Well, you're not suggesting that little horror is capable of manipulating a ruddy great rim lock, then turning the door handle? Though now I come to think of it . . ."

"I don't know what to suggest. All I know is, the door is open and the sweet little thing has gone."

"Well," Newton pounded his pillow. "Shut the door, lock it, and go back to bed."

"Suppose it wants to come in again?"

"It will be a very disappointed little horror."

Celia departed with much shaking of her head and Newton. grinned as he heard her calling from the back door: "Come boy . . . come . . . come." The answer she received was an expectant cry from Tobias, who assumed he was due for an early morning snack. Presently she remounted the stairs and Newton gave a sigh of relief when he heard her door shut.

Next morning she smiled sweetly at her father over the breakfast table and said: "He's come back."

Newton reached for the marmalade pot. "Has he! Who?"

"The little thing. There he was, perched on top of my wardrobe when I woke this morning."

"Indeed! How did he . . . it get in?"

"Through my window. I left it open."

There was a silence of some three-minute duration, then Newton began to frown.

"Look, I've been half-serious about all this up to now, but I've been thinking. There's something—I don't know—something unnatural about that damned thing. After all, we don't know what it is or where it came from. I'm of the opinion it escaped from a zoo or some private menagerie. Perhaps we ought to report . . ."

"No." Celia got up, her eyes blazing. "It's not doing you any harm. If it did escape from some zoo, I'm glad, and I'll be damned if I'll see you or anyone else take it back again."

"Now, see here," Newton pushed his chair back. "Don't use that tone to me. I'm not one of your pansy boyfriends. This happens to be my house, and if I say that miniature horror goes—it goes."

"And I'm telling you—it won't. I'm not a kid for you to order about."

They were interrupted by the sound of flapping wings; in the gradually increasing rustle of disturbed air, the winged creature flew into the kitchen, glided round the ceiling and finally settled on the table. There it sat with folded wings and looked at the two antagonists with gleaming eyes. Newton's anger drained away and was replaced by a feeling of utmost dread. There was no disregarding the look of intense pleasure on the minute face. The head was turning from side to side, the eyes raking each face as though to absorb the maximum satisfaction from the flushed features, while the tapered ears were pricked so as not to lose a fragment of angered sound. Newton put his thoughts into words.

"The damned thing is getting a kick out of us having a row."

"Don't be so silly."

"For Pete's sake, look at it. It's licking its lips. Just as though it had just eaten a good meal."

"It's pleased to see us."

Newton laughed like a man who is not amused.

"You can say that again. There's something weird about this."

He stopped short, let the sentence trail off into oblivion and kept his eyes on the grimacing creature. There was no avoiding the fact; it was unique. Moreover, the tiny face, the slender form and, above all, the exquisite blue eyes, were indescribably beautiful. He wondered why he had not realized this before. It was an evil beauty, combining the repellent fascination of a venomous snake and the sinuous charm of an infant beast of prey, but there was beauty. Or to be more accurate, an extreme prettiness. He felt a sudden, ridiculous urge—a well nigh overwhelming need—to stroke its head, to take it on to his lap and tickle its ears. He turned abruptly away and snapped: "Do what you like, but keep it out of my sight."

During the next few days it became apparent that something was missing from their normal relationship. Gone was the slightly mocking, affectionate comradeship that at times, though neither suspected, bordered on the flirtatious. Now there was politeness; words were marshaled with care, before being uttered. They were like two people walking through a gunpowder factory, knowing that a wrongly placed foot could cause a spark. Newton appeared to have forgotten about the existence of the creature, and Celia was careful never to mention it. Nevertheless, he was acutely alive to its continued presence in the house. Several times, when the kitchen door was open, he heard the strange twittering sound, and once, the rustle of air as it flew up the stairs. There was a terrible urge to go out and watch that slow, graceful flight, feast his eyes on the evil, pretty little face. But he continued to sit resolutely behind his typewriter, vainly trying to make his fingers cooperate with his brain. But the brain was not at all prepared to manufacture sentences, play with plots, create fictional drama, when the bizarre was in his own house. He decided to break through the barrier of suspicion and doubt which had come into being during the past few days.

"I'm going back to town," he announced one morning at breakfast. "I've finished work on the rough draft and I'd like my agent's advice before I go any further."

Celia said, "Oh!" and poured a fresh cup of coffee.

"What are your plans?" he enquired with a carefully casual air. "Would you like to drive up with me?"

"No, thanks. I'll stay on for a bit."

He felt a surge of irritation that threatened to sweep aside his carefully erected defense: Words bubbled to the surface of his mind and demanded release. But for a while he retained control.

"By yourself? It will be a bit lonely."

She shrugged and picked up a newspaper.

"I'll be all right."

Irritation blunted its sharp edge against his self-control and became a blast of anger.

"Don't be so damned silly. How the hell can you stay down here by yourself?"

"Easy. I'll lock the door and stop anyone coming in."

"Look." He slammed his cup down. "This place is meant to be a place where we get our breath back. We've been down here three weeks, and I think it's about time both of us got back into circulation. Haven't you got any work coming up?"

She shrugged again. "So so."

"What is that supposed to mean?"

"I intend to stay on."

"Why?" He shouted and sensed the flutter of wings, but the door was shut and his anger was clamouring for outlet. "You've never wanted to before. If you had someone with you, I would understand. Wait a minute . . . I've got it . . . you've got some man coming down. Just waiting until I'm out of the way."

"If I were, it's no business of yours." Her eyes were now blazing pools of hate. She was shouting, betraying signs of coarseness that shocked him, even while it reinforced his anger. "I don't have to ask your permission before I take a man to bed. If I invite an army down here, it's no damn business of yours. It's about time you remembered you're my father, not my husband . . ."

His hand swung out and struck her left cheek with such violence that she went hurling against the closed door. The door trembled, and from beyond came an excited twittering and the pulsating thud of wings on wood that strangely kept in time with his furious heartbeat. Lying there on the floor, she swore at him, using words he was not aware until that moment she even knew, and a lingering spark of reason made him spin round and run from the room. He flung open the front door and ran blindly to his car, anger warring with a submerged sense of intense danger. It was not until the car was roaring down the main road that he realized what that danger had been. In that moment of mad rage, when the thing had beaten the door with its wings, he—Newton C. Hatfield—had been but a heartbeat away from murdering his daughter.

Newton spent the remainder of the day in the town flat.

He tried not to think, but thoughts scurried across his brain like marauding rats. Since the death of his wife some seven years before, the relationship between him and Celia had been one of almost perfect concord. Whatever disagreements they might have had were without rancor and soon forgotten. But now, on two occasions, there had been undiluted hate, and he had struck her, too. The only conclusion was that either they were both going mad or that horrible little monster was, in some inexplicable way, responsible. He remembered the look of joyful lust when they had quarrelled and the sound of beating wings as it tried to force its way through the door. But what was it? His imagination tried to explain an animal—but was it an animal?—that could stir up the basic instincts, and then—he dared to face the implication—draw strength from the resulting storm. Now, safe in the heart of London, the idea was fantastic; it scarcely merited consideration, but every argument that he presented to refute it was destroyed by the facts as he remembered them. He now went a little farther down the path of forbidden knowledge. If—whatever the thing was—drew strength from the black silt that lies at the very bottom of human nature, then it surely followed that he and Celia had been—feeding it. And, as everyone should know, the end result of feeding is *growth*. Having given this conclusion his full consideration, Newton tore downstairs, jumped into his car and drove back the way he had come.

*   *   *

Newton stopped the car and looked down upon the cottage and the great army of trees that stood in the background. The moon lit up the countryside and made every object stand out as though it were a figure freshly painted on a canvas. He was struck by the stillness, the complete absence of sound, and it seemed to his by now fevered imagination that he had somehow strayed into a plane that was either a little above or some way below that of normal existence. There was a dreamlike quality about the scene laid out before him: the motionless trees, the solitary cottage with its gleaming windows that resembled four watching eyes, and the grey ribbon that was the road, which looked as if it had never known the tread of solid foot or the hum of revolving car wheel. But suddenly, as though in mockery of his fanciful supposition, there was movement. The right hand casement—Celia's bedroom—opened, and a black shape slowly emerged into the moonlight. It perched on the windowsill for a full minute, then, opening black wings, rose gracefully into the air. Newton felt the horror slide down into his stomach like a lump of black ice. The flying creature circled the cottage, then began to flap slowly towards the forest, but before it was lost in a sea of shadow, the moon highlighted it for an awful moment, so that every feature stood out in stark relief. They were all perfectly recognizable: the narrow head with its pointed ears and mane of black hair, the slender body, the wide-spread wings—but there was a terrible difference. It had *grown*. At least three feet from wingtip to wingtip, and possibly thirty inches from crown of head to rear, and the tail was coiled up between the hind legs. Newton made a sound that was midway between a shout and a scream as he pressed the self-starter, then drove swiftly down the hill and screeched to a halt before the front door.

The hall was empty, save for the lingering ghosts of

sated fear: the living room was a deserted battlefield, where overturned furniture lay like the dead of a defeated army: On the stairs he found a piece of torn dress, and three steps up, a discarded shoe. Celia's bedroom door was open, and beyond was the gaping window, with a tattered nylon curtain hanging limply like the wedding veil of a violated bride. She was lying across the bed, the clothes ripped from her body, deep scratches disfiguring her face and white skin. When Newton, crying like a child who has come to understand the meaning of darkness for the first time, leaned over her, she opened her eyes and murmured sleepily: "It is growing up."

They argued long into the night. Newton shouted, threatened, walked out several times, but he always came back. Finally he begged.

"Come away. You can't . . . no one can stay in this place. Please listen to me."

The angry scratches were fading from her face and arms, and that in itself was a matter of fearful concern. But worse was Celia's smile, her cool refusal to discuss what had happened and her emphatically stated intention not to leave the cottage.

"You go," she said. "We don't want you. You're much too goody-goody."

"For heaven's sake," he stared at her with alarmed eyes. "What have you become, girl?"

For a moment she looked wistful, almost sad; then she smiled. "I thought I knew what I was. Now . . ." She shrugged. "Now I know I was wrong."

"That thing—" He jerked his head towards the window. "It is beast; more, it's evil."

"Don't play with words." She moved to the window and stood looking up at the moon bright sky. "It is the seed from which we sprang. As the coal is to the fire, so

that is to man. What is evil anyway? Don't you realize it is
the anagram of *live?*''

"It is also the anagram for *vile,*" he retorted. "You . . .
you are sick. Please believe me, you must come away
now. Don't even wait to pack a bag. Just jump in the car
and we'll be off.''

Her smile was scornful and suddenly he was afraid of
his daughter.

"You haven't got the message yet, have you? Don't you
realize wherever we go, it will follow us? There is a bond
that can never be broken.''

"Tell me," he pleaded. "What the hell is—*It?*"

She shook her head. "It is so hard to explain, and I
can't communicate very clearly—yet. There's no voice in
our sense of the word. It talks to me in my head. But I
have been promised power. Unlimited success. To someone
who has always been on the losing end, that's really
something. I suppose a few centuries ago I would have
been burnt at the stake.''

And she began to laugh as the moonlight turned her hair
to silver-gold, and it seemed to the horrified father that he
was listening to the laughing child of long ago.

During the days that followed Newton watched his daughter with terror-inflamed anxiety, and never did he dare ask
the question that haunted his waking and sleeping life. Where
was it?

Whenever he ventured into the kitchen, it was not there.
Or in the living room. He had not the courage to go out at
night and watch Celia's bedroom window, and no sound
now came to disturb the long, dark hours, but he knew it
was still nearby. Tobias no longer brought his prey home,
but seemed content to sit by the window, curiously alert to
every sound and apparently watching something or someone that was not visible to Newton's eyes.

Celia appeared to have forgotten that there had ever been cause for friction between them and treated her father to the old bantering good humour that disturbed him more than the former bad temper. She had revealed to him a face that had undergone a terrible change, and now that the veil had been resumed, he could only guess at what further deterioration had taken place. But he began to listen and watch for any clues as to the creature's whereabouts and habits. One evening he was rewarded.

"I left my handbag upstairs," Celia exclaimed.

"I'm going up." Newton waited for the angry refusal. "Would you like me to fetch it?"

She smiled sweetly. "Thank you. You're a pet."

Her bedroom was bathed in moonlight; the window was open and he detected a faint musty aroma. Two of his questions were answered. The thing spent the day in Celia's bedroom, and it flew by night.

Next day what could have been further information came from another source. Celia left him alone in the house and an hour later returned with a bundle of newspapers and magazines. Newton, for want of something better to do—his work was sadly neglected these days—seized a copy of the *Daily Mail* and began to skim through it. The possible information was on page four. A little paragraph in the right-hand bottom corner of the page.

MYSTERIOUS BIRD

Several eyewitnesses have reported seeing a strange and very large bird in the vicinity of Clavering in Kent. Descriptions vary from "a batlike creature with pointed ears and a vast wingspan," to "something resembling a giant crow."

Reliable sources think it likely this is some form

of freak bat, particularly as it is only reported to have been seen at night.

The other item had possibly no connection with the thing that flew by night at all, but it still afforded Newton some further disquiet.

RISING CRIME WAVE IN KENT

There has been an unexpected outbreak of crimes against persons in Kent during the past few days. Several cases of robbery with violence, rape and one attempted murder have come to the attention of the police. All have been committed by people who have, up to now, led seemingly blameless lives.

Chief-Superintendent Hargraves, of the Kent Constabulary, said in a statement last nig'
"Television and films depicting violence have much to answer for . . ."

Newton put down the newspaper and forgot that there was a subject he must not mention.

"Celia, for God's sake, where . . . ?"

She turned on him savagely: "Shut up. Don't . . . don't . . ."

She broke off suddenly, then quickly regained control.

"Don't ask questions that I cannot answer."

Well aware that another outburst of mutual anger might mean the flutter of wings, Newton lapsed into silence. But a terrible resolution came slowly into being.

He allowed weeks to pass while the resolution grew into awful maturity, and during that time living with constant fear became a natural state of existence. It was then he realized that hell could not be such a dreadful place, because in time, the damned soul would get used to it. Cold dread entered his bed and became a sleeping partner; nagging anxiety robbed him of appetite; black terror came out of the past and pointed a skeleton finger towards the future. But at the same time his brain, well trained in the art of manufacturing plots, creating problems that must be solved, devised a plan that was based on cool reason.

The thing—whatever its original state—was solid: There must be a form of flesh which coated a framework of some matter that was akin to bone. Therefore, it followed the creature—now a title, an easily recognizable name, began to frequently cross his crowded brain: Fly-by-Night—could be destroyed. Perhaps it would quickly recover from wounds; it might well be beyond his strength to inflict any kind of damage, but there was an element that no solid creature could resist. Fire. The resolution mated with the plan and became an operation.

So that his precious stock of courage should not be reduced by sights and sounds, he deliberately did not look out of the window once the sun had set, and he plugged his ears with cotton wool after retiring to bed. Then, when the moon had begun to wane, he went into purposeful action.

Eight sleeping pills powdered and mixed with cocoa made a near lethal drink, but the situation demanded drastic measures. He watched Celia sip from the earthenware mug, then trembled when she put it down with freely expressed disgust.

"Horrible!" She wiped her mouth, then glared at him with sudden suspicion. "What the hell did you put in it?"

He got up and moved towards her, grimly determined that nothing should delay or impede his great plan.

"Drink it," he growled, and she shrank back, for he was now like any animal that has been driven into a corner. "Drink it."

"No." She shook her head wildly. "No, I'll not let you do . . ."

"Damn you, drink it."

He grabbed her and, made brutal by his great rage, flung the slender form on to the sofa, where it lay with staring eyes and gaping mouth. Then Newton took up the mug. He gripped her lower jaw with one hand while he poured the liquid down her throat with the other. Then he stepped back and waited.

"You fool." She was ugly now; her face twisted up into a mask of hate, her brown-smirched mouth spitting out words. He knew if he had not killed her body, he had at least slain any regard she might still have retained for him. But it was not important—not now. "You can't fight him. Whatever you do, he can't lose. Get that into your sanctimonious head. You cannot possibly win."

"I can try," he said softly. "My soul would be damned if I did not try."

"Your soul!" She laughed. A loud, harsh sound that crashed across the room and went echoing round the house. "What makes you think you've got a soul? A speck of awareness: an atom of intelligence, which will never withstand the shock of death. Immortality is only for the brave."

Still he waited, and presently he saw her eyelids droop, while her tongue released words that had drifted from a mist-shrouded brain.

"My love flies in on the night wind . . . his breath is fear . . . he speaks with the voice of desire . . ."

The voice trailed off; the words died; Celia slept and Newton was now free to prepare for the coming battle.

From the kitchen dresser he produced a gimlet, screwdriver and a bag of three-inch screws. He then went upstairs and entered Celia's bedroom, where he sought for fresh signs of the creature's tenancy. They were not hard to find. On the floor, by the right-hand side of the bed, was a thick eiderdown and a pillow. On the dressing table stood a bowl of greyish water and, of all things, a razor and a tube of shaving cream. Somehow, this commonplace evidence of personal hygiene seemed both horrifying and obscene. The thought of that creature (and oh, my God, how it must have grown) scraping the bristles from its face made Newton feel sick. And hard on the trail of that discovery came another—it was imitating the habits of man. Blindly perhaps, for no other reason than this was one of the customs of the air-breathers.

The casement window was wide open, and beyond, the moon looked down on sleeping countryside. Newton closed it; then setting to work with his gimlet, he drilled holes in window and frame before inserting his screws. When he had finished, the room was sealed up and only by breaking the glass would the creature enter. As an afterthought, inspired more by hope than judgment, he drew a large red cross with Celia's lipstick on each windowpane. It took him three hours to screw up every window in the cottage, and during all that time he kept looking up at the steel blue sky.

Locking both the back and front doors, he went over to the small garden shed and there prepared the firetrap. It was simple and, he hoped, effective. A mixture of paraffin, creosote and petrol was sprinkled over walls, a pile of dead wood, and placed in cans, bucket and a small barrel. After making a torch from a length of thick wood and padding one end with paraffin soaked rags, he sat down on the garden seat and waited.

The night was so beautiful: The sky was at peace and was a perfect setting for the crystal moon and the cold star-diamonds that spread out into infinity. He had a ridiculous feeling that he was the focal point for a billion eyes—a miserable biological specimen that was under a

mighty multi-galaxy microscope and was now being watched
to see how he would react in the coming battle.

Tobias came ambling across the garden and rubbed his
body against Newton's legs. He picked the cat up and
deposited it on his lap, where it purred loudly, then settled
down for a short sleep. Newton grinned ruefully when he
remembered that Tobias was the innocent reason for him
sitting here in the small hours, with his daughter drugged
in a locked house and the garden shed full of inflammable
material waiting for a match.

The first pale fingers of dawn were clawing the eastern
sky when Newton stiffened and then gently lowered Tobias
to the ground. A large black shape was slowly flying out
from the shadows cast by the trees. It circled the house,
and as the monstrous shape passed overhead, Newton
gasped when he realized the extent to which it had grown.
Even allowing for the bent hind legs, it must be all of five
feet tall, and what was even more alarming, the wingspan
was almost as wide. Gripping the unlighted torch in his
right hand, Newton edged his way round the house, being
careful to keep well within the shadow, and watched the
creature's flight with fearful anxiety. What would be its
reaction when it realized that the house was sealed up?
There was always the possibility that it might break the
glass and, once inside, his plan would be frustrated.

After circling the house three times, the winged shape
sank down and glided towards Celia's window, where it
hovered while the wings flapped with intense rapidity. The
ensuing shriek made Newton cringe against the wall, for it
was a cry of baffled rage: an almost frantic scream of
disbelief. Two long, thin arms emerged from behind the
pounding wings, and a pair of taloned hands pawed the
moon-bright windowpanes where the red crosses gleamed
like blood streaks.

The shriek was terminated by a hoarse cry, and the

creature, as though it had been electrocuted, fell heavily to the ground. There it crouched while, the wings half-folded, it examined its hands while twittering with pain or rage. Then it hopped up and down and blew on the extended claws like a schoolboy who has been caned. Newton dared to move a few paces nearer, still hugging the wall, but when he came to the corner of the house, the protecting shadow abruptly terminated and one more step would have brought him out into the full moonlight.

He stepped back and the heel of his shoe clicked against the wall. Instantly the creature became still—changed from a hopping monstrosity to a black frozen statue. Suddenly the head jerked round and Newton was staring at the sinister, pretty face, the exquisite blue eyes and the out-stretched claws. He knew it could see him, but there was a completely silly thought that if he kept perfectly still, it would forget all about him. The clawlike feet moved apart and it was bounding towards him like a giant winged-bullfrog. The hind legs acted as springs, the half-folded wings as stabilizers, and doubtless behind the blue eyes lurked something that did service for a brain. Newton for a while forgot his plan, ignored the dictates of reason that stated now was the time to make a stand; instead, he surrendered to a blast of pure terror, turned on his heel and ran.

From little horrors, mighty monsters grow. Such was the impromptu thought that went with him as he ran. If only he had crushed the little thing that Tobias had brought home, now he would not have been running from something that leaped like a frog and twittered like an overgrown sparrow. A flapping sound told him the Fly-by-Night had taken to the air and the attack would come from above. His foot became entangled with a root and he went sprawling on the ground, where he lay waiting for the end. A minute, perhaps more, passed; then he ventured to look up. The creature was flying in rapidly decreasing circles, and it was in obvious distress. It made a strangled cry, then dropped a few feet, rather like an aeroplane that has hit an air pocket, and it took Newton some while before he realized the reason. The first golden spears from the rising sun were gliding across the clear sky. At once fear receded before a wave of new hope: The Fly-by-Night was a thing of darkness; it did not like light. It would be ridiculous to suppose that, like the legendary vampire, this monster would disintegrate with the rising sun, but it was uncomfortable and had a problem that could only be solved by finding shelter in a very short time. The house was sealed up; on the other hand, the garden shed was waiting—its door wide open. Newton fumbled in his pocket, found his cigarette lighter, then lit the torch.

The Fly-by-Night came down for a bumpy landing. It dropped the last two feet and rolled over while emitting a series of hoarse shrieks that made the newly awakened birds in the nearest trees rise up on fluttering wings. It regained an upright position and began to leap towards the house, presumably still instinctively regarding this as a natural place of protection. Newton ran forward and, with courage he did not suspect until that moment he possessed, stood in its path waving his flaming torch while moving slowly forward.

The Fly-by-Night, confronted in mid-leap by what it most feared, fell over, and Newton took advantage of the situation by thrusting his torch directly into the grimacing face. An ear-splitting shriek and it was flapping, creeping, lurching across the ground, oblivious of the growing light of day, fired only by the need to escape from the searing flames. Newton guided his quarry into the desired path by waving the torch to left and right, until the open shed door was in the creature's line of vision. It managed to fly the last few yards, a kind of flapping run; then it disappeared through the opening, and Newton, his courage by now dangerously low, flung the torch onto the pile of oil-soaked wood and closed the door. He hastily fastened the padlock, then ran towards the house.

There was first a roar, than an explosion, and when he looked back, the shed was one gigantic flame. Such a fire would have gladdened the heart of an arsonist; it crackled, sizzled, spat out little gobbets of spluttering flame and reached upwards, as though to lick the stars, with yellow- and blue-edged tongues of flame. The roof fell in; the walls collapsed, and presently flame gave way to grey-black smoke and it was all over. When Newton at length walked slowly over to the smouldering ruins, there was nothing to see but grey ash, charred wood and a few pieces of twisted iron.

Then he broke down and cried.

It was late afternoon before Celia awoke. She did not speak until her father had prepared a cup of sweetened tea and a few slices of hot buttered toast; then she asked: "What have you done with—with him?"

"Don't talk about it now," he pleaded. "Wait until you are more yourself."

She smiled. "I will never be more myself than I am now. What have you done with him?"

"I—" He paused, then for better or worse, announced boldly: "I burnt it. I burnt it in the garden shed."

Celia daintily sipped her tea, then put the cup down. She nibbled the toast and, after waiting until her mouth was empty, said simply, "I see."

He was at first puzzled, then encouraged by her calm acceptance of the news. Hope came to him.

"It's all over now," he said. "That creature is utterly destroyed and can never influence you again. Now we will begin to forget."

She took another bite of toast and shook her head.

"No, we won't."

He knelt down by her chair and took her disengaged hand in his.

"Darling, you must try to understand. The creature has gone—burnt to a cinder—nothing remains."

She finished her slice of toast, wiped a butter-smeared mouth on the back of her hand. Then she smiled again.

"Yes it does."

"Celia, dear, please listen . . ."

She giggled and tilted her chin with the tips of her cool fingers.

"You listen, daddikins. They will grow very fast and very big."

He brushed her hand to one side, then stood up.

"What will?"

Laughter clogged her throat, made her eyes water, but somehow the words came bubbling out.

"His . . . his children. The ones I'm going to have any minute now."

Where do you go when you die? For believers, it's an easy question. For nonbelievers, it's an easy question. But where do you go when you don't die?

Thomas Sullivan is a midwestern writer who, like many others in dark fantasy, teaches English. This is his first publication, and it won't be his last.

THE EXTENSION

Thomas Sullivan

It rang and rang. The old house fairly echoed with it. And even after it stopped, a fraud of sound like a scream poured through the room.

The master was calling.

But there was no one home to answer. The cook had left immediately after the wake and the housekeeper the next day. A bottle of milk was souring in the chute, and the mantel clock had at last reached equilibrium after sixteen years of relentless posting. It was 1928. Time itself seemed caught in that house, as if the lightning and the thunder had driven it inside to be stilled by the clock.

The master could hear the thunder, too. Out in the backyard. It crackled in the receiver and shook his tomb.

"For God's sake, help me!" he cried in a voice hot with panic.

And the operator answered: "Number, please."

"I need help . . . I'm trapped." This against the thunder.

"I beg your pardon, sir; did you say you were 'trapped'?"

"Yes. Trapped. Yes!"

"Where are you?"

"I'm . . ."—static in the line—". . . coffin."

"Sir."

"I said I'm in my coffin! I called my wife, but she's not home. She was supposed to be; they were all supposed to be for a week after I died—" More crackling in the line.

Then the operator said, wearily, "Yes, sir."

"Listen; listen to me. My name is Frederick French. I live on Sheridan and Fifth—the house with the big mausoleum in back. I'm in that mausoleum now and—*oh, God, are you listening to me?*"

Thunder.

"You said you were in your coffin before."

"Yes, that's right—"

"I really don't appreciate this sort of humor at all, you know."

"Oh, no, no, I swear on my immortal soul—" Thunder again, and this time when it coiled away, the voice from the mausoleum was in tears. "Please . . . I can't stand this much longer. Don't you understand . . . I'm inside my coffin!"

"With a telephone?"

"Yes!"

"Say, did someone put you up to this?"

"Oh, God . . ." He was moaning in terror now.

"I don't like this, mister. You sound creepy. I guess I know people don't get buried with telephones, but you sound awful creepy. You know what your trouble is?"

"It's a special phone. It runs to the house—"

"Your trouble is you've got a warped sense of humor."

"*Help me*," he husked.

"We have our instructions, sir," squirmed at him like a handful of worms.

And the line went dead.

He was sinking in a quicksand of silk, but he had enough presence of mind to slow down, to think it out. The thing he had feared most in his mortal life had come to pass—though the phone was in the coffin with him, and they hadn't embalmed him, and there was enough air to make his calls, if he kept calm. Only, where was Doris? How could his wife not be home? She knew about his seizures; she should be waiting for his call. Unless the doctors had convinced her it was pointless . . . or she couldn't bear to stay in the old house alone.

Clutching the thin neck of the phone, he hooked his finger awkwardly over the base and dialed.

The voice that squirmed like worms said: "Operator."

"Get me the police."

"You again."

"Get me the police!"

"There's no one at the station this hour, mister. Why don't you call it a night?"

"This is an emergency. You must have a number; wake someone up!"

"I know all about your emergency, sir, and I'm not going to roust Chief Miller out for it."

"You have no right to judge me."

"Sir—"

"An emergency. This is an emergency."

"Sir—"

"I've been buried alive!"

"We have our instructions, sir." And she hung up.

He had the feeling now that each time the phone went dead, it stopped the flow of air in the coffin, because the silk seemed to rise around him a little more and his breath fell back on his face like a web. He had never known such darkness, darkness so complete that the mind went out to wander in it.

"Doris!" he screamed.

He needed to protest, needed a witness to the unfairness of fate. She had always been his witness.

"Doris . . ." he whimpered and suddenly resumed dialing.

Random numbers this time. There was a whole living world literally at his fingertips. No need for insecure operators and sleeping guardians of the people.

"Hello."

"He—hello . . . with whom am I speaking, please?"

"Johnson's residence."

"Hello . . . hello, Mr. Johnson, my name—"

"I'm not Mr. Johnson. You wanta talk to Johnson, just a minute."

In the background: "Al, for you."

"Who is it?"

"Some guy."

Pause.

"Hello."

"Al? How are you, Al?" The tremor provoked a keen silence on the other end. "Listen, Mr. Johnson, you don't know me. My name is Frederick French. I own the brick colonial on Sheridan and Fifth . . . the big one? With the iron fence?"

"What do you want, Mr. French?"

"Have you ever heard of catalepsy?"

"You sound funny, French. All wheezy and muffled. You have trouble breathing or something?"

"Yes, yes, as a matter of fact."

"You want an ambulance or something?"

"Something . . . yes. Actually, I'm trapped. I need someone to get me out."

"Out of what?"

"A mausoleum." He said it quickly, mumbled it, as if it were the most common thing in the world.

Long silence. "A mausoleum, you said?"

"Yes. A family mausoleum in back of the house. You must have seen it."

"And you're inside. With a phone."

"That's right, Mr. Johnson. I had the phone installed because of my seizures. It's not all that uncommon—wasn't all that uncommon in the nineteenth century, before embalming practices changed. Grave alarms of all types were popular—"

"Eddie! Eddie, you son-of-a-gun!"

"Eddie?"

"Don't play innocent, Eddie. Jeez, you had me going!"

"No, no, no!"

"Come get you out of a mausoleum! Yeah, Eddie."

"I swear to you—"

"*Seizures!* Oh, that's jake—"

"*I'm not Eddie, damn you! I'm Frederick French! And I'm suffocating, you hear me? Do you hear me?*"

"Hey!" Judgmental pause. "Enough's enough."

"I'm not Eddie," French gasped.

"Okay. But whoever you are, you got a screw loose, mister."

And then he sank a little more into the silk and his

breath fell back on his face like a web, because the line was dead again.

There are darknesses you enter like an ether and darknesses that form walls. Frederick French knew the difference now. His mind had briefly wandered this one, a foretaste of death, but the dying yet remained, and the closeness of the walls provoked a sudden tirade. The sweaty earpiece popped from his ear with a vacuum lisp as he kicked and twisted. He clawed and pushed his elbows against the silken sides of the coffin while the cords of his neck swelled. And when his atrophied muscles were spent, he began to scream, screaming until the coffin resonated and turned red with sound and he was temporarily deaf. Then he lay very still.

Still as death.

Thunder broke the equilibrium. He had no idea how long he had lain still, not hearing, not thinking. But his head ached and his muscles threatened to seize up at the slightest strain. The phone was alongside his leg and the earpiece by his ankle. He couldn't reach it.

When he realized that, he shut everything out again. The next time he came around, rain was hissing over the mausoleum, rain that seemed to make his flesh wetter there inside the coffin. It made the silk he had shredded with his fingernails on the underside of the lid stick to his face. There was nothing left but the phone, he understood now, that and slowly dying.

Shrugging one shoulder, he groped down as far as he could on the other side. But the phone remained out of reach. He tugged on his pantleg, jiggled his knee. That only made the instrument lodge deeper into the crevice alongside his leg. He flipped his foot, but the earpiece wound around his shoe. A drop of sweat rolled slowly down his cheek. Then it stopped. Then it rolled back up again and onto his lip. He spat furiously and threw his head from side to side. It was a spider!

He was deathly afraid of spiders.

Afraid. Fear was already at its quota.

There would be other spiders. Coming through the air tube at the foot of the coffin. Crawling all over him. Little, venomous spiders. Large, hairy spiders. Scores of them. Crawling silently . . . so many legs, drumming over his body. And then he was thrashing again in another fit of rebellion, and the phone moved suddenly into his hands, and he was dialing furiously.

"Hello." A woman's voice. *Hello*. Why not leave it at that? A note of hope. Rain tingled over the mausoleum like the febrile drumming of thousands of tiny legs.

"Hello," he answered in a pale whisper.

"Who is this?"

"My name is Frederick French. If I tell you where I am, I'm afraid you'll hang up."

Static crackled over the line.

"What do you want?"

"I need help."

"Why don't you call the police?"

"I don't know their number."

"Then call the operator."

"Listen. I want to call my niece. But I can't look her up. I need someone to look her up for me. Her name is Anne Fairchild."

"Who?"

"Fairchild," he croaked.

"How do you spell it?"

"F-A-I-R-C-H-I-L-D."

He heard the thrum of pages. She read him the number. And hung up.

The closing of the open line was like a hand on his

throat. He felt his ability to speak wither as he began to count over the dial. Five rings, six—

"Yeah?" Muffled.

She was drunk. He knew it as surely as if he smelled her breath.

"Anne," he gasped hoarsely. "It's Uncle Fred."

"My Uncle Fred's dead." She said it thickly.

"I was buried alive, Anne. For God's sake, I have seizures, you know that."

She said something else then, but it was unintelligible, and the momentary clarity that had brought her to the phone was fading.

"If you don't help me, I'm going to die, Anne."

"Diane? Go ahead and go to her. What the hell do I care?"

Sick, guttural laughter fluttered deep in his dried throat when she hung up. The sides of the casket shook with triumphant thunder, and he could see himself as he was— hair snow white, unseeing eyes starting from his head—as if lightning had illuminated his mind.

He dialed again.

And again.

And again and again.

There was an old lady, nearly deaf; a sleepy man who wanted to beat him up; another who spoke broken English; a child; busy signals; endless ringing; rude warbles. Breathing was an agony, and his pulse thudded in the coffin, but he was still alive. Unbelievably, he was still alive.

Unbelievably.

He dialed the operator.

"Hello, may I assist you?" Same operator.

"You know who I am, don't you?"

"Sir?"

"What happens," he wheezed slowly, "when the phone bill isn't paid?"

"Would you like me to check on your bill, sir?"

"*What happens, damn it?* Do I get disconnected?"

"Have you received a notice, sir?"

"You've got me in the middle of the stream, halfway from either shore . . ."

"If you've received a notice from the phone company, we'll be glad to set up terms—"

"But this *isn't* the phone company."

Silence.

". . . And you're going to keep this up."

"If you're having trouble, sir, arrangements can be made to maintain our service indefinitely."

Indefinitely.

Absolutely hellish. Because he would have to go on trying. Even though he knew better, he would have to go on trying. And here and there a phone would ring in the middle of the town in the middle of the night . . . forever.

The most tiresome question a writer hears attempts to determine where the ideas for the stories come from, especially when those ideas deal in dark fantasy. There are two answers—the real one would bore people to tears, and saying that one has a direct line to midnight isn't always clear, until it's too late.

Julie Stevens, who lives in Oregon, has appeared in OMNI, ISAAC ASIMOV'S SCIENCE FICTION MAGAZINE, and in FEARS.

THE SACRIFICE

Julie Stevens

He is writing a mountain. The air is so thin our words come in short spurts and we stop and take deep breaths long before we get to the end of any sentence. The threat of avalanche is ever-present and we cling to a tiny iced ledge, planning carefully our next moves. Our faces hurt and, worse, our fingers don't, and we are frightened that we have risked frostbite once too often. But the exhilaration! How to explain that the pain and the numbness and the pervasive fear are nothing compared to the other emotions we are feeling now? I look to the man and he has his head thrown back and his eyes are closed, and I know he is savoring the sensation, even now putting it into words which will find their way into stories which may or may not become a novel, which will almost certainly bring him new acclaim.

Now, I think to myself. Now is the time!

The knots slip, or the pins don't hold, or perhaps the ledge breaks loose under our weight. The exhilaration gives way to terror. He didn't mean to write this! He fights back with words, clings desperately to the ledge, willing himself to hold on and, thereby, to live. Does he remember that I am here? Has he spared me a single thought?

Consider J. Alasdair Courtney. The initial stands for James, in itself a fine name, but one given to diminutives such as Jim or Jamie, which are not at all Alasdair's style. You can guess from this example that Alasdair is a bit on the conceited side. It's hard not to be when one has been hailed as the literary beacon of the twentieth century, and conceit is no handicap in the circles in which Alasdair moves. He is greatly admired here in New York, admired for his writing, for the way he holds his liquor despite prodigious consumption, and for his devotion to Poor Madeline Courtney.

Capitalize the P in Poor because it's been years since anyone has spoken Mrs. Courtney's name without calling her Poormadeline. She *is* poor in a physical sense, as an object of pity. But monetarily it is quite the opposite. Alasdair may have been born without money or impressive credentials, but he is not so foolish as to believe that starving artists are, as a matter of right, superior to clever artists who have the foresight to marry well.

He writes each weekday morning in longhand on yellow legal pads, which work he then types out after lunch. He has abandoned the mountain, frightened away by the stink of terror. He begins again, this time near an ocean cove on an Oregon beach he found in a back issue of *National Geographic*. This is a winter beach, beset by high winds and violent tides, where driftwood crashes against wave-racked bluffs. There are no swimsuits here, no sophisticated martini sunsets. The man walks along the wet and pebbled sand. He tries not to catch up with the woman ahead of him, though the writer that directs his every move brings them inexorably closer. His hair is black and wind-tangled, fanning out over the collar of the khaki jacket. She moves to the right, toward the water, and the man follows. He continues to follow even as she strides into the surf. The waves sweep past him, raising the water level to his knees but soaking him to the thighs, and still he keeps walking. A particularly large wave is forming ahead of him. The fabled ninth wave, perhaps? Or is that the seventh? The woman knows, he is certain, but he knows, too, not to ask her.

As the water strikes, he stands rock-solid against it, exulting in the pull of the undertow as it sucks the sand around his boots. He is facing nature, daring her to bring him down, and he is glorying in the contest.

I wait for an appropriate moment to take the pencil.

A small eddy around his ankles, a touch of the vacuum at his heels, and he is on his knees, then on his face in the water, gasping for breath and flailing his arms, his joy lost in the reality of drowning. The writer struggles for him. *Breathe!* he wills his creation. *Find your footing. Hold nature at bay.* And what of the woman who has led them here? I am still present, but he has long forgotten. It does not occur to him that I am important.

Madeline Louise DuPre was something of an anachronism even for those postwar, prefeminist times. She had little concept of self. Hers is a family whose riches go back many generations and whose only occupation is the full-time job of philanthropy. Her father chaired the DuPre Foundation, while her uncles served on the worthiest of charitable boards. Her mother raised her to know both her place and her duty. Madeline took on the task of "good works" the way she approached any other moral obligation— she bared her soul to it. It was not surprising, then, that she should enter romance in the same manner. She had talent of her own, creativity over and above her selflessness, but no one was ever to know. So captivated was she by the genius of J. Alasdair Courtney that she completely subordinated her desires to his. He found this admirable, especially when embodied in the lovely and wealthy Miss DuPre, and thus rewarded her devotion with marriage. While he finished his graduate studies at Columbia and communed with New York literati, Madeline decorated their West Side apartment to suit his needs and threw midnight soirees that only appeared to be the spontaneous gatherings of kindred souls. Alasdair knew what a treasure he had, and lost no opportunity to sing her praises. He had written well before he met her, but with Madeline at his back, he produced work possessing new depth and compassion. He was becoming the writer he had always wanted to be.

His first novel was published to critical acclaim and modest success the year he accepted a teaching fellowship at a midwestern university. "I am moving my muse to Michigan," he proclaimed, amused at the alliteration. And while he was there, his muse thrived.

Is it possible to explain what it is about his writing that so excites the critics? Perhaps I could compare it to a painting, though that makes for a deceiving analogy. He does paint, with blank pages for canvas. But more than that, he can draw the reader into those pages in a way that few have equaled. One starts a paragraph and becomes immersed, unable to respond to the outside world. The events are so real, the emotions so intense, that upon closing a book by Alasdair, the reader is off-balance upon discovering that it was only fiction. The dullest of readers find their imaginations conjuring worlds to fit Alasdair's descriptions, and even his most scholarly critics cannot describe just how he does it.

Did Madeline know? I think not, but it is impossible to guess. She sits in the recliner chair, her face slack and her eyes blank. A succession of private nurses attend to her needs. If she once knew, she no longer has the wit to reveal it.

Madeline's decline began in Michigan, or at least it became noticeable there. She was as charming as ever, but she had curious lapses of memory. She talked more frequently about the invisible friends she had fabricated in childhood. Alasdair was engrossed in the first volume of what would become his Brentwood trilogy and could not or would not help. As Madeline's behavior became more bizarre, he began keeping later and later hours. Several times, he didn't bother to come home at all. Madeline never complained, but neither did she get any better.

Some people find it odd that none of Alasdair's books or short stories deal with death. There is despair aplenty, and hopelessness, and a great deal of anger. *The New York Review of Books* ran an analysis pointing up this lapse and opined that given the intensity of his prose and the emotions it evoked in his readership, it was good that none of his characters died, for one might then expect readers to find themselves drawn into the death and unable to find a way out.

What, I wonder, will the reviewers make of Alasdair's next book? For it will confront death; I have made that my goal. He avoids death, writes pages around it, but I bring him back to the edge. He calls out to Madeline in his dreams; he drinks to forget. How can she help him? She is confined by the bed and the recliner and the wheelchair.

Madeline would help him if she could, I think. It is in her nature. He doesn't always understand that. Sometimes he thinks she is the source of his inspiration, and his pain. It is true that as his writing has gotten stronger, Madeline's health has deteriorated. He sees the connection, but he draws the wrong conclusions.

He will stay with an ocean scene, but he changes the locale. Now the man is on a gentler coast, with coarse white sand and blue-green water and postcard vistas in the distance. Perhaps this will be a romance—Alasdair does them quite well. He writes in a companion for the man. She has black hair, as do most of the women he writes. Madeline once had black hair. There are traces of it still in her thin grayed locks. The woman is swimming, and she is smiling. The man is entranced and scarcely notices as he scrapes his heels against the broken coral.

Blood poisoning, I think. Slower, not as exciting, but he is less likely to notice before it is too late. I see now where I made my mistake in the past—he wants the sensation of death approaching, but when he feels it, he knows I am near. He knows to be wary.

Ah, Madeline, every word he writes is one he believes he is taking from your very being. He knows you were aware of his indiscretions, as of course you were. He imagines that you blame him, as well you should. He knows you never asked for anything on your own behalf except to please him, and he let you because it was so easy. Worst of all, he knows it would do no good to go back and relive it because the work he produced inspires awe even in its author and he cannot relinquish that power.

Such nonsense! Even in his guilt, the man is a fool. Madeline has a simple, incurable, wasting disease. It has a long medical name that need not concern us, and she has carried the genetic predisposition since birth. One of her uncles had died from it, and her youngest brother is even now exhibiting the symptoms. There is much for which to blame Alasdair, but this is the least of it.

Observe J. Alasdair Courtney in his New York apartment, at work in the alcove overlooking Central Park. He is writing swiftly, enveloped in his creations, uneasily certain that he takes his muse from his long-suffering wife. The conceit of this is laughable—who is he to think that he has the power to take another's muse? He has his own, one that is silent and unassuming and not at all a match for me. For it was Madeline who gave me life, and Madeline to whom I have always been faithful. I never belonged to him, and if I have helped him, as I sometimes have, it was at the bidding of my sweet Maddie. She did indeed protect Alasdair, in ways he can never know, but she can't help him now, and if she never wanted vengeance upon him for his treatment of her, the same cannot be said for me.

The clichéd fine line between reality and whatever else there is does not, in the minds of those who draw that line, take into consideration the notion that reality never has had a decent definition. And at midnight, the line simply doesn't exist.

Dennis Etchison, hard on the heels of his best-selling collection THE DARK COUNTRY and of his World Fantasy Award, is preparing, with Scream Press, for the publication of his second— RED DREAMS. He is also in the process of completing a new novel.

Mark Johnson is an illustrator, cartoonist, and collector of movie memorabilia. He is a nostalgia buff.

THE SPOT

Dennis Etchison and Mark Johnson

The van crept up Elevado Way, its headlights stabbing like ice picks at the encroaching darkness.

Martin kicked at the debris on the floorboard, but the cans and paper bags were all empty; he tried to put the thought of food out of his mind. He rolled down the window and peered out at the old Spanish-style houses, at the sun as it disappeared like a tired eye behind the tops of the palm trees that rimmed the horizon of the city below.

"Better step on it, Rog," he said. "The Old Man doesn't like it when we get in after seven, remember?"

"I guess he doesn't have much of a choice, does he?" said Roger, bulldogging the wheels around a steep curve. "He gave us three buildings to do today—and overtime is overtime. We're the best team he's got, aren't we? If he doesn't like it we can always go back on unemployment, right, Jackie? Am I right?"

Martin leaned his chin on his hand and watched the flickering tile roofs, which glowed now with a deep ochre stain from the setting sun, as he kept track of the house numbers with one half-closed eye.

He was thinking of the time he and Kathy had bought a map to the stars' homes, that first week in California. Now he felt that he might be following the endless bifurcations of one of those same winding streets with pretentious, foreign-sounding names. The only thing they had found

116

that seemed alive that Sunday, however, was an old man with an Indian blanket over his legs, his wheelchair planted in the sun on the other side of an enormous lawn fronting a house that looked suspiciously like a misplaced Southern mansion. They hadn't got close enough to be sure, but he could not help wondering if there had been more to it than a false front, an old movie set installed around a modest house with a view, perhaps to improve the land value. They had waited there under a shade tree, eating their picnic lunch in the car, but the old man had never moved. For all they could tell, he might have been nothing more than a made-up skeleton set out as a prop on the too perfect grass.

Martin heard his stomach growl. He gave up. "Hey," he said, "you don't have any more of that Kentucky Fried Chicken stashed in back, do you, Rog?"

Roger glanced reflexively at the equipment in the rear of the van. "Aw, tighten your belt. We'll be able to cop something when we get inside—this neighbourhood's full of fat cats, I can tell. Anyway, I hear it's supposed to be good for people in our profession to stay a little bit hungry."

Martin recalled the rotten stench from the refrigerator in the last place they had cleaned, and shuddered.

Our profession, he thought. And what profession is that, Roger? If you do that sort of thing, you become that sort of animal, don't you, Rog?

He remembered to check the numbers. He blinked and turned his head, almost missing one.

"Hey, I think that was it," he said, and then Roger was downshifting and swinging around a gravel circle and braking with a noisy ratcheting in front of the Carlton Arms.

It was another of those buildings taped and glued together back in the fifties around an indeterminate number of cracker-box apartments, somehow always more than you would guess from the outside. Martin thought of the architects for these quiet horrors, all right-angles of powdering stucco and rust from hidden drain pipes, as the ballpoint-pen boys: They could be relied upon to make an infinite number of copies, but no originals.

The manager, a pale, nervous man who treated everyone as a potential process server, scrutinized the work order as they stood shifting their weight from foot to foot, as they studied their shoes and said nothing, and directed them at last to the elevator.

They passed an overweight housekeeper in a white uniform on her way out of the building. She picked her teeth and watched them suspiciously, as if they were in some strange way competitors. They ignored her and unloaded the west-and-dry vac, the buckets and mops and cart full of cleansers and disinfectants from the van, clattered it all through the garage and up to the third floor, to what were undoubtedly still described in rental ads as penthouse apartments.

The tenant had probably moved out within the last couple of days, possibly within the last few hours; Martin noticed a half-loaf of not yet mouldy bread on top of an old copy of *Variety,* a can of crystallized honey and a plastic bag full of Blue Chip stamps. Martin pocketed the stamps as Roger screwed a 250-watt bulb into the kitchen ceiling, and they set to work to make the place habitable for the next occupant, whoever that might be.

Who knows what else got left behind? he wondered. In closets and back rooms, in cupboards and under sinks, on top shelves and in forgotten drawers, so much overlooked or perhaps simply and conveniently disremembered by those on the move, as though on purpose, as a way of shedding the collected burdens of a life gone on too long in one place. Like snakeskins, he thought, or the dead casing of gypsy moths. Still, when he thought of it at all, it always surprised him just how much they left behind, some of it inexplicably valuable.

There was a lingering smell about the room that Martin could not quite place. Another housekeeper or maid in a tight white uniform passed by outside. From time to time, as they worked, muffled sounds penetrated the paper-thin plaster, the echo of delicate movements as of mice busy under the linoleum or behind the peeling latex paint on the walls.

Martin had just begun cleaning the chipped metal grooves of the sliding windows with a toothbrush when a door on the opposite landing swung slowly open. A beam of dingy light cut through the twilight, tracing faint yellow streaks across the discolored bottom of the empty swimming pool in the courtyard below.

"I think we're being watched," he said, pausing between strokes.

The window frame had not been cleaned in years; a residue of soot and unidentifiable particles from the air had settled along with piles of sharp, corroded filings like insect droppings within the cracks. It was difficult to get rid of, even with the large wire brush and the chemical solvent.

"How much longer do you figure, Rog? We only have one unit to do in this building, don't we, and that's it?"

"Two more," said Roger.

"You've got to be kidding."

Martin swore under his breath, aware of the woman in the opposite doorway. Her features were lost in darkness, but he could see jagged points of hair sticking out from her head in the backlight like the spokes of a broken wheel.

"Get a load of that pose," said Roger, mixing the rug shampoo. "I wonder what she's waiting for."

Martin made a quick mental note of the proportions, of the odd cant of the limbs. "Do you remember *The Bride of Frankenstein?*" he said.

"I worked with Elsa Lanchester once," said Roger. "Did I ever tell you—?"

"You did." Many times, he thought. "Listen," he said abruptly, dropping the brush. "Will you tell me something? What in hell are we doing here?"

"About three-thirty an hour," said Roger.

"Seriously."

"Seriously," said Roger. "It's my latest role—it's called 'paying the rent.' Do you know that the average SAG member makes like seven hundred dollars a year?"

"But you didn't decide to be an actor for the bucks," said Martin impatiently. "You couldn't have. You'd have been a fool."

Hell, he thought, the average guys I went to school with, the jocks, are all managing supermarkets or selling Porsches now. I could have had a piece of that. So why didn't I? Why did I turn my back on Kathy, a house, kids? There must be a reason. Or maybe I'm just a fool. Maybe that's all there is to it, after all.

Roger unwound the cord and tried to find an outlet. "You may not believe this, Jack," he said, "but there are times when I'm glad to be pushing a broom for a living. Like right now." He groaned and stretched. Martin heard bones crack in the empty room. "My mind's still my own, you know? I mean, when we leave here, we're through. And I'm my own man. Till my agent calls for me for another reading. A commercial, anything, I'm not particular, so long as I have the chance to practice my craft."

That's crap, thought Martin, but didn't say it. Because he didn't know why. But there was something basically wrong with the equation, though it had sounded reasonable enough for him to take this job himself until his next commission until . . .

Roger was staring across the courtyard. The woman had left the doorway and was now making her way tenuously towards them, one hand on the railing for support.

"That one's about ready for the bone orchard, if you ask me," said Roger. He backed up and fumbled with the cord reel, as if he recognized her, as if he did not want to. His hands were shaking. Why is he so upset? wondered Martin.

"Did I ever tell you about my next project, Jack? It's a real departure for me. I've been working on the treatment in my head." He was talking too fast, rattling through the words as if they were beads. "*The Adventures of Reggae Rat*. It's a children's story. Bet you didn't know I could write, too, did you? My agent's been after me for years to put together a property of my own. Naturally, there'll be a part in it for me, so that when I sell the film rights—I'll need an illustrator for the book first, of course. Why don't you see what you can come up with when you have the time. I know you're doing that other thing on spec right now, what's it called—*Pipe Dreams*? That's it, isn't it, Jackie? Am I right?"

Roger stopped talking as the woman arrived at their door. Martin stood to one side to let it happen, whatever it would be.

"How's it going, ma'am?" said Roger. "Nice evening, isn't it?"

"Young man," began the woman.

Martin stifled a laugh. How many more years can we get away with it? *Young men on the way up. Promising talents. Ageing enfants terribles,* he thought. Very rapidly ageing.

"You simply must help me. I have a terrible, terrible problem!"

Roger reached for the work order. "Let me see here," he said. "What apartment was that now?"

"Number twenty-six," she said. "I'm only staying between engagements, you understand, until I can find more suitable quarters. But you must come at once."

"I don't see it," said Roger, scanning the clipboard. "Are you sure—?"

"Oh, the colored girls come in and clean around me once a week, or is it once a month? I've so much on my mind these days, you know. But you really must help me. Why, I've called and called to complain, but it never does any good!"

Roger exchanged glances with Martin. He seemed to be forcing himself to a decision.

"Now just you calm down, ma'am. We'll see what we can do, all right? I'll be over in a jiffy."

The old lady wandered away, clutching her housecoat, muttering to herself.

"What . . . ?"

"It's good PR," said Roger, grabbing a boxful of cleansers and sponges. "See, we spend five minutes with Baby Jane here. She tells the manager; the manager tells the Old Man. The Old Man gets a lock on the building. She's satisfied—and we get a raise. That's called 'priming the pump,' my boy. 'Greasing the pig.' " He shouldered a broom and started out. "Do what you can with this dump in the meantime, but don't knock yourself out. I'll be right back."

Martin watched as Roger disappeared into the opposite apartment, ahead of the old lady, holding the screen door for her.

He shook his head. Great, he thought. Who knows when we'll get out of here now? He withdrew to a corner of the living room and leaned against the wall.

He looked around at the floor polisher, the scrub brushes,

the plastic jugs of cleaning solution and germ killer, and the packet of paper bands for the toilets that said SANITIZED in cheerful script.

He sighed.

He sank down so that he was sitting on the floor and took out his sketch paid and a Pilot Fineliner pen. He opened to a blank page. The sketches he had been working up for his *Red Dreams* concept were all grotesques; she would fit in nicely. All together, they would form the core of a fantastic one-man show, if anybody in the La Cienega galleries were into that sort of thing yet.

He was trying to reproduce the lumpy outline of her coat when a scream sounded from the other apartment.

He tapped the cap of his pen on his teeth. He squinted into the darkness and started to get up. At that instant the other door opened and Roger came running with his supplies, looking like a Fuller Brush man who has just been bitten by the family dog.

He stumbled in, out of breath. "Jesus Christ," he said with a wild look in his eyes. "I feel more like I do now than when we got here!"

Martin put away his notebook. "That bad, huh?" She had seemed like a candidate for the cackle factory, all right. "What happened?"

"The usual. She wanted me to kill the rug."

"What?"

"The lint, rather. On the rug. She says it's really bugs—cockroaches or something."

"Is it?"

"Are Donny and Marie Osmond sisters?"

"I don't know."

"My point exactly! I tell you, man, I had to get out of there. I thought I could handle her—I'm used to dealing with people. But I should have trusted my instincts. There's something about that old bird that gives me the creeps.

Another minute and I wouldn't have known my own hole from an ass on the ground.''

Martin considered Roger's face. He was trying to make sense of his partner's overreaction when the screen door slammed open across the way and the old woman staggered out, making unintelligible sounds in her throat.

"Here we go again," said Roger. "I can't do it, Jack. You try if you want to. Hey, maybe you can bring us back some eats. She's got something cooking in there; I could smell it. Just don't take too long, okay?"

Martin tried in vain to get a good look at her. Probably just an old Hollywood crank, he thought. There must be a lot of them around here. Maybe the whole building's full of them, who knows? Some sort of retirement set-up. There were no children visible, no pets, no tricycles. Now that he thought of it, the manager down below had had a certain thespian fussiness about him.

"I can pay you," she said as she came up.

"Don't worry," said Martin, stepping forward, feeling sorry for her in spite of himself. "A regular service of the Sunshine Cleaning Company. It's all free and it won't hurt a bit."

He left Roger, walking behind her at a respectful distance. As he followed her into her apartment, he was finally able to see her bright orange hair and the eyes that bulged like poached eggs through flesh caked with accumulated makeup. There was something vaguely familiar about her, even under the wan light that filtered through the dusty tassels of the lamp, but he still could not place her.

She collapsed onto an overstuffed sofa, reupholstered in purple crushed velvet, as if the exertion had been more than she could bear. She was silent for a moment. Then her eyelids unfolded, twitching thickly as she caught him staring at her.

"It's there, by the table," she said, pointing a long arm that would have been graceful if not for the arthritis.

He felt himself bow slightly.

Her hand retracted to cover her eyes, shielding them from the light that came through the burnt lampshade. Her chest began to rise and fall, as if she were sinking into a deep slumber.

He went to the table, realizing after a few steps that he was on tiptoe.

It was a fine old Chippendale with years of wax rubbed into the surface, but with an incongruous sample of frayed pink velvet thrown haphazardly over the top. There was a small open box of tarnished antique jewelry, a copy of *TV Guide*, and a framed photograph of what appeared to be a flying saucer.

His attention drifted automatically to other photographs and certificates on the wall, glossies gone sepia with age and news clippings and hand-lettered commendations. He recognized one of the faces, that of a young actor who had been killed tragically in a car crash when Martin himself was a teenager.

"It moves," she said.

He turned, startled. "I beg your pardon?"

"It goes away and then it comes back. I've told them to clean it; I've pleaded and begged, but they won't do anything about it. It always comes back. Small in the afternoons and then larger in the evenings, but it always comes back. I used to clean it twice a week with the carpet sweeper, but lately I've been so terribly, terribly tired; I don't know why . . ."

Her voice failed. Even now as Martin watched her, the last of her strength seemed to leave her body and seep into the cushions and pillows.

What was she talking about?

He heard the clinking of silver on dishes and low voices

from the next room. He took another step and saw a doorway that led to the kitchen.

The old woman moaned and got to her feet. He felt her brush past him, trailing an aura of cheap perfume.

"Why, it's as plain as the nose on your face," she said. With a crooked finger she directed his eyes to the floor, holding the door frame with her other hand. "Will you help me? If you won't, I don't know what I'll do."

"Of course I'll help you," he said quickly. "That's what I'm here for."

That seemed to pacify her. She nodded shakily and went on into the kitchen.

Martin turned his attention to the carpet at his feet. It was a worn Oriental design, with bone-white threads showing through. In the middle, extending outwards from the legs of the table, was a long, spiderlike spot. It ended at a dark oval outline in the shape of a stomach sac.

He knelt and suspended his hand above the pile of the carpet, as if trying to detect something from the feel of it, the texture.

The spot flowed over and covered his knuckles.

He drew back.

The spot returned to the carpet.

He stood up and stepped carefully around it. As he did so, the spot enlarged, bleeding off the carpet and onto the floor.

Suddenly he let out a chuckle.

He looked at the lampshade, the curtained window behind it, the end of the sofa between the lamp and the table.

That was all there was to it, then.

The spot? It was only a shadow, growing as the sun went down, disappearing and then reappearing when the lamp was snapped on. A shadow. Nothing more.

He shook his head.

He walked around the room, strangely relieved, and again heard voices from the kitchen.

"None of the dead has been identified . . ."

It was a radio or television set, he realized.

He found himself back at the table. He noticed signed photographs on the wall of a man in a grey suit shaking hands with various minor celebrities. One of them was an old-time actor who had appeared in most of the cheapjack science fiction films of the fifties. Martin had seen them all, or most of them, either in theatres at the time or on *The Late, Late Show* in the years since. One of the certificates was inscribed, "To Albert Zugman, From the Baron Frankenstein Society in recognition of his Contribution to the Genre."

That was it: The man in the grey suit was none other than the late Albert Zugman, king of the "B" Pictures. His movies had been Martin's absolute favorites as a boy. Perhaps they had even been the original source of his taste for the bizarre. How many times had he sneaked into the old Rialto Theatre on Saturday afternoons to see them over and over again?

He traced the edges of the publicity stills with genuine affection. *Robot Invaders*, circa 1953, if he remembered correctly. And *I Was a Teenage Dracula*, about 1958. Even *Hippie High School*, from 1967. That one had been Zugman's last attempt at another kind of exploitation picture; it had failed. So, apparently, had Zugman. As nearly as Martin could recall, Zugman had died quietly in the early seventies, all but forgotten.

The flying saucer? That would be from *Mars vs. Earth*. Of course.

And the old woman would be Mrs. Zugman herself, the former model and actress. In person.

My God, he thought.

There must be something he could do for her, some way

of repaying even a small part of the hours of pleasure he had received.

Then he remembered.

He lifted the end of the sofa and moved it twelve or fourteen inches and set it down so that there was no longer a direct line between it and the lamp. There. Now there will be no more shadows to bother her, he thought.

It seemed so little.

Well, wasn't there something more he could do before he left, some other detail, perhaps, further to ease her mind?

He waited, but she did not come out of the kitchen.

He circled the room, a patternless array of objects and memorabilia, a sad mixture of quality furnishings and the dreariest chintz. For the first time he noticed cardboard cartons along one wall, some of them containing odds and ends of statuary, vases, pictures. She—or someone—was in the process of moving her things in or out; he couldn't tell which.

He turned into the small hall.

It was a cracker-box apartment, all right, with two tiny rooms, a kitchen and a bath. He flicked on the bathroom light.

The imitation-porcelain basin was coated with layers of spilled face powder, hardened into cement over the years.

He switched off the light.

In the bedroom was a transparent mask attached to an oxygen tank. Rays of light from a street lamp outside slanted through the adjustable louvered panels of the window, casting sharp vertical shadows over her bed.

He heard a sound somewhere behind him. Feeling like a trespasser, he turned back to the living room.

She was standing by the table.

"Oh!" she cried. "Oh, my dear! What have you done?"

"Excuse me," he said hurriedly. "I was just wondering if there was anything more I could . . ."

"You mustn't touch my things!" She pressed her hands to her face, her watery eyes fixed on the sofa. "This is all I have left of the estate. I hear them coming in at all hours like thieves in the night, like ants. Oh, you're one of them, aren't you? You're just like the rest!"

She lunged unsteadily to the kitchen.

"Ma'am?" he called, following her. "I was only trying to help, please believe me. Mrs. Zugman?"

He saw another person with her in the kitchen, a woman in a white uniform.

"Don't make me hurt you," one of them was saying. He couldn't tell which one.

He rapped on the doorjamb. "Ma'am, if you'll let me explain . . ."

She spotted him and hobbled out in a near-panic. He heard her closing the door to her bedroom and her bony fingers struggling with a lock that would not catch.

The other woman remained seated at the kitchen table. She leaned forward on her elbows, squeezing something in her fat hands. She might have been Mexican or middle-European, he could not be sure. A portable television set was propped across from her. Patiently her lidded eyes returned to it.

They must be cooks, he thought, all of them in their white dresses. That would explain why they're so well-fed, their uniforms taut and bursting at the seams.

A huge kettle simmered on the stove. He smelled a familiar lingering odor and recognized it at last as a mixture of heavy spices about to boil, as if held in readiness for a long time. But why? The refrigerator stood open, the racks inside picked clean. It looked as if it had been empty for days, perhaps longer.

He took a tentative step forward, trying to think of

something to say. There were questions taking shape in his mind, but he did not yet know how to frame them.

Her hands flexed almost imperceptibly in the white light, and he saw that she held nothing in them, after all. It had been only the fleshiness of her own hands, cupped expectantly around each other.

She glanced up at him, her jaws grinding in a steady, regular rhythm. Her lips fell open. There was nothing in her mouth, not yet.

And a sudden dread began to overtake him, creeping up the back of his neck and spreading across his scalp. It was like nothing he had ever felt before.

Her jaws clenched and unclenched, a trickle of colorless fluid starting already from the sides of her mouth, dripping from the corners of her faint but unmistakable moustache. She made no move to wipe it away.

''Was that trip really necessary?'' Roger was saying. He had been muttering for several blocks, but this was the first of his quasi-observations to register. Martin let it go and tried to lose himself in the rush of foliage outside the van.

Can't you step on it? he thought.

Roger tore open a package of Mickey Banana Dreams with his teeth, devoured one and set the other on the dashboard. He pushed it towards Martin.

''Found 'em in one of the drawers,'' Roger said. ''You know, it blows my mind sometimes, the stuff they leave behind when they go.'' He tried to laugh, but it didn't come out right. He licked his fingers and let the wrapper fly out the window. ''Anyway, I just hope the Old Man doesn't find out about those other two units, at least not till we get paid for the week. If the manager complains, we'll say one of us got sick and had to split. Which is true, right?'' Roger eyed his partner in the semidarkness. ''She really got to you, didn't she?''

''You recognized her before I did,'' said Martin. Say it, he thought.

The van shook, turning downhill.

Roger took a long time to answer. ''She was Lylah Lord,'' he said wonderingly. ''*The* Lylah Lord. I wasn't sure at first.'' He adjusted the rearview mirror, his eyes glassy. ''But you saw her. That was what got to you, too, wasn't it?''

''I saw her,'' Martin said. He saw her now, in fact, saw her no matter how hard he tried not to: the tattered robe, the spindly wrists, the veins and age spots on her legs. A tired, starved old woman, living with death and waiting helplessly for the end; it was her final, hysterical role, one in which she had awakened to find herself trapped and from which she could not escape. He tried, but he could not put her out of his mind.

''You want to get drunk?'' said Roger.

''It's late.''

''That it is. And we have a big, new apartment complex over on the east side first thing tomorrow morning. I saw the order. But I just thought, when we get back to the valley, away from here—''

Unexpectedly Roger's voice, the trained instrument that it was, failed him.

''I know,'' said Martin.

''I used to wonder what happens to old actors in this town. Now I wish I'd never found out. Did I ever tell you, Jackie, that I had quite a crush on her? She was the love of my life for years. I collected her pictures on trading cards. Even carried one around in my wallet. I wonder if it's still there? Lylah Lord! Jesus Christ.''

They approached the base of the foothills, where Elevado Way merged and became one with the plain of jewel-like streets and traffic signals and dimly lighted windows, each the tired eye of another private residence within which one more sad melodrama was playing itself out, alone, to the end. And among the lights, Martin knew, were the bright, cold flowers of theatre marquees and television screens where the faces of people long dead and forgotten spoke and gestured from another time and place, and where they would continue to do so, forever perhaps, or until even the last remaining record of their lives would itself break and decompose into remnants to be carted away with the rest. Like the actors whose photographs were even now curling and disintegrating on the walls of her apartment. He reached for the pack of cigarettes on the seat.

"I didn't know you smoke, Jackie."

"I don't."

Martin lit up and sat watching the cigarette flare in the darkness and then subside to an ember. He inhaled deeply, but it did no good. Cars passed them on either side, taillights braking and then growing weak in the distance. Once a huge truck roared by, rattling the van from a great height, as if it meant to run them off the road, as if it did not even see them. The vibration knocked the ash from Martin's cigarette. He watched the burning continue the length of the cigarette, converting it all to ashes.

"Maybe we're in the wrong profession," said Roger.

Martin looked over at him, trying to see his eyes.

"I don't just mean Sunshine Cleaning," said Roger. "I mean—" He cut the wheel sharply and they mounted an on-ramp. "Look, the first thing I had to learn as an actor was to eat shit. Unsalted. You know? And it isn't much better in your field, am I right?"

Martin thought: Why is consensus so important to him?

"So what are we breaking our balls for? Can you tell me that? I mean, being an artist is fine if you get the breaks. But why should we waste our whole lives waiting for some kind of—I don't know—" Roger's hands trembled on the steering wheel, under the strobing of lights that passed above. "I'm sure as hell not going to let myself end up like her. I know that now. The way I see it, we've just been fooling ourselves."

What, then? wondered Martin.

"Let's get it together, Jackie. Who do you think hires those maids or whatever the hell they are, for example? Somebody, right? He must be raking in the dough, enough to make some kind of a life, you know? I bet he has guys who do nothing but haul them out in the morning, pick them up at the end of the day. You figure he needs more drivers? That's what we ought to be into, something with a future. What do you think?"

Martin was thinking about what he had seen at the Carlton Arms. Whether it was true or not in its particulars didn't really matter; the sense of it was the same. It was big fishes eating little fishes, consuming and being consumed, just as we feed and are fed upon in turn by the Old Man. And so on.

The feeling returned then. The feeling that had made him want to be out of there. I have to break the chain, he thought. And, feeling an even greater fear, he thought: *It stops here.*

They were nearing the end. The cigarette had burned down to the filter and was sputtering dangerously close to his fingers, but he was not aware of it. For some reason he was thinking of the young actor who had been killed in the car crash when he himself was only a boy. He felt pain, and his eyes filled with tears.

A shadow passed over them as an illuminated road sign swept by overhead.

"I want out," he heard himself say.

Roger smiled at him. "I know. Believe me. I've got to get home and get something to eat myself. But, hey, I think there's a Bob's Big Boy coming up. If you don't want a drink, maybe we could grab a bite before we go back. Man, I sure wouldn't mind having one of those maids' jobs right now, let me tell you. I'll bet they sneak whatever they want right out from under those old birds' noses. Am I right, Jackie?''

''My name's Jack,'' said Martin.

Roger drove on in silence. They left the freeway and headed along the main street, the restaurant logo becoming clearer until it dominated the night sky.

''You sure you don't want to stop?''

Martin did not answer.

''Well,'' said Roger, ''you give the idea some thought, okay? This racket's for losers. Now, a port-a-maid or whatever they call it, that's the kind of scam we should be into, I'm telling you. One thing about it—we'd never go home hungry. At least see if you can find out who they work for. You can do that, can't you?''

No, thought Martin. No, I can't. He was hungry, all right. But not that hungry.

It's the small things that are the most frightening—those things which we either take for granted because we see them every day, or those which we don't think about because we don't always see them. In combination, in fantasy, that's a lethal mistake.

Craig Shaw Gardner is one of the finest of the newer writers of dark fantasy. He lives and works in Cambridge, Massachusetts, and is currently working on his first novel.

OVERNIGHT GUEST

Craig Shaw Gardner

Did he really look like that?

George stared at himself in the bathroom mirror. It was the lighting in these places, always much too bright. It made you look one step away from rigor mortis. "The

Curse of the Hotel Bathroom!'' He smiled at the thought despite himself. His teeth looked yellow in the glare.

"George, honey? What's taking you so long?"

Julie's voice startled him from his reverie. She was so young, so cheerful, so fresh—so different from his wife.

"Be there in a second, honey." He allowed himself one last masochistic glance. Those bags under his eyes weren't always that dark, were they? Those smile lines on the sides of his mouth were long and well-defined, like half-circles chiseled in stone. Remember when he had hair all the way across his head?

"I'm coming!" he called, and turned away. He shouldn't pay any attention to the mirror. What should these little things matter, anyway, now that he had found Julie?

She sat on the edge of the double bed, her pale pink negligee a pleasant contrast to the light blue of the bedspread and the walls. Her dark brown hair framed her pale face, so white she might be made of porcelain. Her eyes, more almond-shaped than oval, gave her features a slight Oriental cast, and made her one of the most beautiful women George had ever seen. A perfect picture, he thought as he approached her, my love in pale pastels.

She closed her eyes as he leaned down to kiss her.

"What took you so long?" she whispered when he paused for breath.

"Foolish vanity," he replied after a moment's pause.

"But I can't wait. I need you so much now."

She wrapped her arms around him. "Kiss me," she whispered. "Free me."

He did as he was told.

It was funny, sometimes, how your life could change overnight.

George stared past the red glow of his cigarette, held out against the dark. Shadows fled across the room as cars passed on the road below. A window of light played across the pale wallpaper, flowing by the TV, a dresser with a knob missing, and a picture of the sea. Julie slept beside him. Her soft breathing mixed with the distant voice of crickets. Together, they spoke of peace and warmth and love.

George put the cigarette to his lips and breathed deeply. He thought of his wife.

Life with Alice wasn't really so bad. It was just so ordinary. He realized that, now that he'd found Julie.

But he hadn't told Alice where he was going or how long he'd be gone. Thoughts of Julie made it difficult to talk. He hadn't had time to explain, only to go. How would he explain this weekend to Alice?

Maybe he wouldn't go back.

The thought sliced through him like a cold wind, disturbing and exciting at the same time. How could he leave his wife, his kids? What would the guys say down at the plant when, day after day, he didn't show up for work?

If he never showed up for work, what did it matter what the guys said?

He held back a laugh. He mustn't wake Julie. He had heard of this sort of thing before, men who vanished completely and left their entire lives behind. Marriages, mortgages, jobs, obligations: Poof! He'd heard about it, but this was the first time he'd really thought about the implications.

Right now, the idea rather appealed to him.

Another car rushed down below. He rose from bed with the headlight's glare drawn by the pale pattern sweeping across the wall. Somehow, thoughts like this required movement.

He found himself standing in front of the dresser, surrounded by the night. He felt a little foolish now, alone in the darkness. He needed to calm down and get some sleep. Maybe a glass of water would help. He stumbled to the bathroom.

The light hurt his eyes. That damn yellow glare again. It was those two old light bulbs overhead, the kind with clear glass. You could stare right at the filament and blind yourself. He should have found the faucet in the dark somehow. He squinted into the mirror as he poured the water. He really didn't look that bad. He wouldn't call himself old. Distinguished: That was a much better word. It was all a matter of attitude. Having a girl like Julie changed your whole world around.

There was a buzzing in his ear as he swallowed the water. It was a low, level sound, something he couldn't even be sure he heard. Insects, maybe. There could be crickets in the walls. He wouldn't be surprised at anything in the walls of a place as old as this one.

He set the plastic cup by the sink and walked the three steps to the door. The buzzing was fainter here. There was probably something wrong with the light above the mirror. An old bulb, maybe, or something wrong with the circuit. He thought of insects trapped in that garish glowing bulb, flying frantically, looking for escape that wasn't there. Serves them right, he thought, for coming to a hotel like this.

The smile stayed on his face all the way back to bed.

"Good morning, lover!"

George opened his eyes. Julie's eyes stared back at him, less than a foot away. They were beautiful dark eyes, brown with flecks of green, and he would have been content to look at them for hours if her lips hadn't been so close as well.

Her kiss aroused him, and they made love in the early morning light. The sheets beneath them glowed yellow with the sun, and Julie's soft skin seemed to glow as well under his caress. He found himself filled with a vitality he thought he had lost years before. Her touch was magic. He could make love to her a hundred times and never tire. She laughed, bright and warm, when he touched her just so, and her laughter filled him with a joy that could only be contained when they were in each other's arms. If he could not touch her, could not kiss her, if they could not make love, he would surely burst and shatter into a million pieces.

But her kisses were there, and her love was there, and when it was over, he found that his tension was gone, and all it left was peace.

"What should we do today?" Julie asked after a while.

He wanted to say "make love," but he suggested breakfast instead.

Julie hummed to herself as she dressed. George went into the bathroom to shave.

The yellow, glaring light was good for this sort of thing. It showed every pockmark and wrinkle, but it showed every chin hair as well. A clean shave every time, you handsome devil, George thought as he pushed on the electric razor. It was no wonder Julie was crazy about him. He was getting better-looking every day.

The hum of the razor reminded him of the buzzing he'd heard in here the night before. He flipped the razor off. The buzzing was still there, faint but definite. He could hear it clearly now that he was awake.

Well, he wasn't going to let a little buzzing noise ruin his weekend. His electric razor swallowed the lesser noise again. He and Julie had been lucky to find this place, getting away at the last minute, and in tourist season, too. This was the first time he'd been this far north, but Julie knew the area a little, and she had remembered this place just out of sight of the main highway.

Julie called him from the other room. He followed her downstairs and across the courtyard to the motel's coffee shop.

A little bell rang as they opened the door. There didn't seem to be anyone in the place. They walked to a booth with faded green seats. There was a little jukebox over the table, the kind you hardly saw anymore. A hand-written note taped on the top informed them: "Don't waste your money! Out of order!"

A woman with a bright yellow cap appeared in a doorway behind the counter. "With you in a minute!" she chirped, and then she was gone again.

"I want my eggs sunny-side up." Julie smiled as she rose from her seat. "Be back in a second." She grabbed her purse and walked across the room to a door marked "Women."

George stared after her for a moment, then turned his attention to the old jukebox. It was awfully quiet in this place. It was too bad this old thing didn't work.

Look at these songs! Apparently, the jukebox had been out of order for some time. He flipped through the selections row-by-row. There wasn't anything here even close to current. George never paid that much attention to the radio, but he couldn't remember hearing any of these songs for years.

There were a couple of titles he recognized—old standards, the kind that got recorded over and over again. He remembered, with sudden clarity, listening to one of the songs in the kitchen of their first home. Alice had sat across the table from him. Jane, their youngest, just a baby then, sat on Alice's lap. It was late afternoon in early autumn, and the sunlight streaming through the open window had a golden tinge you only saw at that time of year. It had shone on his wife and child so they looked like they were filled with the sun. It made them more beautiful than anything he had ever seen.

He looked across the table at a neon sign that snapped and buzzed in the window. He wanted to talk to Alice. Maybe there was a phone in here someplace. If he could just hear the sound of Alice's voice . . .

He could ask the waitress. What was taking her so long, anyway?

Julie stepped out of the ladies' room. Even in the harsh fluorescent glare of the coffee shop, she was beautiful.

The waitress appeared right behind her. They both ordered ham and eggs. George wasn't quite sure when the waitress left. He was too aware of the pressure of Julie's foot against his ankle and the way her fingers played against his open palm.

This would be their day.

Julie led him into the room, but he hurried her to the bed. He needed to have her now. He felt like he hadn't made love in half a year rather than half a day. All afternoon, as they walked along the beach into town, when they poked together through the little shops, while they ate lunch in that overcrowded sandwich place, all he could think about was her touch, her laugh, the way her eyes looked into his.

Now, at last, they were alone. He laid Julie across the bed. She laughed, a warm, welcoming laugh. He laughed in response, a sound that came from deep inside. He used to laugh like that, long ago. When had he forgotten about laughter?

He laughed again as she pulled him down to join her, a laughter full and warm and young. Julie has given me this, too, he thought as their lips met. And then they were clutched tight in each other's arms, and there was no more breath for laughter.

The buzzing was far worse in here now. He could hear it clearly, even over the noise of the TV Julie so avidly watched in the other room. Oh, well. For a woman as wonderful as that, he supposed he could forgive a weakness for sitcoms. They couldn't make love all the time, after all.

God, was it noisy here! His ears seemed to become more and more attuned to it every time he turned on the light. At first, he hadn't been sure anything was there. Now he was listening for nuances of sound.

There were three noises, really, in this bathroom. That clicking buzz was only the most prominent. There was a knocking somewhere far off, the kind you always heard in old houses. Or old hotels. And he heard another sound, too, an alternate sighing and whistling, surely the wind finding its way through this not-too-well-made structure.

He flushed the toilet and walked over to the sink. Maybe if he hit the old bulb a couple of times it would stop its racket. Looking at the flickering light, he remembered fifth grade. The fluorescent tubes had never been very good in that classroom. One had flickered worse than this. He and his classmates, who were very much into outer space at the time, decided it was the Martians trying to contact them. Absently, George wondered who was trying to contact him now.

He forgot about the bulb when he looked into the mirror.

He had all his hair. His receding hairline was gone. And the hair was deep, curly brown, not the wispy grey so prevalent the last couple years.

So it wasn't his imagination. He was getting younger.

"Julie!" he cried as he ran from the bathroom. She looked up from the TV.

"What's happened?" he asked.

Her smiled turned to a half-frown. "You saw yourself in the mirror."

He nodded.

"Your younger self," she said. "It's something that happens here."

He stared at her. The warm, giving woman had suddenly become a stranger. What was she saying? What was happening to him?

"Come." She smiled again and patted the bed beside her. "Sit by me."

He moved to turn off the television, but Julie shook her head vehemently. She waved him forward.

"I haven't told you everything," she said as he sat down beside her. "I've been here before, with other men."

He pulled away from her. Her eyes stared into him— wide-open, innocent eyes, eyes maybe a little afraid. What did he expect, anyway, after the way they had met in the park?

She stroked the side of his face. "You're different, though. Stronger than the others. I could leave here with you. With you, I could be free of this place."

She kissed him, slowly and tenderly. In a voice just barely a whisper, she said, "Let's leave this place forever."

He kissed her again. "Anything you say." And again. "In a minute."

"One more time, then," she replied. "Then we must go."

He should have turned off the bathroom light. He could hear it as they made love, even over the television, and in that moment before climax the sound filled his brain, as if small flies nested in his inner ear.

They made love this time all in a rush, and at the end they lay exhausted in each other's arm, the sheet beneath them drenched with sweat.

He freed himself from Julie's embrace with a groan. His head was pounding with the noise of the TV and that constant rustling buzz behind it. He rose from the bed on shaky legs and flipped off the television, then stumbled to the bathroom. If he could get rid of that other noise, maybe his headache would go away.

It was funny how your head could amplify things at times like this. The noise sounded like a chain saw, as if someone was trying to cut through the walls. The pounding was there, too, slamming against his skull. The sighs of wind sounded like urgent whispers, as if someone had a message that George had to hear.

He looked at himself in the mirror.

He had lost twenty years from his face. All the age had dropped away. The eyes of a man barely out of college stared back at him.

If only this damned noise—oh, who cared about the bulb! He looked the same age as when he had married. He didn't know how it had happened, but it was a gift.

His first years with Alice filled his head. He needed to see his wife again.

How would he explain this change to Alice? What would she think? She'd be happy for him, wouldn't she?

He stepped from the bathroom and saw Julie watching

him. She was afraid of this place for some reason. She looked as if she wanted to say something but couldn't. There was a lot here that he didn't understand. But he'd get Julie out of here now. He owed her that much. After they were free of this place, he'd figure out what to do about Alice.

"Come on," he said. "We're going."

He hurried into his clothes as Julie gathered hers about her. He grabbed her hand and rushed her from the room. They didn't stop until they reached his car outside.

"Where do we go now?" Julie was smiling.

He paused to catch his breath. "We'll have to find a place for you to stay." He leaned down and unlocked the door on the passenger side.

Julie looked horror-struck. "Aren't we going to stay together?"

"Sure," he said, walking around the car. "We would, if this were a perfect world. But I don't think we can, not for a little while at least. I don't know, really. I have to go see my wife."

He got into the car beside her. She was crying. He looked at her and sighed. "There are weekends like this, and then there's the rest of life."

He started the car and saw his eyes reflected in the rearview mirror.

His wrinkled eyes, set in a fifty-year-old face, with too little hair on top of the head. He looked old, older even than he did before.

"Julie?" he whispered.

"I'm sorry," she said. "We left so suddenly. I wasn't ready. There are things you have to do if you want to stay that way."

"I'm old."

"You can look in the mirror again, if you want to." She opened her car door.

He followed her up the stairs. There were liver spots on the back of his hand that he had never seen before. How old was he now?

Julie opened the door to the room. They had turned off the bedroom light when they left, but the light in the bathroom still burned, spilling across the room, a pathway to the magic mirror.

George walked forward, surrounded by the noise. The walls groaned as he approached; the wind screamed with a hundred voices, all underscored with that grinding, like stone trying to escape stone, like a hornet's nest behind his eyes.

He looked in the mirror at an adolescent boy. Younger still, then? He reached out in wonder to touch his image and saw the liver spots still on his hand.

The mirror was a lie.

He wasn't getting younger. The mirror only told him so. He was old, then, older than he ever imagined. He'd never realized how much age had changed him, until he looked into this mirror.

Anger rose in him. Everything was a lie; the image in the mirror, his weekend of passion, his life with Alice. It made him furious. The sounds filled his head. He thought he heard a hundred voices laughing.

He raised his fist to smash the mirror.

It was cold and it was dark. As much as he tried, he could not really speak.

He was old, but not as old as the others. There were many of them, hundreds perhaps. There was no way for him to know.

Then there was light, and he could see after a fashion, although not as he was once used to seeing. And a man stood there and looked at all of them, but only saw an image of himself, a false image.

And he who was inside tried to call out, to scream with all his will. And the hundred around him screamed as well, but none of them had voices as they once did, and their cries could be taken for a whisper of wind, a groan of wood, a buzz of wings.

Then the light was gone, and there was nothing but distant laughter—Julie's laughter, and that of a man, a man who sounded a lot like George, when he was younger.

Midnight, in one of its forms, marks the shadowed alley that separates madness and reason. Because of the dark, however, it's impossible to tell which is which, if indeed there is a difference.

Janet Fox has had her stories appear in every major publication where quality fantasy is prized. For her fans, she simply doesn't write enough.

INTIMATELY, WITH RAIN

Janet Fox

The land had a barren, torn-up look, the dark soil churned up by workmen and their machines, native brush cleared away to the last ragged stand of timber along the creek. Annmarie clutched her black plastic patent purse against herself, shivering a little in the raw March wind, for all the portliness of her figure. Her matching shoes squished ridges of mud as she stood staring off toward the creek; she knew those bends, the sluggish trickle of mud-brown water dimly mirroring overhanging foliage. She knew where to seine for minnows and knew the deeper spots where skinny-dipping had been possible. Her heavy bosom heaved a little as she remembered.

She felt a hand on her elbow. "We can go inside. Nothing's finished in there yet, of course." She looked at William Dudley with almost a sense of shock—his round face, chins doubling down to a white shirtfront, a laurel wreath of thin gray hair garlanding a bald head, a permanent red flush beneath the skin. She was surprised, not by the fact that he seemed so old, but that she could remember him in no other way.

"It's cold out here," she said, hearing the whininess of her own voice, but unable to alter its tone. "I must get back soon. I have a Women Workers Club meeting at four."

They entered the unfinished house that would be their new home when it was completed. There was the woody smell of new lumber and a rawness to it, though she could not have said it had an empty feel. It was as though the place were already inhabited by something—something shy, but ineffably present. "A good omen," she told herself, even though she knew it was imaginary. She fancied something almost childlike about it, creeping about unseen with a suppressed giggle. It had been twenty years since Angela, her youngest, had been a child. Now the children were all grown and gone, and she couldn't really say she was sorry about it. There were always so many worthwhile uses for one's time.

She wandered away from William, who was inspecting the basement, and walked from room to room, trying to imagine how these bare chambers would look when all was complete. She supposed her nerves weren't all they should be, for the feeling of someone else in the house wouldn't go away, even though she knew it was only imagination. She could almost have sworn she was being watched by wide, wondering eyes, that there had been a blur of motion at the window. So strong was the impression that she rushed to the window, a glassless frame, gripped the sill and looked out. The sun was bright, making everything appear terrifically real. Nothing was there except a small brown lizard, its back as rough as tree bark, sunning on a pile of bricks. Disturbed, it lifted its head to survey her out of one bead-black eye and then slithered down into the pile between bricks. Leaf shadows fluttered under one vulnerable tree left standing by the work crew.

She looked down and saw that a splinter of wood had pierced her wrist when she'd grabbed the sill. She pursed plum-colored lips and, with a shudder of distaste, drew out the sliver; a thin line of blood was drawn down her arm, almost reaching the cuff of her best gray dress. Somehow the day seemed spoiled. "Let's go, William, my club meeting—"

"Calm down, Annie," he said. (He'd begun calling her that after the last child had left, she realized. Odd how it startled her now.) "We've got plenty of time. This is a nice place. A nice place to settle in. You'll have to agree now that I had a good idea there. And for you it's coming home."

"Things change. In over thirty years people die . . . people leave. I can't really say it's home."

"But look how well you fit in, even though we've only been living here for six months."

She smiled. One learned things—what to join, whom to cultivate. Money helped too, and William had plenty of that.

*   *   *

The decor was a bit stodgy, even to her taste—fat chairs and divans with chintzy prints, pictures of children and grandchildren propped everywhere—but William liked it and it was comfortable. Annmarie sat by the window in her housecoat, warming her hands on a coffee cup. The mornings were still cool. The house was becoming familiar now, though sometimes she awoke in the night and thought she was in older homes, the contours of these rooms a shock until she remembered. The feeling that she was never alone in the house had deepened with residence, though she'd never said anything about it to William. He lived in such a matter-of-fact world; he'd simply deny that anything like that existed and probably he was right.

She looked away from the sun-filled window back into the darkened room. Her vision filled with dancing spangles; she thought she saw something by the fireplace, a slight figure poised for flight, the suggestion of glossy dark hair. When her vision cleared, of course nothing was there except a dusty-winged moth that fluttered a moment and then darted up the chimney. Still, there was that impression of a childlike figure—a kind of sprite. She finished the bitter dregs of coffee with a grimace. She hardly had time to sit here dreaming. There was the church bazaar to manage.

She smiled as she put on the layers of undergarments that strapped her bulk into a firmer but no slenderer package and applied the makeup that did nothing at all to hide the lines of her face. She had been a little afraid to come back here to her hometown, though she would never have admitted that to William. She had been terrified that someone would remember Annie Byrd, the daughter of old Crikbank Ed—Anytime Annie. She had heard the name, always in whispers and giggles. And there were those who should have remembered, stolid old citizens whom she passed in the streets or greeted in church with a circumspect nod. It must have been the time that had passed and the way she had changed in the meantime. Perhaps it was almost as if that other person, that other life hadn't existed at all.

Full summer made the scraggly trees along the creek bank swell with layers of foliage. Annmaire had begun, now that it was warm, to walk here. The shack where she and her father had lived, now long torn down, was some miles from here, but she had no desire to return to that place. It was pleasant to walk among the trees, and she never walked here alone.

She had accepted it because there was literally no one she would talk to about it. She could see it now, in the undulant green-gold shadows under the trees—a figure, straight, slender, barely female with breasts that were no more than bud-swellings. The skin was butterscotch-brown— all over. The hair, with the color and texture of moss, hung raggedly in peaks about the small face, and the eyes were large and luminous, the color between sunlight and leaf shadow. A wood spirit—sprite—dryad.

For all its lucent beauty, the thing still made her uneasy as it paced her through the trees. She knew that if she tried to approach it, speak to it, it would be gone and a squirrel or garter snake would disappear into a tangle of underbrush, so much had it grown to be one with the natural life of this wood. She felt she could almost run with it through the aisles of forest, bare feet intimate with soil and moss, diving into the tepid brown water on a sultry dog day evening, the water a long coolness against the skin—a sheath of silk—then, toward morning, to be dressed in the rough garment of the tree, just peering out a little to see the sunlight falling in slanted shafts to the forest floor.

She shook off the feeling and turned back toward the house. There was something wrong about her thoughts running free like this; she pulled them up, as if she were approaching memories she didn't dare relive. And she had to get sandwiches ready for her bridge club which would meet that afternoon.

The Country Club was decorated with streamers of red, white and blue, but they were drooping and wilted as the dance drew to a close. Smoke wreathed a few somnambulant dancers. While William was enmeshed in interminable talk of politics, she stepped outside a moment to get out of the smoky atmosphere. A bulky shape approached her, and for a moment, she thought it was William; then she saw that it was not.

"Mrs. Dudley?"

She nodded, frostily, as this kind of meeting didn't seem exactly proper.

"Annmarie; Annie Byrd?"

She searched the sagging gray face with its dewlaps and eye-pouches, but she couldn't remember a name.

"David—Davy Brubaker." He stood a trifle unsteadily, leaning toward her to exhale a breath of stale alcohol. "Don't you remember me?"

She felt she should deny any acquaintance; yet somehow she couldn't.

"We had us some good times back there in those woods," he said hoarsely. His poor, time-broken face tried for an obscene wink, but couldn't quite bring it off. "Us guys never knew where you went after—"

She pushed him away from her and went back to the dance and crossed the floor, feeling in one sense naked, humiliated, in another almost relieved. Was there an undercurrent of such talk, she wondered, that she'd been unaware of all this time? William greeted her loudly, having had too much to drink. She managed to get him to the car, to drive him home. A slight free figure seemed to fly before them in the beam of headlights. She put William to bed, but was herself unable to sleep. As she roamed the house, she felt an awful constriction and a desire to be free of it. It was as if she were slipping from the confines of her tree, her body light and firm, her hair vegetable cool when it blew against her cheeks. She ran lightly to the deep pools and waited there. Through an endless twilight they came to her, one by one, shaggy boyish satyrs, the moon bringing coppery highlights from the curling hair of chest and flanks; young forest gods, their faces and bodies as self-consciously perfect as those of Greek statues. Her buttocks had squirmed their shape into the moist earth of the bank, not once—many times. They were all young, all beautiful; no wonder she had difficulty distinguishing one from the other. She supposed one of them had been Davy Brubaker, ludicrous as that seemed now. Sated, she returned to draw the substance of the tree close about her, and in the morning she awoke on the divan, struggling to draw the rough blanket over her against the morning's coolness.

The following day wasn't as difficult for her as she had thought it would be; there were all these things to do. She visited the beauty parlor, had lunch with several of the girls. After lunch there was her volunteer work at the hospital in a nearby city. She had gone through the day like a sleepwalker; there were ways to let routine take over and the time passed very quickly, but as she undressed in her bedroom, removing the tight layers, the bindings, she was remembering things. She heard herself mouthing platitudes at a woman who was in the process of dying, a little at a time, and who had looked vaguely amused. She had read greeting-card type verse to a man in a body cast.

William was sitting open-mouthed and snoring in front of the TV set. She turned off the set without waking him. It seemed there was a tension in the air, the wind blowing in the scent of rain. She remembered that smell. A few fireflies blinked above the grass as she hurried toward the shelter of the trees. It didn't seem odd to her to be running out barefoot, dressed only in the thin housecoat. The wind whipped stingingly cold drops against her skin, but she ran on. She knew she would recognize the glade with its soft floor of forest debris and its single great twisted oak. A dryad could never lose its own tree. She thought as she ran, panting, that she'd almost forgotten what it was like to feel this free—not since the days when she'd gone skinny-dipping with the town boys, one and then another, in the deep pools. She knew now that it had been done in true innocence, not in guilt as they had made her believe later, and if she ran swiftly enough, she might yet recapture that innocence.

Breathless, she reached the glade at last and fell exhausted to the dark forest floor. Lying there brought back that other time.

She'd escaped another of her father's fits of rage, the names he'd called her still burning in her ears. She'd blundered clumsily along the bank till she'd come to this place, where she'd collapsed, the pains beginning in earnest, as the midwife had warned they would. All the other tales the ignorant old woman had told her were in her head, too, and she'd been sure she was going to die as the pain washed over her, coming and going in waves and rhythms that had nothing to do with what she wanted. Some old knowledge she hadn't known she possessed had taken over then; must have, for she'd survived.

The rain was quite steady now, comforting, a kind of release. She rose, the thin robe gaping, pieces of brush and straw clinging to her doughy white flesh. She approached the tree with a rapt expression. There was a hollow there, and the dryad lay cocooned in rough bark in organic-smelling darkness. She reached in; her fingers scraped brittle wood pulp, felt a dry, twisted mass. "How strange to realize now,'' she thought, ''that you are all I ever had of beauty or of innocence. I'll make them wear the name—bastards—and give them back their guilt!'' She cradled the dark object in the crook of her arm; it was shriveled and brown like some old earth-buried tree root. ''Won't William and the others be surprised,'' she said, ''when they see how beautiful you've become?''

Nostalgia is seldom connected to the band of influence generated by our uneasiness about midnight. Yet there is a distinct danger to dwelling too long in the past that was not, ever, as good as we remember. Nostalgia can too often lead to self-pity, and self-pity too often leads to more than a simple case of psychological destruction.

Susan Casper lives and works in Philadelphia, and though she has been writing for only a couple of years, she has already made a name for herself as one to be watched eagerly.

SPRING FEVER

Susan Casper

The clock showed nine already. She'd overslept. Sandy couldn't believe it. By the time she woke up, the kids had already made their lunches and taken off for school, leaving a worse than usual mess behind them. Sandy yawned and combed her fingers through her hair. Hadn't even brushed the tangles out yet—she must look like hell. And what was worse, she didn't even care. Usually, she'd have the house half done by now, instead of wandering around aimlessly in a stupor, half-asleep. All she really wanted to do was go back to bed, but Amanda wasn't due until tomorrow; she'd have to do the cleaning herself. Wake up, kiddo, she told herself, time to get to work. She yawned again as she started the coffee maker, then drifted lethargically to the front door to see if the paper had come yet.

She opened the door—and suddenly it was spring. She'd been subconsciously prepared to be greeted by the same cold, gray, blustery weather they'd endured for weeks, but suddenly the sun was shining brightly out of a clear blue sky, and the air was balmy and warm. The big maple tree out front had broken out with tiny new green buds, and there were birds hopping about and squabbling on the lawn. No doubt about it—all at once, winter was gone. It was spring. She just stood there in the doorway for a moment, suddenly wide-awake, breathing in the velvety air, the breeze bringing her that wonderful smell of freshly cut grass, a smell that pleased and excited her, a smell that she always associated with bright April mornings from her girlhood, when the world was fresh and new and anything could happen. Instinctively, her eyes went to the burgundy Mercedes shining brightly in the driveway, and she frowned. Somehow, it was the wrong sort of car for the day. It had been a gift from Steve, but she had really wanted a white Trans Am. Now that was the right kind of car for a day like this, a car that would really *move*, that gave a feel for the road under your wheels. A hot car, the kind you could scream along in with the wind whipping through your hair—as different as could be from the calm stately bulk of the Mercedes, which sailed along so smooth and stolid and safe that it didn't even feel like you were driving. What was there about the first real spring day that made her want to get in her car and . . . go. Go anywhere. Just take off, right now, right this second, and not come back until . . . until she felt like it.

She wondered what Steve would say if he came home to find that she'd gone out and left the house like this. He certainly wouldn't understand. The Protestant work ethic gripped him like a vise. First you get your work done, and then—maybe—you can play. Nor would he understand her impulse to just pick up and *leave*, going no place in particular for no particular reason. Steve was about as spontaneous as a rock. She recalled the time, right before Michael was born, on a day very much like this one, when she was still working at Ridgeway. "Why don't we both call in sick today?" she had asked. "You can take me to the zoo, or something."

He'd just stared at her uncomprehendingly for a moment, then shook his head. "Sandy, I have a lot of work to do. And you . . . well, you'll be out of a job soon enough." He'd patted her bulging abdomen. "Give your boss a break, huh? Be a good girl and maybe I'll take you to a movie tonight after we get the place cleaned up." They never had gotten to that movie, though; he'd had to bring work home from the office . . .

She picked up the paper and went back inside. The coffee was ready. She drank it quickly, and then got to work. She pulled the vacuum cleaner out of the closet and went into the living room. She plugged it in, clipped on the attachment, and then, ignoring Steve's perplexing component set, snapped on the little portable radio that sat on a shelf in the bookcase.

The Beach Boys were harmonizing about having fun in Daddy's T-bird and she could almost feel the breeze through her hair, the gentle vibrations of the steering wheel under her fingers. . . . If she could get her work done in a hurry, maybe she would take a little ride this afternoon. Drive down to the old neighborhood and take a look around. Let the old nostalgia out for an airing. Why not?

She turned off the vacuum and began to plump the sofa cushions. There was something sticking out from behind one of the cushions, something bright, metallic, and pink against the muted beige and brown. She fished it out. A well-chewed pen. Probably Jennie's. But just for a moment, it had *meant* something to her. She associated that color with a funny taste in her mouth. What was it? . . . Her eyebrows wrinkled together and she ran her tongue over her teeth. Something her body had remembered before her brain . . .

Got it! The drinking glasses at Carol's house. Those horrible aluminum glasses that set her fillings off and made everything taste like icy metal. They had been just that shade of metallic pink. . . . Good old Carol. She'd married Ben Wickert about a year before Sandy married Steve, but somewhere she'd heard that they'd gotten divorced. And Carol stuck with three kids. She wished they hadn't lost touch. What good times they used to have together. Carol and Ben, Sandy and Ray.

Ray. . . .

They say your first love stays with you forever. She could see him now, just as clearly as if he were standing in front of her. The boy she had almost married—with his gorgeous black Sal Mineo curls, his shirt open halfway down to show off his hairy chest, and those magnificent blue eyes that put even Paul Newman's to shame. The "little greaseball from Venango Street," as her mother had called him. But nobody could dance like he could.

The D.J. played "I'm Your Puppet," and Sandy stared hard at the radio. Almost as if he knew what she was thinking, he had played their song. The song that had been playing that night when they sat in the back of his souped-up

Ford down at Beechers Point . . . the night she had almost let him go "all the way." She could still feel his lips, hard and demanding, painfully pressed against her own. His hands on her body were clumsy and much too rough . . . and yet, how she had *wanted* him. It had never been the same with Steve. Steve was too tender, too considerate, too gentle. Making out with Ray had filled her with wild, breathless, all-consuming passion. She had never felt that kind of excitement again. She wondered what it would have been like with Ray if she *had* let him "go all the way," and she felt a shiver of illicit excitement go through her.

The hell with the house. Amanda was coming tomorrow, wasn't she? That's what they paid *her* for. As far as Steve was concerned . . . well, she was "calling in sick" today, and if he didn't like it, that was just too bad.

The Mercedes had been sitting in the sun. The leather upholstery warmed her legs through the thin double-knit slacks, and the steering wheel felt good in her hands. Too bad this wasn't a convertible; she felt claustrophobic in here, cut off from the wonderful spring air by all this steel and glass and chrome. She rolled the windows down to get as good a feeling of motion as possible, then let out the clutch and stomped down on the gas pedal. Houses whipped by on either side, and she fumbled a fresh pack of cigarettes open with one hand. There was never much traffic out here this time of day—she could afford to let the horses out a little.

Steve must have used this car last. The radio was tuned to an easy-listening channel. The Montovani Strings— elevator Muzak. She fumbled with the knob, trying to find the station she'd had on in the house, the one that played nothing but golden oldies. Yes, that had to be it. The announcer was extolling the virtues of Batter Fresh Bread, but she recognized his voice.

The breeze felt terrific. She pulled the combs from her hair and let the wind whip through it as she turned up the ramp to the expressway, leaving suburbia behind.

To the strains of the Dovelles singing "You Can't Sit Down," she eased down the Croton Avenue exit ramp and onto Rudman Street. Here was street after street of two-story storefronts with apartments overhead, interspersed with blocks of row houses and semidetached brick homes. The old neighborhood. She breezed through it, cruising down Moravian Street. There were no good memories here. She turned right on Castor, then right again on Eastwood. Out past her old high school.

Northeast High. She'd worn the pale blue satin with spaghetti straps and lace edging, her hair lacquered up into French curls, Ray's pair of orchids strapped on her wrist. She had felt the eyes on her that night; even Carol had been jealous of the way she looked, the way Ray had strutted with her on his arm.

She turned right on Cottman, speeding up as she hit the little-used back streets behind the school. She roared around the Boulevard and out to Decatur Road. The old drag strip—a wide, smooth strip of highway only three blocks long, where the factories belched their black smoke during the day and where nobody, but *nobody*, came at night, unless they were looking for a little action.

How many nights had they picked up someone at the Big Boy and driven up here to race? Too bad that the restaurant wasn't there anymore. That was one place she'd really like to take a look at.

She spotted the cyclone fence that Ray had run into once while he was trying to see just how fast her daddy's car would go. He'd had too many beers and just thought the big dent in the Chevy's fender was funny, but she remembered how scared she had been. Daddy was so mad he'd grounded her for a week, and Carol told her that Ray had picked up some little redhead. She thought the world would come to an end. But the first day she was allowed out, there was Ray, still waiting for her.

Her blue jeans were riding up on her, making her uncomfortable, and she tugged at them as she turned onto the twisting dirt trail that led up through the park.

Beechers Point was empty. She circled slowly around the tree-lined path. Tonight the place would be jammed with cars, their taillights burning so that the cops wouldn't come and shine spotlights through the steamed-up windows. She had seen them shining their lights into the next car over on the last night she had spent here with Ray. That was the thing that had made her break away from him at what was certainly the last possible instant. She had been grateful at the time, after she had cooled down and had a chance to think about it. Now she wasn't so sure. . . . Later that night she had gone out with Steve for the first time, putting temptation behind her. . . .

The sun was directly overhead now, and it had gotten quite warm. She hit the knob just below the dashboard and watched the top rise up into the air and slide down into its compartment. That was the thing she liked best about the old Chevy. She squealed around the corner, out of the park, and turned left onto the Boulevard, beating time to ''The In Crowd'' on the steering wheel.

She turned into the lot past the Big Boy, not slowing down until she was behind the restaurant. There it was. Her favorite stall, right at the end of the very first row, where she could see everything and be seen *by* everyone. She backed in and pressed the button on the speaker. ''I'll have a Big Boy and a chocolate Coke,'' she said.

She heard the car before she saw it. It was an old car, its motor exposed, dual pipes gleaming along the sides, its tail jacked up into the air. Orange rust paint dotted the bright green door. It backed into the adjoining stall and the motor gunned twice before it died. Sandy smiled. She checked herself in the mirror, applying a fresh coat of pale pink lipstick. As she blotted her lips together, the car door opened and Ray slipped inside.

"Order for me, babycakes," he said as he threw her white leather bag on the floor and slid over close by her side.

Oh, how her stomach fluttered whenever he sat this close! He put his arm around her shoulder and gestured with his other hand. "See that red Plymouth over there? Thinks he's really hot shit. Straight off the lot and he thinks he can take me with it. Look at the way he's staring." She looked over at the other car; the driver of the Plymouth had short hair combed down in bangs, Beatles-fashion, and his nylon windbreaker looked new and expensive. An uptown kid, slumming for a lark. He was sneering theatrically at them between bites of his burger, his girl hanging adoringly on his arm. It would be fun taking him on.

"I've got to get back early, Ray. Mother's making me go out with this son of a friend of hers tonight. A college boy," she said mischievously, teasing him. She saw Ray's hands tighten into fists, and relented. "I can't help it, honey. Honest, I don't *want* to go, but Mom says I can't see you anymore if I don't go out with Steve tonight."

"You can go home *now* if you want to," Ray said sullenly, "I'm sure Adele would just love to take on this porker with me."

"I'm sure she would," Sandy said, smiling thinly, "but the Bear would break both of your arms off and feed them to you if you tried to date his girl. And besides"—she moved over and put her arms around his neck—"we belong to each other, don't we?"

"Just see that you remember that when you're out with

that dip tonight.'' He still sounded sulky, but he glanced at
her speculatively as he spoke.

Sandy left her car in the back of the lot and slid into
Ray's. They toured the lot in an S pattern, checking out all
the stalls, then stopped in front of the Plymouth. The
driver smiled nastily and gave them the finger; his girlfriend
giggled and clapped. Ray's eyes narrowed to slits, but he
said nothing. He nodded his head to the driver to follow
and pulled out of the lot without looking back.

They took the drive up slowly. This was an insult to the
challenger, implying he couldn't keep up if they went any
faster. He pulled up beside them at the next red light. ''If
that's the best speed you can get out of that bucket,'' he
shouted, ''I'll be done before you even *get* there.'' The
Plymouth tore off, laying rubber as the light turned green.
Ray smiled, but kept his speed down. His smile was hard
and mean, and suddenly Sandy shivered and wished she
didn't have to go home when they were through. After a
race, when they were both excited, was the best time to go
to the Point. And the worst time, too, because then it was
the hardest to stop.

The car was waiting for them as they got to Decatur.
The plump little blonde slipped out of the red car and went
over to the side of the road. Sandy moved over, pressing
as close to Ray as she dared, and kissed him once for luck.
A wave of excitement went through her. Feeling flushed
and dizzy and almost drunk with excitement, she rested
her hand on the dashboard and riveted her eyes on the
blonde's arm, which was raised now, ready to drop. Ray
gunned the motor. The vibrations sent a shiver up her
spine.

The girl's arm dropped. Sandy heard the squeal of the
tires, felt the sharp surge of acceleration press her back
into the seat. The roaring wind snatched her breath away,
pulled her hair back from her head and slammed it down

into her face, stinging her forehead and cheeks. She could feel the road sliding by beneath them. The standing lights in the factory began to tick rapidly by and the cyclone fence became a translucent gray blur.

Ray was grim and intent, looking more gorgeous than she'd ever remembered seeing him. His clear blue eyes studied the road ahead and his sure, steady hands worked the gears and guided the wheel without hesitation. She glanced at the other car. It was steady beside them at first, then gradually began dropping behind. "We got him, baby," Ray whispered beside her. The curb rushed toward them, and she pressed her hand into the dash as a brace.

Ray hit the brake. The car screeched to a halt, bouncing on its springs for a moment before becoming still. Sandy squealed. She threw her arms around Ray's neck and kissed him. Her mouth opened under his, and she felt the hot, hard touch of his tongue. Heat shot through her again, flattening her stomach and tightening her thighs. Her whole body seemed to be aching, and she wanted him more at that moment than she ever had in all their time together. She began to tremble.

After a few moments, she broke blindly away and moved over toward the door. He looked at her, angry, hurt . . . she couldn't tell which. His face was like stone. "Come on, I'll take you back to your car," he said. "You've got a hot date with a college boy tonight."

She stared at him from across the car—his clear blue eyes, that little curl hanging down on his forehead, his clean-lined jaw. "Ray," she heard herself saying breathlessly, "don't take me back. I don't want to go out with anyone else, honest. You're the only one for me. Let's go up to Beechers Point . . ."

He turned and stared right into her face. He still looked hard and mean; a vein ticked in his cheek. "Uh uh," he said deliberately, shaking his head. "No way. I'm tired of being teased. I'm tired of going home at night feeling like I'm gonna bust. I need a *woman*, not a little girl. If I take you out to Beechers Point tonight, it's not gonna be like all the other times. It's gonna be put up or shut up. No changing your mind.''

She was very quiet for a moment, and then she sighed and melted against him. Trembling at her own daring, she put her hand on his thigh. ''Take me to Beechers Point,'' she said, her own voice sounding husky and strange in her ears. Her face felt like it was on fire. ''Way down deep in the back where nobody will find us. I'm not going to change my mind. . . .''

Sandy threw the breakfast dishes into the sink and ran out to get the morning paper. Yesterday someone had stolen it, and Ray had been hopping-mad. One of the kids had left his lunch bag lying on the hall table, she saw. Well, good—let him do without. It would serve him right. Sometimes she got so tired of the kids she could scream. She opened the front door and unlocked the screen . . . although, with that huge hole in it, why they bothered to lock it in the first place was beyond her. The boy had left the paper all the way down on the bottom step, again. She made a mental note to speak to him about it when he came around for collection, and went down to get it.

What a beautiful day! After that long, grim winter of wearing sweaters and keeping the heat turned down to save money, after suffering through what seemed like a decade's worth of gray, slushy, blustery days packed into one season, after all that—suddenly it was spring. There was no doubt about it. All at once, winter was gone, and she was standing in the balmy, velvety air, feeling the warm hand of the sun on her shoulders, drinking in that wonderful springtime smell of freshly cut grass . . . a smell that always pleased and excited her, a smell that she always

associated with bright April mornings from her girlhood,
when the world was fresh and new and anything could
happen. She glanced at the secondhand Beetle that Ray
had gotten her to drive the kids around in, and she felt a
sudden urge to go for a ride. Get away from the damn
housework for a while, and the kids, and her sullen,
miserable husband. Better than breaking her butt while he
spent the day flirting with every broad who brought her car
down to the garage, anyway. Hell, she *would* go for a ride,
just take off, right now, right this second. What was there
about the first real day of spring that made her want to get
in her car and . . . go. Go *anywhere*. And not come back
until she felt like it.

The strongest emotion one feels at midnight is fear; the strongest emotion one feels when one is in love isn't love—it's fear.

Leslie Horvitz is the co-author of the best selling novel, DONOR, and is currently working on a new thriller for NAL.

PICTURES OF A WOMAN GONE

Leslie Alan Horvitz

The single-engine Aerocondor plane dropped lower in the immense blue sky so that its passengers could better glimpse the curious tapestry of lines etched four thousand years ago into the landscape of Nazca.

Glen Margolin aimed his camera, a Canon AE-1, not at the earth below him, but at his wife of six months, the former Kelly White. She, more than any ancient relics or incomprehensible designs fashioned by extinct Indian tribes,

169

was what truly compelled him. She was endlessly beautiful to him, maybe too much so; every time he looked at her, he found something new to discover.

Kelly registered the click of the camera going off, but paid it no mind, by now used to her husband's incessant picture-taking.

"Look out the window, Glen; you're missing everything."

He looked; below him there extended to the horizon a patchwork of geometric patterns: straight lines intersecting obtuse triangles, spirals running tangentially to rectangles and squares. From the maze flowers emerged, and insects, fish, birds, whales, even one figure which resembled an ancient astronaut.

Kelly was fascinated, just as Glen had expected she'd be, which was why he'd proposed coming to Peru for their belated honeymoon. Like almost all the women of Glen's acquaintance, she was ready to believe in fortune-tellers, tea leaves, Tarot cards, and writers like von Daniken who ascribed to such phenomena as the Nazca lines an extraterrestrial origin.

Glen, who at thirty-five was four years his wife's senior, assumed that sooner or later she would grow out of these things. And to try to hasten that day, he did what he could to interest her in science: astronomy, physics, geology—he didn't care what enticed her so long as it was based on hard, rock-solid fact. None of it succeeded in capturing her imagination, however; her body might be bound to the laws of science that Glen was always talking about, but not her mind.

The single-engine was making a racket, almost drowning out the voice of the guide, a short, cocoa-colored man with slanted eyes that lent him almost an Asiatic appearance. His command of English was uncertain at best. "The people here," he was saying, "call this El Calendario because there are those who think these lines mark out the months of a calendar.''

"What's he saying?'' Kelly asked, straining to hear.

Glen listened for a while longer and tried to put into his own words what the guide had said. "Apparently, the way some of these lines are drawn, they're oriented towards the sunrise at the time of the solstices—on June 21st and December 21st. The June solstice is the beginning of winter down here.''

"I see,'' Kelly mumbled. Her eyes focused on the terrain, but she seemed unable to distinguish the particular lines the guide was referring to.

"What's he talking about now?'' she asked Glen.

"He says that the Inca used to call the Pleiades of November the Collca. It means the granary.''

"Harvest time?''

"Right.''

"But the Pleiades of June,'' he went on, "is called the Oncoy.''

"And what does that mean?''

"The Disease.''

Glen had first met Kelly White on his way to work, a year before, early summer in the Northern Hemisphere, a day on which a great deal of nubile, college-age flesh was on display.

She was headed in his direction, magnificent of bearing, her walk deliberately paced; the rhythm of it, were it set to music, would have been marked *andante*. His eyes caught on the lilting movement of hips, then of the suggestion of her well-rounded breasts, loose within an agate-blue silk shirt that floated over her hips, and finally they rested on her face, and he was lost.

He stepped up to her, raised his camera, and snapped her picture.

He told her the truth, that he was with a small ad agency which he'd founded and was now managing, though he was having to struggle for every success he achieved. He noticed that she was carrying a portfolio. She said she was studying art at one of the small colleges the city of Boston abounded in. He suggested that she consider doing freelance work for him; he was so determined not to lose her that he resolved to keep giving her assignments, even if it should turn out that she possessed no talent whatsoever.

She did have talent, though it was raw and in need of development that only time and unceasing patience could bring. Glen doted on her. It had been his conviction that men generally ended up with women who were neither much better nor more intelligent than they were themselves. He'd heard of people who married believing they were soul mates, two lost spirits in corporeal form trying to somehow become one again, but in his opinion, these people didn't have their heads screwed on too tight. It was more a matter of genes, he felt, of one person's chromosomes crying out in the night for another's.

Which was why he, a man of modest looks and twelve pounds overweight, with a paunch he vowed one day to be rid of, could not understand why Kelly so responded to him, why one day three months after they met on Boston Common, she agreed to marry him. It was enough to make him think that there was a God, after all.

The morning following their expedition to the plains of Nazca, Glen and Kelly left for Lima. They weren't spending any time in the capital; they had a problem with time. A month was all they'd allotted for this trip and they wanted to see Brazil once they'd finished their tour of Peru. So all they saw of Lima was its airport, a dull, gray place, which in the afternoons could have doubled as a ghost town of sheds and empty terminals and runways on which no plane ever seemed to move. Only as the sun began slipping towards the west did the airport come alive again, and it was then that the Margolins departed for Cuzco, eleven thousand feet high in the Andes.

"The air's a lot thinner here than where we've been, Kelly," Glen said as soon as they stepped off the Faucett Airlines plane that had brought them to Cuzco. "So you'd better not run around or drink any alcohol tonight. Otherwise you'll have a hangover like you wouldn't believe. I'm told it's like the bends that divers get if they come up too quickly."

Kelly shot him an irritated look. She didn't like being told what to do. And, as Glen knew, she especially didn't like secondhand wisdom. She seldom read, except for magazines and junk novels she'd tear through and forget as soon as they were discarded. She seemed to be under the impression that anything not experienced directly was not worth paying attention to.

She only pretended to comply with his wishes. After a few hours she grew bored, and refusing to stay in their hotel room so long as she could hear people walking around, talking and laughing, enjoying the warm June night she said she was going out for a walk. "Why don't you come along?" she urged him.

He agreed, but suspected that it would not end with a walk. The central square of Cuzco was known as the Plaza de Armas and when they reached it, they were assaulted with booming music: Donna Summers, Peter Tosh, the Rolling Stones, all coming out of a second-floor window over one of the colonnaded walkways flanking the square. A discotheque.

"Let's go take a look," Kelly said.

"You know you're going to do more than want to take a look."

He felt he was with a child who had to be restrained for

its own good, but when she insisted, he didn't take long to capitulate. He always lost when he fought with her.

He refused to dance, but that didn't stop her. A man with a beard the color of rust peppered gray approached her and, reaching out his hands to take hold of hers, virtually pulled her onto the floor. She didn't resist.

"Kelly!" he shouted, but it did him no good. She probably didn't even hear him with the music.

Glen watched, angry, resentful, and jealous, too, he supposed. When Kelly invited him to dance, he declined, but not because he feared what effect it might have the next day on his health. Rather, he was defending a position he'd staked out; he couldn't very well make a mockery of his own words. Besides, he wasn't much of a dancer. Not like this man who, from the looks of him, was possibly Dutch or Belgian, certainly European.

Glen imagined that her nameless partner was the sort of man that truly appealed to Kelly, that all he was was an aberration among her lovers. There was, for instance, Hal Maburn, whom Glen had never met. Nor had he ever wanted to meet him.

Hal and Kelly had lived together for fourteen months, an interlude in Kelly's life that culminated in heated arguments and mutual recriminations, all punctuated by a great many slamming doors and shattered dishes.

What caused them to break up, Kelly told Glen, was drugs. Hal was consuming them and pushing them; Hal was recreating the world with them—and in the process recreating Kelly herself with them, until she'd mustered the strength enough to pull away.

But Glen was convinced that whatever had attracted Kelly to a man like Hal Maburn must be still at work, dormant, but ready to return to operation given the right stimulus. For all he knew, this man with the rust-colored beard could be just that.

*   *   *

In the morning Glen woke to the sound of Kelly groaning. Her face was contorted with pain. "Oh, God," she said, "everything hurts like hell."

She looked flushed and haggard, as if somebody had come along during the time they slept and aged her by twenty years.

"Don't tell me you told me so," she said. "I'm paying for my crime, I know. Just let me sleep."

He asked if he could get her something, but she refused. "Later maybe I'll order up some tea." With that, she burrowed herself back under the covers, seeking escape from the daylight that penetrated into their room.

So Glen, armed with camera and guidebook, went out to explore Cuzco himself. He took some pleasure in being on his own, with no need to justify his selection of sites to Kelly. For when she went touring, her idea was to get a sense of things, to absorb the atmosphere; details didn't interest her and Glen's fascination for ruins and old churches was incomprehensible to her.

From cursory observation, Glen was struck by how, in the midst of tourists and the local Spanish population, the Quechuas wandered, dark, brooding people with high cheekbones and eyes whose slant told of Asiatic races that had centuries before crossed land bridges which no longer exist. They were proud and impoverished, the men and women both with wide-brimmed black hats shadowing their brows, their torsos blanketed by mantas of red, black, and the bright gold of the sun they still worshipped. They were everywhere on the Plaza de Armas, squatted on its periphery, imploring passersby to stop and inspect the jewelry, antiquities (some genuine, others newly created), and gold coins they'd put out for sale.

They lived in the slums of Cuzco and in the mountains that surrounded the valley on which Cuzco was situated.

Glen understood that they still looked upon Cuzco as their religious center and yearned even at this late date for the return of the Inca emperor. It was rumored that he was still locked up in one of the towers of the great cathedral which dominated one side of the square. In 1950, after an earthquake, the Quechuas had come down from the mountains to wait in the plaza in expectation that the tower would collapse and free the emperor. It was likely that after all these years, many of them were still waiting.

The site Glen most wanted to see was the Corincancha, the great Inca temple which once was covered by seven hundred sheets of gold. But of course, the gold was gone, stripped by the first Spaniards to arrive in the city in 1533, and there was not much left to see, just an undistinguished courtyard set inside the convent of Santo Domingo. Even someone prepared to be disappointed would come away from this place feeling cheated.

"One vital aspect of Corincancha, however, has been almost forgotten," Glen read as he stood in the middle of the courtyard, trying to imagine what it must have been like with four thousand priests and attendants running about, performing improbable rituals. "It was the Inca's principal astronomical observatory."

Glen recalled the lines at Nazca, the manner in which they'd been aligned to the stars, to the solstices and equinoxes. It was June 19th, two days before the solstice. Two days before the dawn rise of the Pleiades, the Oncoy. Disease.

The guidebook noted the presence of three holes bored into the outer walls of Santo Domingo. He would never have found them if he hadn't known where to look for them. Although the true purpose of these holes was unknown, it was suspected that the blood of sacrificial victims was somehow channeled through conduits leading to these holes. Without having any idea why, he tapped the holes, one after another, and to his surprise, produced three notes of a musical scale. The result was the beginning of a tune that he thought he knew very well but which had now slipped out of his mind.

Glen was obliged to go off on his own again the next day while Kelly was laid up, recuperating. When he returned early in the evening, though, he discovered her gone. "Cabin fever," she'd written in the note she left on the bureau top for him. "I just had to get out. Be back soon. K."

Since she'd neglected to mention at what time she'd gone out, he had no idea what soon meant.

He sat down to wait for her, assuming she'd be back in time for dinner. But she was not. He grew frantic, but tempted as he was to go and look for her, he remained where he was, certain that he would miss her otherwise.

Close to midnight she did come back. "What are you doing in the dark?" she asked, flicking on the light.

"Where were you?" His voice contained no anger, only resignation—and relief. At least she did return. That was something.

"I was out walking."

"Walking?" Cuzco wasn't so very big that you couldn't walk from one end of it to the other in an hour, unless you roamed into its suburbs, and he doubted she'd do that. "You didn't go dancing, did you?"

"No," she said. "I went walking. And I got lost. I wandered into the Quechua district. At least I thought it must be the Quechua district. And I couldn't find my way out again for quite a long time."

"Why didn't you ask someone?"

"I don't speak Spanish and I certainly don't speak Quechua," she said. "No one would understand me."

"And then you found your way out?"

''That's right,'' she said. ''And then I found my way out.''

''You must be starved.''

She shook her head; she was already in the bathroom. He could see through the doorway the image of her in the mirror, her fingers undoing the buttons of her blouse. He tried to see if her eyes were dilated the way they'd be if she'd smoked too much grass. But when he stepped up close to her, by the basin, and looked into her eyes, he could see nothing there that he could fathom. It was as if no one was at home.

It was drizzling on and off all during the journey to Machu Picchu, but when Glen and Kelly arrived at the small train depot on the other side of the river from the ruins, it began to clear. A ribbon of yellow light peered out from under the mist way towards the east.

A fleet of minibuses was parked by the depot, ready to transport the tourists across the Urubamba River and up the steep, granite slopes of Machu Picchu, depositing them all in front of the hotel—the only hotel on the mountain— that would serve as the Margolins' home for the night.

Once they'd registered and secured their room, they went together to the entrance of the ruins and paid for the tickets. It was only then that Kelly said that she thought it a better idea if they each went off and explored the ruins on their own and then met back at the hotel for a late lunch.

''Are you angry with me?'' Glen asked.

Kelly got a surprised look on her face. ''Why, no. What makes you say that?''

She kissed him and, guidebook in hand, started down a path that descended in the direction of a cluster of rock lintels which had once served as the homes of Inca royalty.

Machu Picchu had had to wait until 1905 to be discovered by the outside world; before then it had been lost to history, a city that even the Incas had obliterated from memory by the time the conquistadors came to Peru. Of the skeletal remains unearthed at the site, most belonged to women and children. Something had happened to the men, but no one knew what.

Hundreds of tourists were picking their way among the walls and pillars and terraces that constituted the whole of this remarkable site. Glen tried to concentrate on what he was seeing, diligently consulting his guidebook (a different edition from Kelly's and more exhaustive), repeatedly taking pictures with his Canon, but all the while he was tracking Kelly as she moved from one spot to another.

A momentary panic would seize him whenever he'd lose sight of her. But then she'd reappear, her blonde hair, blue rain hat, and tan coat far below him.

The clouds, gray and swollen with rain, scudded overhead, propelled by a northerly wind. The sun was a pale copper penny in a milky-white atmosphere.

Kelly was now standing in the middle of a towerlike structure that enclosed a natural rock formation on which a rectangle had been carved. In one of the walls a hole could be discerned.

Glen hunted through his guidebook, interested in finding out what purpose the structure had served. When he redirected his gaze at her, he saw that she was no longer alone.

A man was standing next to her, apparently talking to her. He was obviously a Peruvian, a Quechua, with an alpaca manta thrown over his chest and a black straw hat rising from his head.

As he watched, a peculiar thing happened. The sun broke through the cloud cover and cast its light over the granite ruins. A single ray shot through the hole above Kelly's head and, for an instant, struck both her and the unknown Quechua beside her. Then the sun was blotted out by clouds again.

Glen understood what had happened. Kelly had—by chance? by intention?—wandered into the Intihuatana, the astronomical observatory of Machu Picchu, in time for the winter solstice to occur. The Intihuatana had been built specifically to calculate the date of the June solstice; Kelly could very well have discovered this information, just as Glen had, from her guidebook. Nonetheless, Glen didn't like it. He felt that she was becoming a part of something that he could not penetrate, could never in a million years hope to reach.

At lunch he suspected that she would mention nothing about the man she'd spoken to in the observatory, but to his surprise, she brought him up almost immediately.

"His name is Luis," she said. "He's a guide and he's looking for people to take with him on the Inca Trail."

The Inca Trail, as Glen knew, was an ancient Inca highway that extended through jungle and high sierra from Machu Picchu in the direction of Cuzco. It customarily took four to five days to complete its entire distance.

"You told him that we don't have the time for a hike, didn't you? We're due in Rio the day after tomorrow."

"I know the itinerary," she said. "We planned it together, remember?"

The fact was that she did not tell Luis that they lacked the time. What she told him was that she would have to ask her husband, but that she thought it would be fine with him. Before giving him a chance to reply, she added that Luis could lead them to Vilicabamba, the last redoubt of the Incas after they were driven by Spanish incursions deep into the jungle.

"But, Kelly, no one knows exactly where Vilicabamba is. I've read a couple of books about it and no one's in agreement as to its location."

This logic was not about to carry the day with her.

"The Indians knew all about Machu Picchu before an American discovered it in 1905, right? So maybe the Indians know where Vilicabamba is, too. It's just that maybe no one ever bothered to ask them."

To Glen, whether Luis could or could not find a lost Inca city in the middle of a jungle—and in a government-restricted area, to boot—was irrelevant. It was one thing to visit sites that were accessible to the public; it was quite another to strike off on a wild goose chase.

"We're going to Rio, and that's final," he declared.

In the morning, when Luis met them in the lobby of the hotel, he'd brought with him all the equipment that they would require for the hike: backpacks, sleeping bags, tents, water bottles, first-aid kit, and a provision of food that included dried meat, dried fruit, cheeses, and tins of sardines, pâtés, and tuna.

Luis struck Glen as a sullen, quite possibly illiterate man, whose air of deference was only a cover for his disdain for both of them, Glen more than Kelly. He was not tall of stature—none of the Quechuas were—but he was handsome in a dark, sullen sort of way, with deep-set eyes that hinted at a knowledge of passion and brutality that would forever be denied Glen.

Glen was not only embarking on this hike against his will; he was also not feeling very well. He wasn't sure what was wrong with him; it seemed to be a combination of malaise, an incipient cold, and altitude sickness. Whatever it was, Glen concluded, it was undoubtedly psychosomatic in origin, although that made it no less difficult to endure.

Were it not for fear that Kelly would have done everything to spoil the rest of their vacation if he hadn't consented to this trip, he would never have given in to her. He wasn't certain that he didn't hate her that morning for holding him a slave to her whims and emotions.

By the end of the first day of the hike, Glen had only a dim memory of heat and dust stirred up from the baking earth underfoot. For a time Kelly and he had walked side-by-side, with Luis gamely forging on ahead. But after several hours had passed, Kelly tired of the slow pace he was maintaining and joined Luis, leaving him to bring up the rear.

Luis observed his discomfort and offered him Microren for altitude sickness, but he refused, asserting that there was nothing wrong with him, that he just liked to go slow to have an opportunity to savor the sights and snap some pictures. Luis shrugged and went back to setting up camp for the night; it made no difference to him.

The second day, they passed through groves of eucalyptus and palms threaded through with irrigation canals, and while Glen felt no better than he had the previous day, he took heart from the bucolic setting and the easiness of their path.

But by noon, after traversing a small, noisy ravine, their course took them up an incline marked by massive boulders and bluffs where it was practically impossible, at times, to get any sort of purchase at all.

What particularly astonished him was how tireless Kelly appeared to be; she showed no sign of faltering even after several hours of arduous climbing, and only once or twice did she seem to have difficulty keeping up with Luis who, after all, was obviously experienced in making treks of this kind.

It then occurred to him that what she'd been chewing so incessantly in the last two days was not gum, as he'd supposed, but cocoa leaves provided to her by Luis, whose generosity to Glen was confined to altitude sickness pills. Not that Glen would have accepted the leaves in any case.

He asked her if he was right.

"So what? The worst thing that happens is, if you do it long enough, with this yibie stuff here, you ruin your gums." The yibie she referred to was the lime-rich substance which activated the alkalis in the leaves and liberated the high from it. "It's not like doing cocaine, Glen."

He wondered about that, but he didn't care to press her. It was the wrong moment.

"Something's bothering you," she said. "What?"

"I'm just not feeling well, that's all."

"No, it's something else."

You should know better than I, he thought, but he held his peace and eventually she stopped asking.

The climb so much exhausted him that by sunset he simply got inside his sleeping bag with the intention of reading a bit. The book fell from his hands and he was out almost instantly.

The sound of a woman's laughter brought him awake. It was the middle of the night, as dark and impenetrable as he'd ever seen it, and the woman who was laughing was his wife, Kelly Margolin.

She was not next to him in her sleeping bag; she was with Luis somewhere in the darkness—not far, he judged by the direction of the sound, from the campfire which had, while he slept, burned itself out.

Again he drifted off and again he woke, perhaps minutes, perhaps hours later.

This time she was much closer to him, not laughing anymore, but talking. He strained to hear.

"It's all right," she kept saying over and over, "it's all right; relax—there, you're coming down now; you'll be fine, you'll see."

She was standing maybe half a dozen yards from him;

at one point he could make out her eyes: how incandescent they were, but how far away they were too. Then she began to walk around, this way and that, making small circles.

Glen looked for Luis, but he wasn't there. It appeared as though Kelly were talking to herself or to some presence that she imagined to be there beside her.

"Kelly?" he said softly, afraid somehow of intruding.

But if she heard him, she did not acknowledge it. Instead, she continued to talk, but not quite as distinctly, so he couldn't follow her words. Four or five minutes went by like this, and then, abruptly, she dropped down on top of the sleeping bag. He thought he heard a sob escaping from her, but maybe not.

She lay there, quiet, exposed to the chill. Glen got up and carefully draped his extra blanket over her. She stirred, but her eyes remained tightly sealed.

When she rose in the morning, Glen was already awake. His health was somewhat improved, but his disposition was not. A permanent state of panic had gotten hold of him, and try as he might, he could not shake it off.

While he drank the tea that Luis had prepared, the guide sat like a melancholy Buddha, his eyes fixed on the valley that lay below their campsite. What he was thinking was anyone's guess.

Glen deliberated as to whether he should ask Kelly about last night, but he needn't have bothered. She volunteered to tell him without any prodding.

"It was uncanny, Glen," she began. "I was talking to Hal. I had the feeling that I was right there with him."

"Right where?"

"In Boston, where he lives. But we weren't at his apartment; it was somebody else's apartment—I didn't recognize it."

It's Hal she really wants, he thought.

"He was in bad shape," she continued; "he was suffering from a heroin overdose. I don't know how I knew, but I did. There were some other people in the room with us, friends of his, and they were giving him cold compresses to try and bring him down. He was unconscious, but he was talking to me and pleading with me. And I was trying to answer, trying to talk him down."

A question sprang to his mind then.

"Did Luis give you something last night, a drug of some kind?"

"The cocoa leaves, you mean?"

"No, not cocoa leaves. Something stronger than that, a hallucinogen maybe."

Her silence told him what he needed to know.

"Hal," he said when she didn't immediately reply, "is five thousand miles away."

"I'm not going to argue with you," she told him, and got up and walked over to where Luis was sitting.

On their third day they were obliged to cross terrain that was dense with overgrowth and where birds screeched unceasingly and legions of bloated winged insects rustled among the brush and tendrils at their feet.

By the trail a fast-running stream suddenly appeared; it forked some distance up ahead, then vanished into the promiscuous vegetation.

Luis gestured to this stream and said, "There, that is where Manco's wife was sent."

At first neither Glen nor Kelly had any idea what he was referring to. Then he explained that Manco had been one of the last Inca emperors, the ruler of Vilicabamba. When he'd rebuffed the Spanish offers to surrender, his kidnapped wife was murdered and thrown into the stream so that its currents could convey her corpse past Manco's position.

"So Vilicabamba is in that direction?" Kelly asked, clearly excited that they were approaching their goal.

Luis nodded, but said nothing.

Glen only thought of the blood draining from the woman's wounds as she was borne home to her husband on the water's crest. He hoped never to lay eyes on Vilicabamba.

That afternoon they came, after ascending a series of stone steps dug into the flank of a mountain, to a natural rampart formed by slabs of rock and the surrounding wood. Here they found a confusion of stones that had once been part of a fortification. And it was easy to see why; below, there stretched a valley which an enemy army could use to make its approach to Machu Picchu. This point commanded a sweeping view of the valley, and, if Luis was to be believed, for many years was employed by the Incas as a strategic outpost.

"Tomorrow," Luis told him as they stood there, gazing down into the valley, "I will get horses for us and we will ride out to see Sayacmarca."

"Sayac-what?" Glen asked.

"Very important ruins, very beautiful." To Kelly he said, "This is the gateway to Vilicabamba."

Vilicabamba again. It was getting to be like a curse.

"How long will all this take?"

"Not long. We ride out early; we come back early."

From experience Glen knew that what not long meant to Luis was not what not long meant to him.

"And where will you get the horses?" Kelly wanted to know. Looking about, she could spot nothing that would hint at the proximity of a stable or farm where horses might be quartered.

"There is a place not far from here," Luis assured them. "You let Luis worry."

*   *   *

As soon as Glen mounted the horse, he knew he was not going to make it. His mysterious illness, which had never really left him, was back in earnest; attempting to ride for God knows how many hours, across the unpromising terrain he'd viwed through his binoculars, on the back of this nervous horse, was surely the height of folly.

Why couldn't Kelly also be sick? he asked himself. Just this once.

But she was far from sick; she was in as buoyant a mood as he'd ever seen her. "I haven't ridden a horse for ages," she said. "Are you absolutely certain you can't come?"

To his regret, he was absolutely certain. A couple of minutes seated awkwardly on the horse and already he was nauseated.

He watched them ride away. And as they did, he snapped pictures of them with his Canon AE-1. The sun was barely up when they set out, but it caught them in its rays, seeming to set them on fire. Luis was recognizable by his black hat, Kelly by her blonde hair, but otherwise, as they grew increasingly distant, there was nothing to distinguish one from the other.

I should've gone, he told himself; no matter how terrible I feel, I should've gone with them.

He continued taking pictures. He didn't know why, but there was nothing else that seemed quite so worth doing.

Then he couldn't see them any longer. He wondered whether the Canon was better able to keep them in sight than he was.

The sun was much higher now and its white scorching light obliterated the contours of the mountains and the valley. Sayac-what? He tried to remember the name of the ruins, but he could not.

He waited. The only thing that compelled his interest

was the succession of bright red digits that flashed by on the screen of his watch.

At eleven he picked up his binoculars and peered down into the valley, thinking that if they were to return by noon, surely they would have to be starting back. But nowhere could they be seen.

At noon there was no sign of them either. Nor at one. The hours had a remorseless way about them; they seemed not to want to progress. The sun remained obstinately high, burning down until the whole of the valley was bleached of color. And still they did not come back.

For nearly two months Glen remained in Peru, lodging at the same hotel off the Plaza de Armas that he and Kelly had stayed in when they'd got to Cuzco, in forlorn hope that she would one day come to find him there. He spent his days between the police station and the American consulate, beseeching officials to redouble their efforts to locate his wife. The Peruvian officials were at first cordial and sympathetic, but as time wore on, it was apparent that they had little interest in the affair. They looked on Glen simply as an annoyance.

"Come back tomorrow, señor," he was repeatedly told; "by then we might have some news for you."

The American consul, a phlegmatic young man who devoted most of his energies to renewing visas and calling on fellow countrymen who'd been clapped into jail for attempting to smuggle cocaine through internal customs at Cuzco Airport, was willing to listen to Glen for hours. Possibly he had nothing else to do with his time. At any rate, he could offer him practically no consolation. "It happens that people disappear on occasion. There are parts of the country, close to where your wife was last seen, that you need special permission from the interior ministry to visit."

The implication in his words was that Kelly had ventured into the jungle—or whatever was just over the horizon—at her own risk, and perhaps in violation of Peruvian law.

When Glen raised the matter of their guide, the consul shrugged and said, "There are probably a thousand guides in this country named Luis. Do you know this man's last name?"

Glen confessed that he didn't. It had not ever occurred to him to inquire. And what good would it have done? The man could have easily lied to him.

"Do you know where he lives?"

Again Glen had no idea.

"So you see, there's not much I can do. I'll put as much pressure as I'm able to on Garcia to continue the investigation, but I wouldn't want you to get your hopes up."

Garcia was the brusque, extravagantly moustached man who was in charge of the province's police force. Glen rarely had an opportunity to see him in person; usually he had to confine his dealings to bored functionaries who, without exception, insisted on serving him coffee before allowing him to explain his problem.

From noon to three in the afternoon, it was impossible to find anyone in authority anywhere; everyone was at home, at lunch, or asleep. In the evenings and through the nights, when all offices were shut down for the day, Glen lingered in bars and discotheques, among a mixed crowd of tourists, expatriates, and indolent Peruvian youths. He consumed amounts of alcohol that would in the past have put him under the table. When he woke in the mornings, he would have terrific pounding headaches. The hangovers were worse because he was carrying on his binges eleven thousand feet above sea level.

Not a day passed when he didn't look at the photographs he'd taken during their final weeks together. He felt that unless he had Kelly's face to inspect daily, he was in danger of forgetting what she looked like. In particular he studied the last series of photos he'd made, of her and Luis on horseback, riding out into the valley. It was not every man who had a pictorial record of his wife's disappearance.

He purchased a magnifying glass so that he could be sure to see the last shadow of her, the last hazy speck of her, before she went over the horizon.

Actually, he could not be absolutely certain where exactly the camera lost sight of her. He didn't know why it should matter, but it did.

At first he could not bring himself to write back news of what had happened. He had hope in the first week that she might reappear and that no one else need learn of the incident. But when she failed to return, he had no choice but to let their families know.

He wrote that she'd become lost in the jungle. He said that the American and Peruvian authorities were doing everything possible to find her. He did not mention Luis in any of the letters or telegrams.

He spent one last futile week in Lima, discussing the situation with the American ambassador and a host of lesser bureaucrats, all of whom assured him that they would do their best to follow up on the case. They urged him to go home, saying that there was nothing to be gained by his further presence in Peru.

Going home, he realized, would be tantamount to acknowledging that Kelly was gone forever, but there was no way he could remain away indefinitely. For one thing, he was running out of money; for another, the employees to whom he'd delegated the running of his business were wiring him almost daily, appealing to him to come back; there were problems only he could set right.

As much as he could, he avoided everyone he knew once he got back to Boston. He paid obligatory calls on his parents and on hers. Everyone made a great show of understanding, but it was obvious to him that he was being blamed for Kelly's disappearance. He only fueled suspicions by obscuring many of the details. "There's more to this Luis character than he's telling us," he one day overheard Kelly's mother say to her husband.

At work he found more sympathy, but even that didn't last very long. He was so aloof, so miserable, that he exerted a demoralizing influence on the people who worked for him. His heart wasn't in the business any longer; he committed grave errors, failed to woo new clients, and did nothing to stop old ones from leaving. Even his employees began bailing out. But Glen was so despondent that it made no difference to him.

Friends of Glen's tried to help him; they invited him to dinners and to parties, broadly hinting that there were intriguing young women to be met at these events. Glen declined practically all of these invitations. It struck him that he was becoming a recluse, but he thought he actually preferred it that way.

He stayed at home nights, drinking and watching slides. He lived with Kelly in his head and he lived with her on the screen.

One night in April, around ten, the phone rang. The phone so infrequently rang during the nights that it jarred him. People had long since given up on trying to rescue him from his depression; they figured that he must deserve it.

He was drunk on scotch; a mist was seeping pleasantly into his brain.

"Hello?"

There was a long silence on the other end. Glen thought he could hear the honking of a car. The call must be coming from a public phone booth.

"Hello? Who is this?"

He was about to hang up when he heard the familiar voice.

"Glen. Glen? This is Kelly, Glen."

He didn't believe what he was hearing. His first reaction was that this was a hoax, a cruel joke. But the voice was right; the voice was Kelly's.

"Kelly? Is that you? Is it really you?"

"Yes, it's me; it's really me, Glen. I'm home; I came back. I want to see you."

"Where are you calling from?"

"I'm not far away. Can I see you tonight? Now?"

"Yes, yes, of course," he was stammering, his words barely audible even to him.

"Do you have company?"

"No, I'm alone."

"Good. I'll be there in a little-while."

"But where are you? I'll pick you up . . ."

But she'd already hung up.

Glen could not sit. He paced through his house, his drink gripped in his hand, thinking, not thinking. After half an hour had passed, he thought that maybe she hadn't phoned, that maybe he'd been hallucinating, his imagination fired by longing and scotch in equal measures.

Then the bell chimed, once, twice.

He ran to the door, threw it open.

Kelly was standing there, her face silhouetted by the glow from the lantern fixture hanging over her head. She was wearing a long white raincoat and a rain hat into which she'd tucked her hair. It was not raining, though; perhaps, Glen thought, it had been wherever she'd come from.

He beckoned her in. In the fuller light of the hallway, she looked a great deal tanner than he remembered her being, but also much more tired, weary actually, depleted.

She tossed off her coat and hat, carelessly depositing

them on the couch as soon as she stepped into the living room. She stopped, her eyes searching; surprise was slowly gathering on her face. "You haven't changed anything, have you?"

"No," he said, "why should I?"

He was trying to sort out his emotions, to orient himself to her; he did not know how to act with her, whether to erupt in rage or fall at her feet in tears; he didn't know anything. He was struck dumb in her presence.

"You were waiting for me," she said in a very quiet voice.

"Yes," he admitted, "yes, I was."

She took his hand in hers.

Her hand was cold. It was not so cold outside.

"Where did you come from?"

"Could you get me something to drink—whiskey, vodka, whatever you have, I don't care."

He hurried into the kitchen and prepared something for her in nervous haste, fearful that when he got back to the living room she wouldn't be there.

But she was there. "You didn't tell anyone I was in town, did you?"

Why was she so worried about other people knowing? But of the thousands of questions he wanted—needed—to ask her, this was one that mattered least. He told her no, no one else knew.

She appeared to breathe easier. She slumped down in the couch, a long sigh escaping from her. She was clearly exhausted.

Maybe, he thought, she's been on a flight from somewhere and was suffering jet lag.

He sat down beside her, handed her the drink.

For several moments she didn't speak. "God, I missed you," she said.

The last thing he expected to hear. Missed him?

She gazed up at him, her eyes full of appeal. "Please don't ask any questions; I haven't the strength to answer any questions."

"Just one, just one, and then I won't ask any more."

In fact, he didn't know which question he wanted to put to her. What did he want to know above all else?

"All right, but only one."

"Did you run off with Luis or did he take you away with him?"

"That's not fair; that's two questions . . ." But she decided to respond anyway. "I ran off with him. That is just what I did, Glen; I ran off with him."

"And now?" Another question. He quickly apologized.

"Now; now, I don't know. I'm here. And if it's all right with you, I'll stay here for a while."

"It's all right; sure it is. I don't ever want you to leave again."

He believed that he could absorb her disclosure about running off with Luis if he could be certain that she had truly come back to him. It meant that he had bested Luis, emerged the victor.

It was funny how he'd thought about this reunion a million times over, and it wasn't turning out anything like he imagined.

"Do you want anything to eat?" he asked. "I can fix up something in a minute."

Everything at this stage was so tentative that he could operate only on safe ground. Food and drink were safe ground.

What struck him as particularly odd was that he felt that he was the one who should be doing the explaining, that he was the one who should apologize.

"I have a confession to make," he found himself saying. They were maintaining a cautious distance, sitting together on the couch—a distance of inches, a distance of thousands of miles.

She gave him a curious stare, but said nothing.

"I was the wrong man for you, the wrong husband. I've had a lot of time to think about this, and that's the conclusion I've come to."

The way she looked at him now he realized he'd shouldn't have said this. Maybe he shouldn't have said anything. He understood, deep down, that he was seeking her sympathy and also still seeking her love.

Abruptly she rose from the couch. He wondered what she was going to do.

She took his hand, threading her fingers through his. "Come," she said. "Come with me."

Six months in a far-off land had done nothing to erase her memory of the house she'd lived in. Confidently she led him up the stairs and into his—their—bedroom.

All at once she was standing in front of him, naked, her limbs glistening, her clothes heaped about her ankles. In the absence of any light, he could hardly discern the features of her face. But her eyes seemed to glow preternaturally.

"I don't know who you are," he said.

But at that instant he didn't know who he was either. When he approached her, it was with trepidation, with a strange, sad fear of a kind he had never felt before.

Time seemed not to have any part in what ensued. He would wake to discover himself entwined with her on the bed, with no recollection of what had happened earlier. Blankets and sheets had swirled about them one minute and lain in a tangle on the floor the next. Their skin was hot and wet; he smelled of her, but the smell was unfamiliar; it was not how he remembered—in her breath she exuded the odor of a jungle and another man. When she woke, suddenly, with a small cry, surprised possibly to find herself where she was, she gave Glen a long, enigmatic look. He thought that she might be trying to place him.

Then, without a word, she guided him into her, but when she thrust her hips up hard against him, at the same time running her broken nails down his back until she drew the pain from him she wanted, he was bewildered all over again. She had never made love like this before; she had never exhibited this fervor, this madness. She swore into his ear, in English and in Spanish and in a language that he couldn't at first recognize, but later decided must be Quechua.

It was Luis she was fucking, he thought; it must be Luis, not him. She was lost, much further lost in his bed, with him, than she'd ever been in the overgrown interior of Peru.

He despaired and his erection died.

But she was not daunted, not that night, nor the following day. She seemed not to want to let him go. She appeared to have no need for food, only water from time to time to relieve her of her thirst

He was too exhausted, too spent, to get his anger to the surface, to demand that she tell him what was happening, where their destination lay. Besides, he was afraid. He was afraid of her answer.

When they didn't sleep they plundered each other.

The April afternoon light seeped in through the windows, then faded and grew dim. Glen could not understand why the telephone hadn't rung, for surely somebody at work would want to know what had happened to him. But then he discovered, while Kelly was asleep, that she'd unplugged the phone. He did nothing to restore the connection.

Tomorrow, he thought, he would have a talk with her and settle things. For now this was enough, sating himself on her and, maybe if he was in some way lucky, getting her out of his system.

He fell into an uneasy sleep filled with agitating and incomprehensible dreams. Every hour his eyes would open and he would look to see whether she was still there.

He'd catch sight only of a portion of her in the gloom: a single leg extending out from under the sheets; the gentle slope of a breast, the nipple stiffened like a small, nubby finger; a blur of blonde hair against a white cloud of pillow.

Once he saw that her eyes were open, too, and that she was staring right back at him. She whispered something to him he couldn't quite hear.

"What was that, Kelly?"

"Do you forgive me?"

"Forgive you?" He thought that he would have no difficulty saying that he did, that forgiveness after all this time would be no problem. But he could not get the words out; he simply could not speak at all.

She was waiting, her breathing shallow. It was important to her that he say something, that he give her the answer she'd come all this way for, but he could not.

She sighed and turned over in silence.

"Kelly? Kelly?" he said. But it was too late; she did not reply.

The six o'clock sun brought him awake. Kelly was no longer in the bed beside him. The impression of her body, though, was still visible on the sheets; they were gray and stained and there was, he saw, an oddly shapen spot that might have been dried blood.

When he could not locate her anywhere in the house, he was not surprised. He wondered whether she would have stayed had he told her he'd forgiven her. There was no way of ever knowing, he supposed.

He plugged the phone back into the socket and waited to see if she would call.

But when the phone rang, it was not Kelly on the other end. It was a man whose voice was unknown to him. The man said that his name was Kenneth Hibler.

"I'm with the State Department," he added.

Glen was mystified. "What can I do for you, Mr. Hibler?"

Hibler hesitated before replying. "I'm afraid, Mr. Margolin, that I have some very bad news for you."

"Yes?"

"Your wife, Kelly, has been found in Peru. I'm very sorry to have to say this, Mr. Margolin, but she was found dead."

Glen laughed. A nervous laugh, a bit hysterical. Hibler must have thought him mad.

"I think you must be in error; my wife was just here. She came back from Peru."

Now Hibler probably thought that he was refusing to accept reality. But he went on: "Of course, there's always a possibility of error in identifying the remains. The body is being shipped back to you and should reach you by Wednesday. You can verify the identity then. But I must tell you, Mr. Margolin, that we double-checked the fingerprints and dental records before we let you know. In something like this we do everything we can to eliminate the possibility of error."

Glen was so lost in thought that Hibler raised his voice to get his attention. "Are you there, Mr. Margolin?"

"Yes, I'm here. I'd like to ask you a question."

"Anything."

"How did she die?"

"I was going to get to that. Evidently some locals in the area came on her body in a place not far from the spot you reported her lost. I regret to have to say that it appears as if she had fallen victim to foul play.''

"You're saying she was killed?''

"It looks that way. To be honest with you, Mr. Margolin, the job the Peruvian authorities did in investigating this was not all it should be. It's a lot different down there than it is in America.''

"I know,'' Glen said wearily, "but tell me something, Mr. Hibler, how could you possibly identify any body that's been lying out in the jungle, in all that heat and rain, for over six months? I'd expect that it would have decomposed in that time.''

"Under those circumstances, I'd have to agree with you, but we're not talking about six months here. The body was found about forty-eight hours after death occurred. There was no decomposition to speak of. The local police made the identification on the basis of the photographs you left with them.''

The funeral parlor where the body, after its long journey back from Peru, came to rest was slightly garish and much too bright for Glen's liking. The walls were a variety of Pompeii red, with full-length mirrors set into them. Glen had a glimpse of himself standing over the bier; his face was paler than he'd ever seen it, and he realized his shaving must have been sloppy, for a conspicuous stubble was visible on his chin.

To the Whites and all the relatives who appeared, he had little to say; cursory acknowledgments seemed to be all that were expected and they were all that Glen could possibly manage in any case.

He was the last to look into the casket. It was a moment he'd been putting off as long as he could. Everyone expressed surprise at how alive she looked. Still, Glen advanced towards the casket with trepidation, like a man who's bet all of his money on one last hand of poker but hasn't the nerve to see what cards have come up.

He looked in. She was thinner; she even seemed to have shrunk, but it was definitely Kelly. Either her or her exact double.

What he found so odd was the expression on her face; it was almost one of serenity. He never remembered her looking so calm when she was with him. Was the other woman a ghost, then, and this the real one? How was he to tell?

For in truth, he'd never known Kelly White, not on the day he'd met her on Boston Common, not on the day he'd married her, nor on the day she'd ridden off on horseback with Luis beside her. Maybe it was not in his capacity to know a woman like her.

There was only one thing he regretted, and that was that he had neglected to take any pictures of the woman who'd come to his door a week ago, disheveled, in her white raincoat. Even if he could not separate what was real from what was not, surely the camera could have done so. Just one picture would have been enough, he thought; just one picture so that he would never forget.

Introduction to Kelvin Jones

It isn't easy, being a pillar of society, even if, as a cleric or a policeman, it's by default. There are standards to maintain and beliefs to foster, and there's no use asking for divine help when you learn that you've been wrong—from the start.

Kelvin Jones is a fine British writer making his first appearance here in an American publication.

THE GREEN MAN

Kelvin Jones

As the Reverend Bear opened the stout door to the west entrance, a gust of wind swept inwards. He stepped back, startled by this sudden intrusion of the elements. Past the porch he could see the dark shapes of the cedars, their branches laid bare, against the black sky. He had forgotten how late it was.

He drew the heavy brass key from the ring attached to

his belt and inserted it into the door. As the lock engaged, he had a sudden image of the church's interior, the solid round pillars ranged either side of the nave, the great hammerbeam roof shadowing everything beneath it. St. Helen's was not a church he liked to linger in, especially in the winter months. Not only was it difficult to heat, but its Norman builders had allowed little light to penetrate the dark interior, even on a day of brilliant sunshine. The deeply recessed windows gave a cloistered feeling to the interior and no amount of polish or ventilation eradicated the cloying fustiness of the central tower. It was not, to his mind, the most suitable of places for Christians to worship in.

He shivered, suddenly aware of the chill night wind. A procession of thoughts wound its way through his tired mind, ecclesiastical obligations, each more dreary than the last. His sermon was not due until tomorrow, yet he had not even the faintest idea of his subject.

Not that it mattered, he thought cynically. He could always choose a ready-made one from his countless volumes. Besides, of late his mind had been otherwise preoccupied. Workmen had been carrying out extensive restoration in the clerestory, stripping away the layers of whitewash, the legacy of sober Victorians and their Cromwellian ancestors.

Already they had revealed a series of remarkable wall paintings, patterns of interwoven flowers, their colours fresh and vivid as the day they were painted over eight hundred years before. The Reverend Bear paused at the entrance to the porch. It was almost unbelievable that Christian worship had been practised here for such a period. What would the subject of tomorrow's sermon have been then? The seven deadly sins, perhaps?

He shut the outer door and looked upwards. Against the pale halo of the city lights, three distorted gargoyles jutted from the central tower, their faces grimacing at him. He turned, rather more swiftly than usual, and began walking at a brisk pace down the long drive towards the main road.

There was a narrow footpath linking the old vicarage with the main south circular and it was his habit in the summer months to take a shortcut along this route. Of late he had avoided the path since the way was poorly illuminated, a thick wood skirting much of its length. But tonight was an exception. Whether it was the thought of his cozy fireside that directed his footsteps this way or maybe some unconscious desire for excitement, he could never afterwards determine. But he strode purposefully ahead, plunging into an indeterminate well of darkness where all that was visible was the dim strip of the chalk path.

Halfway along the path he stopped. He had no reason to do this. He told himself as much, for he had work to prepare before the evening was spent and already a sense of fatigue was starting to settle uncomfortably on his mind.

Nevertheless, he surprised himself by stopping and lighting his pipe, an action that could only suggest confidence in his surroundings. This was curious, for the Reverend Bear was nothing if not timid and darkness of any kind always seemed to him to be a facet of that alarming world conjured by the medieval mind in which the souls of the departed languished in everlasting perdition.

He stood at the edge of the path, conscious of the wind biting angrily at the trees. It was odd to think that in the middle of the great city there were places like this wood, sealed off from the world, still much the same as it would have appeared in the Dark Ages. Only then, he reasoned, it would have been a place of wild beasts and nameless fears. Now it was something else; it represented that border of the conscious mind where vague shapes flitted . . .

Suddenly, something broke in on his train of thought. He listened. There it was again. The sound of a voice. Something between a sigh and a gasp. A curious sense of excitement began to rise within him. Should he not investigate? What if someone had injured himself and lay there in the darkness in need of assistance? He could not, in all conscience, pass by without offering help.

He began to make his way through the bracken, stopping every so often to listen. Embarrassment prevented him from calling out, lest the sound be the product of his own imagination. No, there it was again, to the left of him, this time much closer, more sustained. He began to wish he had a torch. But slowly his eyes began to adjust to the darkness and he could discern the outlines of the tree trunks.

By the edge of a clearing he stopped. He peered into the gloom. He could hear it distinctly now. The breathing was rapid, but was it not more than one voice that he could hear?

The shadow of a suspicion began to cloud his mind. Then, as his eyes scanned the ground in front of him, realization dawned. Through the bare branches of the trees, a skein of moonlight fell on naked limbs locked in a tight embrace. Slowly the body of the man rose and fell above that of his companion. The sighing of the woman grew faster, more ecstatic. The sight repelled him, yet he could not turn and bolt. He remained there, behind the tree, fascinated, frozen with anticipation . . .

"It is a truly remarkable piece of sculpture," said the Reverend John Waldon.

"Remarkable, yes, but I find it hideous."

They were standing in the clerestory. It was eleven o'clock. Above them, beyond the hammerbeam roof, the sun poured down on St. Helen's, but only a fraction of its power penetrated the length of the nave beneath.

Up here in the clerestory there was a smell compounded of age and disuse which made the Reverend Bear slightly nauseous. He looked again at the huge carving. It was, as his companion pointed out, remarkable. The workmen had discovered it only this morning, hidden away behind three inches of plaster. It was a large motif, probably dating from the thirteenth century, consisting of a grotesque head encompassed by a thick webbing of intertwined leaves and foliage.

The Reverend Bear felt slightly incensed by his friend's obvious pleasure in the piece. To him there was something altogether loathsome about the face. Its high cheekbones, curled saturnine nose and the cruel twist to the mouth gave it a suggestion of menace.

"What on earth does it represent?"

"It is certainly not a Christian image," replied his companion, a man steeped in the architectural trappings of early churches. "I remember seeing something similar in a church in Berkshire. There they called it the Green Man."

"The Green Man? Jack of the Green?"

He recalled a curious figure, clothed in a bush, in a mummer's play he had once seen. It had made little sense to him.

"The same. I imagine that to our pagan ancestors he was like a Roman silvanus, a creature of venery and of the wild hunt."

"All the same, I dislike it."

The reverend John Waldon gave his companion an odd look. There was something in the clergyman's manner, a suggestion of unease, that had never manifested itself before. His normally pallid complexion and watery grey eyes seemed drained of life.

"The restoration work certainly has lightened much of the church's interior," he said, changing the subject.

The Reverend Bear managed a smile. As they turned

and walked away from the scaffolding he felt a sense of inward relief. It was always so cold up here in the clerestory.

"The sun was risen upon the earth when Lot entered into Zoar. Then the Lord rained upon Sodom and Gomorrah brimstone and fire from the Lord out of heaven. And he overthrew those cities, and that which grew upon the ground. But his wife looked back from behind him, and she became a pillar of salt. And Abraham got up early in the morning to the place where he stood before the Lord. And he looked toward Sodom and Gomorrah and toward all the land of the plain, and beheld and lo, the smoke of the country went up as the smoke of the furnace. Here endeth the second lesson.''

The Reverend Bear rose from a velvet cushion bordered with golden tassels and inscribed with the initials INRI. To the left of him the gold-plated eagle which served as a lectern shone, distorting the features of the reader.

"We will now sing Hymn number fifty-two. 'O God Our Help in Ancient Times.' ''

The congregation droned into life. He looked about him. *Men, women and children, all in white and their faces as pale as moonlight.* His grip tightened on the brass rail. He made a conscious effort to concentrate on the words of the hymn. When he came to the words "In ancient times," he stopped abruptly and looked up.

It seemed as if the dark shadows of the clerestory had dispersed, giving way to a yellow effulgence. Although he was some sixty feet away, the head appeared almost brilliantly outlined among the scrolled leaves, the blank eyes bulging, the nose sharp as a razor edge. He looked down quickly at the hymn book, but he was hopelessly lost.

He coughed to cover his embarrassment. He thought of Lot's wife turning to view the forbidden city, her body turning to salt. A glimpse of unbelievable perversions, bodies articulated in death at their moment of ecstasy. Beads of perspiration broke on his brow . . .

When the service was concluded, he hurriedly changed out of his vestments and left the church. Outside, the sun was streaming down, throwing the dazzling greens and browns of the late autumn into startling relief. Compared with the stale air of the church's interior, the excursion came as a pleasant contrast. Outside, standing beneath the tower, was the Reverend John Waldon. He approached rapidly, his face beaming.

"I must congratulate you. That was a most excellent sermon."

"You thought so?"

"I have rarely heard a better one. Such force. And such conviction."

Bear smiled gently. He felt strangely displaced. For the life of him he could not recall the contents of his sermon.

"Good. You must visit us again in the near future."

"Now, if you'll excuse me, I promised to see the members of the Mother's Union at twelve. Good luck with the restoration."

The Reverend Waldon made his way out of the churchyard with firm, unwavering steps. He was a man whose faith never faltered. Bear watched him go, then turned towards the driveway. He was looking forward to his lunch. Certainties of that type gave an added dimension to his life. The sound of the beef as it dropped sizzling onto the plate, the pungent aroma of white cabbage—these things comforted him.

The main road was particularly busy this Sunday morning. Several parishioners nodded to him as he made his way towards the railway bridge. He was beginning to feel like his old self again. Perhaps I should take a holiday, he thought. Maybe the work is beginning to get on top of me.

He disliked doctors. He felt distinctly uneasy in their presence. It was the fear of being analyzed that put him on edge.

At the corner of the bridge he stopped and looked about him. It was a beautiful day, sharp but vivid, the perfect weather for walking. Then he encountered the footpath which he had taken the previous night. He recalled the experience there that had so disturbed him. Still, it was unavoidable. It could not be helped. Today it was a different path, a different setting, he consoled himself.

He made the plunge. Soon he was halfway down the track, walking at a brisk pace. There was no one else about, which surprised him a little. It was such an obvious choice for a morning constitutional.

Halfway along he stopped to sit down on the sawn bole of a tree. To his left, across an open field, a flock of black crows circled silently. He took out his pipe and lit it. Soon the pungent tobacco was swirling about him. His mind felt sharp and vigorous, full of distant thoughts and half-remembered phrases. He tried to recall some of his sermon but found the exercise dull and unedifying.

He was about to reach for his box of matches when suddenly he heard a sound behind him. He turned sharply, expecting to see a stranger there, but he could see nothing except the long line of trees stretching back towards the railway track.

He stood still for some moments, listening intently. There it was again, the sound of a voice, calling. But it was indistinct. He could not tell if it were a woman's or a man's. He stood up, irritated by his uncertainty, and knocked the bowl of his pipe against the tree stump. He moved towards the edge of the wood. There it was again. A sound like laughter this time, a woman's voice.

He felt an urge to continue his route, yet there was a part of him which pushed him over the bracken between the thick tree trunks into the shade of the wood. He moved silently, not wishing to disturb whomever it was who had penetrated the interior, desiring only to remain unseen.

From the depths of his brain words formed, a meaningless pattern, a rhyme he had heard as a child. But now they revived in his consciousness, flew hither and thither about his expectant mind:

> Fly then quickly, make no stay
> For Herne the Hunter rides this way.

The words took on a magical force. They would not disperse, would not shift from his thoughts. He felt puzzled, confused by his own behavior. What was he doing here? Why had he stepped across this threshold into the shade of the wood?

He stopped. It was the same clearing, but now brighter because of the sunlight that filtered through the branches. It was the same couple, he could swear to it. The voices were identical. Even their positions had not altered.

But now the act appeared even more brazen, daringly explicit. The woman lay with her back to him, her knees drawn up almost to her breasts. Above her the man rose and fell, his broad back moving with uninterrupted ease, his face suffused with pleasure. With each stroke the woman clenched her fists, then relinquished them, gasping as she did so. The man increased his speed, lengthening his strokes. Perspiration began to drip from his brow onto the woman's neck.

Bear shut his eyes, trying to blot out the picture, but the sounds continued, penetrating the barrier. His mind whirled chaotically, but he knew that he dare not move, that he was an unwilling witness to the act. Slowly the words filtered back into his tortured mind:

> Fly then quickly, make no stay
> For Herne the Hunter rides this way . . .

He saw himself as if from far above the wood: a silent figure, petrified, cut off from the spectacle that took place before him. Then, from beyond the trees, came a sound like none that he had ever heard before.

Like a cloud of darkness it crashed upon him, heavy and stifling, a nebula of chaos bearing with it the voices of the long-dead. High in the air broke the frenzied neighing of stallions, their teeth champing, their eyes staring and mad, and beneath this was the unleashed anger of the beast tearing at the ground, rooting up trees and bushes, rending flesh.

The Reverend staggered back, stunned and confused by the appalling sounds which had broken about him. His eyes were now wide open. No lingering doubts remained in his mind as to the meaning of this place. Whatever had sought to lure him here, whatever had lulled him into a false sense of security, was now revealing its purpose with unchecked ferocity.

He looked about him. The wood, formerly so tranquil, was now plunged in unutterable gloom. The branches of the trees crashed wildly, locked with each other in a frenzied parody of the act of coition he had just witnessed. The man and woman, their embrace broken by the sudden change, sat staring about them, clutching at their clothes. Leaves whirled into their faces, flung by angry gusts of wind, and above all this the sound of a horn, cold and shrill, as ancient as time itself. It was the summons of the Hunter.

Over the clearing a dark shape fell. From its center there was fashioned a face, something glimpsed when the sleeper breaks from his nightmare, shaking the presence from him.

Burning eyes set in a halo of green and over all this there was the smell of decay, the acrid odor of death. He turned and fled from the wood. Behind him the storm still raged. But now there was another sound, a long sustained screaming. He dare not turn. He must not watch.

The Reverend Francis Bear dried his hands on the red towel that hung behind the bathroom door. He sighed. It had been a long day. But it had been an enjoyable day.

He padded along the corridor that led to his Italiante bedroom in his fur-lined carpet slippers, smiling to himself. Sodom and Gomorrah. It had been an excellent theme. It had fired the imagination of the congregation. He turned the gleaming brass doorknob and opened the bedroom door. Inside, the heavy brown wood panelling was barely discernible in the light of the flickering embers of the coal fire. The landlady must have drawn the heavy velvet curtains in his prolonged absence, for the darkness in the room had a close, suffocating texture to it that he found almost overpowering.

He went to the curtains to draw them back, then thought better of it. The room was snug. Why disturb things? He sat on the coverlet of the bed, staring into the fire. The red coals shimmered with a baleful intensity, sending up occasional flames of an orange hue into the chimney. He looked about him at the objects in the room. Somehow their familiar shapes appeared distorted. The mahogany bureau lay huddled by the bed, its scrolled feet scarcely visible in the shadow. They were like the feet of a giant bird of prey. Above them, the two brass handles glinted in the firelight.

He moved to the fireside and, picking up the poker, began to move the glowing coals into fresh life. He wondered if he should turn on the light. But what reason had he, a man of the cloth, to fear from a room he had lived in for nearly twenty years? He was tired, he told himself, and in that condition his imagination lay open to the suggestible.

Putting down the poker, he changed position so that the

majority of the room's furniture lay to his left. He sank back into the Georgian armchair, feeling the protection of its enormous sides, and smiled to himself. His mind began to wander in the direction of the day's events. He wondered what it was that destroyed the cities of Sodom and Gomorrah. A nuclear explosion perhaps? Was God capable of that? Of course. God transcended moral or immoral actions. God was eternal. He pictured the earth, blasted bare, the trees torn from their roots, legs and arms and broken faces sticking out from beneath the rubble.

Suddenly his hands tightened on the arms of the chair. Barely perceptible, just out of the corner of his left eye he detected a movement. He turned his head, but that area of the room to which his attention was now drawn seemed quite still. Could it have been the reflection of a car in the street outside? Then he remembered that they were drawn. Their heavy texture permitted no light. He sat staring at the corner of the room in the vague dread that something would move there again. The corner, which had a potted plant on a small oak table and a low bookcase, lay silent as the grave.

He tried to concentrate on God, but God seemed remote and disinterested in the heavy Italiante room with its heavy furniture. He said the name out loud to himself: "God," but the word had lost its meaning and once uttered it was instantly lost in the enormity of the room.

He looked at his hands. Across the backs broad streaks of red still spread their telltale stain.

He had tried everything, but not even the strongest bleach could remove the marks. And now there was something else, something that puzzled him, a deformity that he had never noticed before. He held his left hand in front of the flames and curled the fingers towards the palm. It was undeniable. In the course of a day the fingernails had

grown to twice their length. And there was a faint greenish
tinge to them.

He sat in the darkened room, thinking of the clerestory
and the image on the wall there. What had he said to
Waldon? That he found it hideous? What a peculiar remark.
And then there was something else, some other memory. It
frustrated him not to be able to locate it. Yet as he grasped
for it, the imprint evaded him. What had he done today?
Very little. The sermon, the walk along the footpath, the
traditional Sunday lunch.

He looked back again into the fire and the flames leapt
up at him like accusing fingers. The flames were scarlet
now, like the color of blood, like the color of Babylon's
whore in Revelations. The fingers of flame pinned him to
the chair, daring him to move and be damned.

He would never be alone.

Not again.

*The city-dweller often shakes his head in amaze-
ment at the way those in the country choose to live
their lives. Without subways and theaters and high-
rises and museums, how do they manage a full and
enriching life? Very well, thank you, especially
when their clocks are permanently set at twelve.*

*William F. Nolan is currently working on at
least six or seven projects, not the least of which is
a massive collection of his short stories, due soon
in a special edition from Scream Press.*

CEREMONY

William F. Nolan

He hated riding cross-country in a bus almost as much as
he hated *driving* cross-country, but the problem was he'd
missed his rail connection getting into Chicago and just
couldn't wait for the next train. He *had* to be in Provi-

dence by Thursday evening to meet the Sutter woman. So it was the bus or nothing.

Mrs. Sutter was leaving that same night for Europe, and when she returned she expected her husband to be dead. The contract had to be settled before she left and the advance paid him. He didn't ice rich, unfaithful husbands unless he was well paid for the job, half down, the other half after the hit. Funny part of this one, he would have done old Sutter for *free*. Because of the total. He'd dispatched 13 people (would joke sometimes about "working as a dispatcher") since he'd gone into this business and he needed to break the total.

It wasn't that he was superstitious. Never had been. But, in plain, hard truth, that damned number 13 *was* unlucky for him. No question about it. He was 13 the time his father had split out for good, when they were living in that crummy, red-brick, coldwater flat in St. Louis. Not that he loved his old man. Not that bum. It was just that his father was usually able to keep his mother from beating the crap out of him. She beat him senseless twice that week, after the old man had split. Took it out on him. Way she took everything out on him. Always had. He was missing three teeth because of her. Good ole Mom.

That was the same week he ran off to Kansas City and got a job as a stacker in a paper-box factory after lying about his age. He'd looked a lot older than 13.

Then there was a double-13 on the license plate of that big, pink Lincoln convertible the blonde had driven when he'd hitched into Boulder City a few winters back. The blonde had been fun, sure, but she was coked out of her gourd when she flipped the car on a hairpin turn in the mountains and almost killed both of them. She thought it was funny, having a double-13 on her plates. Yeah, funny.

And, in Nam, there was a transport number, 13-something, painted on the tail of that lousy chopper that went down in the rice paddy. He'd been sent back to the States after that, with a Purple Heart, but the crash had killed his best buddy—the one real friend he'd ever trusted. He didn't trust people as a general rule. People screw you up when you trust them. But he'd trusted Eddie . . .

There had been a lot of 13s in his life, all tied into hard times, bad breaks, heavy losses. And now, by Christ, his *job* total was 13. Bad luck. But Mr. Sutter would make it fourteen and everything would be okay again. Life was fine, so long as he stayed away from the 13's.

"The bus will get you into Providence by late Thursday afternoon," the train clerk had assured him in Chicago. "But it's a long trip. Rather exhausting. We'd suggest a flight."

"I don't take planes," he told the clerk. He didn't tell him why.

It wasn't the chopper crash in Nam. Not that. It was the dream. About a commercial airliner, a big 747. Falling, with him strapped inside, staring out the window. Going down fast, people screaming, a jet engine on fire with the right wing burning. Paint cracking and peeling in the fierce heat, with the flames eating at a number on the trailing edge of the wing. A number ending in 13.

The *one* job he'd had trouble with, killing Wendl, that banker in Tucson, when a piss-ass schoolkid had seen him come out of Wendl's house after the job and called the cops, *that* one had been on the 13th. He originally planned it for the fourteenth, but when he found out Wendl's family was returning from their trip a day early, he was forced to make the hit. But never again. No more jobs on the 13th, no matter *how* much he got paid. He'd learned a lesson there, in Arizona. Cops had almost nailed him for sure.

So now he was on a bus in late October, heading for Providence, Rhode Island, ready to eliminate Mr. James

T. Sutter at the personal request of his loving wife, Jennifer. He'd get the advance from Mrs. S. and spend a week in Providence, then ice the old fart before taking a train back to the Coast.

Bringing his job total to fourteen.

He grinned, closing his eyes . . .

. . . and woke with a jolt, feeling cold glass strike his forehead. He'd nodded off, lulled by the rocking motion of the bus, and his head had bumped the window. He straightened, coughing, and wiped a small trickle of saliva from his chin. That's how it was on a long bus ride, with those fat tires hypnotically thrumming the road, setting up a measured vibration in your body, making you drowsy. Your eyelids get heavy, slide down; your mouth gapes, and you doze. And wake. And blink. And doze again.

Time is meaningless. You don't know where you are, what town you're passing through. Don't care. Your back aches, and your feet are swollen inside your shoes. Your clothes itch, tight and sweaty around you. You smoke, but the cigarettes taste sour.

Hours of travel along strange highways, suspended in a surreal vacuum between night cities and day cities, looking blankly out at hills and rivers and passing traffic, chewing on stale Clark bars from paint-chipped vending machines in musty-smelling depots. Riding endlessly through country you'd never seen and never wanted to see.

It was early afternoon on Highway 95. Sun half down along a rolling horizon of green hills. They'd just crossed the state line from Connecticut. He'd seen the big sign with a girl's smiling face painted on it . . .

WELCOME TO RHODE ISLAND!
A Nice Place to Visit.
A NICER Place to Live.

He suddenly remembered a song he'd heard when he was very young. His old man had this classic recording of the Andrews Sisters—Patty, Laverne and somebody—singing energetically about "poor little Rhode Island, smallest of the forty-eight . . ." There had been only forty-eight states when the Andrews Sisters had made the record, and he remembered feeling sorry for the place. He'd been a little kid, shorter than most of his schoolmates, and he identified with smallness. One summer he'd found an abandoned pup, a real little guy, obviously the runt of the litter, and had taken it home. But his mother strangled it. She didn't like pets.

Poor little Rhode Island . . .

They were passing through farm country in the western part of the state. Lots of big rocks, with dirt-and-gravel roads branching off into fields (what were they growing?—he sure as hell didn't know) and with pale white Colonial farmhouses off in the distance. He spotted some apple orchards, and there were plenty of elms and oak trees along the road, all fire-colored. Like passing a circus. He wasn't much for scenery, but this was special—New England in October, putting on a class show for the customers.

How many hours had it been since they'd left Chicago? Twenty, at a guess. At least that long. It seemed like weeks, riding these endless gray highways.

The bus was nearly empty. Just him in the back section and an elderly couple up front. It had been crowded at first—but people kept getting off. More at each depot stop. Finally, it was just the three of them and the driver. Well, nobody in his right mind rode a bus for twenty hours. But it was almost over. Not long now into Providence.

He closed his eyes again, let the singing tires take him into sleep.

* * *

He woke to darkness. Thick black Rhode Island night outside the glass, an interior dark inside the bus. He'd been jarred awake by rough road under the wheels. Nárrow and bumpy. Why had they left the main highway? Jesus! He'd been due into Providence before dark.

He got up numbly, bracing himself against the seat back, then walked forward unsteadily along the aisle past the elderly couple (godawful bony-looking people) until he reached the driver.

"Where are we?" he asked, squinting into the night. "Why aren't we on 95?"

The driver was a thin character, with gaunt, stretched skin. He stared intently ahead at the narrow road, illuminated in floury-white patches by the probing lights. "Sorry, buddy, I had no choice."

"What's *that* mean? How late are we going to be getting into Providence?"

"Won't be there till morning," said the driver. "You'll have to spend tonight at the Mill. We'll be coming in soon. Maybe another ten minutes."

"The hell you say!" He leaned over to grip the driver's thin shoulder. "Turn this thing around and get us back on the main highway! I'm due in Providence tonight, and by God you'd better *get* me there!"

"No can do, buddy. Engine's fouled up. Overheating real bad. May be the carburetor, dunno. Only place to get 'er fixed is at Doour's Mill. They got a garage there. You ask me, lucky we made it this far. Gotta admit it sure beats being stuck someplace out on the road."

"Is there a phone at this garage?"

"Oh, sure. You can call from the Mill. No problem."

He started back toward the rear of the bus, thinking it's 13 again. *That's* why this job has gone sour. He checked his watch. Damn! Won't do any good to call Providence now. She's gone. Off to sunny Italy. Figured it for a chicken job; figured I didn't want the contract. She'll hire it out later, after she gets back.

Unlucky.

Okay, he told himself, ease down. You can score another contract in New York. Just have to put off going back to the Coast for a while. Plenty of action in New York. He had some good contacts there. He'd make it fourteen in New York. Just relax. What's done is done. Don't fight it.

"Happy Holiday!" said the couple, one after the other, both saying it to him as he passed them on the way to his seat.

He paused, gripping an upper handrail as the bus shuddered over a deep cut in the gravel road. "Uh, yeah . . . same to you."

When he reached his seat in the SMOKING PERMITTED section, he slumped down heavily, got out his cigarettes. Dead pack. He tossed it away, dug out a fresh one. He lit a Salem, drew in smoke, sighed, settled back into the cushion.

He'd forgotten; tonight was Halloween! This was it, all right, October 31st. As a kid, it had been his favorite holiday.

He never got presents for Christmas, or for his birthday, and Easter was a drag. But Halloween was nothing but great—the *one* night in the year when people *gave* you things. Free candy . . . cake . . . apples . . . doughnuts . . .

He smiled, remembering.

The bus lurched to a creaking stop. Doors hissed open.

They were at the garage, a weathered building with light seeping from its fogged windows. A dented Ford pickup

was parked in front with the words HARLEY'S REPAIR
SERVICE painted on the side.

"All out, folks! Doour's Mill."

He stepped down onto the gravel roadway. The driver
was helping the elderly couple from the bus. They moved
slowly, cautiously, their bones like breakable china. That's
how you get if you stick around long enough, he thought.

The garage owner, Harley, began talking to the driver.
Very tall, in baggy trousers and a torn denim work jacket.
Then the driver came around to open the luggage door on
the bus.

He reached in for his travel bag. Light, compact, good
leather. Had it custom-made to fit his needs. With a
hidden compartment for the short-barrel .357 Magnum.
Sweet piece of equipment. He'd started with a Browning
.380 automatic, but he'd never trusted it. The Mag he
trusted. Always got the job done. Easy to carry, with a
real kick to it.

"You wanna use the phone, one's right inside."

"No, it's too late now. Forget it. There a cafe around
here?"

"Straight ahead. Two blocks up. If it's open."

"Thanks." He checked his watch. Nine-thirty. "What
time do we leave in the morning?"

"Be here by six," said the driver. "She'll be ready to
roll by then."

"Okay."

He passed the dim-lit garage. In the smoked gloom,
standing next to a high-piled stack of discarded truck tires,
a lean, unshaven mechanic in greased blood-dark overalls
stared out at him.

He continued along the street. The gravel gave way to
concrete, but the ground was still uneven. Tufted grass
spiked up from wide cracks in the surface. The ancient

Victorian houses along the street were in equal disrepair, their gabled bay windows cracked and shadowed. Porches sagged. Roofs seemed hunched against the night. Doour's Mill had gone to seed, a time-worn New England relic of a town that seemed totally deserted.

It wasn't. A pair of teenagers, holding hands, came toward him, heads together, talking quietly. They looked underfed. The girl had no figure at all. "Happy Holiday," they said to him as they passed.

He didn't answer them. No point in it. Terrific town for a holiday.

He had no trouble finding the cafe. It was the only building along the main street with a neon sign. MA'S PLACE. Reminded him of his mother. He didn't like that. When he got closer, he saw that the first two letters had burned out. It was ALMA'S PLACE. Several other letters in the sign were dying, slowly dimming, flickering and buzzing in the air above his head like trapped insects.

He opened the door, stepped inside.

He was the only customer.

The waitress behind the worn linoleum counter was obviously young, but she looked like an anorexic. Pasty skin. Long, bony face with watery brown eyes. She blinked at him. "Hi, mister."

He said hello, asked if she was serving hot food.

"Sure, till ten o'clock we do. I mean, no steaks or specials this late, but I can fix you some eggs."

"Okay, that'll do. Scrambled easy, with hash browns and wheat toast."

"Easy it is," she said, and walked back to the kitchen to fix his order.

He sat down on one of the counter stools, laid his travel bag over another, and glanced idly around. A few greenish-colored tables, some crooked wooden chairs, an old broken-faced jukebox in one corner. Dark, not working. Near the antique cash register somebody had tacked a paper plate to the wall. On it, scrawled in black crayon: HAPPY HOLLOWEEN!

He chuckled. They can't even spell Halloween in this godforsaken town.

The waitress ambled out of the kitchen with eggs and toast. "Sorry, no more hash browns," she said. "But I can give you some sliced tomatoes. As a substitute, no extra charge. Not too fresh, though."

"This'll be all right," he told her. "With coffee."

She nodded, pouring him a cup. "It's kinda strong. You use cream?"

"No."

"Well, it's kinda strong."

"It'll be fine," he said, spooning sugar into the cup.

"I hope the toast is okay. I tried not to burn it."

"It's fine," he said.

He began to eat. One thing you can order safely in a joint like this, he told himself, is eggs and toast. Hard to screw up eggs and toast. These were all right.

He sipped the coffee. Ugh! Bitter. Damn bitter. He spooned in more sugar. Helped some, but not much.

"I toldja it was strong," the girl said.

He didn't say anything.

"Guess you wonder, this being Alma's Place, who's Alma, huh?"

"Hadn't thought about it."

"Alma was my mother."

"*Was?*"

"She died. Little over a month ago. Just didn't last till the Holiday."

He looked up. "You mean—until Halloween?"

"Right. She just didn't last."

"Sorry."

"Well, we all gotta go sometime. Nobody lives forever, right? It's like the Indians used to say—about how when it's your time an' all."

He spread butter on his toast. It *was* burned. "Guess you don't get much business around here."

"Not much. Not anymore. Used to be the cotton mill was open. They named this town after it, Doour's Mill. Owned by Mr. Jonathan Doour."

"What happened to him?"

"He died and it closed down. All the mill folk moved away. We got only a real few left in the town now. Real few."

"Why do *you* stay?"

"I own the place is why." She shrugged, picking at a shred of loose skin on her lower lip. "Mama wanted me to keep it going. Besides"—and for the first time she smiled—"people gotta eat!"

"I didn't see any other lights along the street," he said. "Are you the only one open at night?"

"Mr. Exetor's drug store stays open. Half a block down." She pointed. "He's open to ten, like here."

"Good. I could use some cigarettes."

"He's a widowman, Mr. Exetor is. Wife passed on end of the summer. Just *wasted* away."

He finished eating, pushed his plate back.

"More coffee?"

"I'll pass. Too strong for me."

"Yeah, like I said, it's kinda strong." She looked at him with intense, shadowed dark eyes. "You're invited to the Ceremony."

"What?"

"You're invited. We have it each Holiday. On October 31st, each year. And you're invited."

"I don't go to church," he said. "But thanks anyhow."
He got out his wallet. "How much do I owe you?"

"That'll be seventy-five cents," she said.

"Here's a buck. Keep the change."

"Thanks, mister." She rang up his order on the ancient
cash register. "Ceremony's not in church. Fact is, we
don't have a church here anymore. I mean, we *have* one,
but it's boarded up. They broke all the windows."

"I see." He picked up his travel bag, moved to the
door.

"Happy Holiday," said the girl.

"Same to you," he said, and walked out.

It was raining now. A thin misting foggy rain. The
street glistened like black leather under the pale light cast
by the cafe's overhead neon.

He turned up the collar of his coat and walked to the
drugstore. No sign outside, but the window said EXETOR'S,
in chipped gilt. He walked in, and a tiny bell tinkled over
the door.

Exetor was round-shouldered, cadaverous, with a bald
head and long, big-knuckled hands. A thick vein pulsed,
wormlike, in his mottled neck. Looked as if he'd be
joining his wife soon. Well, in a town like this, it didn't
matter much whether you were alive or dead. The old man
had been fiddling with a box of pipe cleaners and now he
put the box down. "Might I help you, sir?"

"Salem Hundreds. Two packs."

Exetor walked behind a dust-filmed tobacco counter and
got the cigarettes. "You from the bus?"

"That's right."

"I saw it come in."

"Our driver had some engine trouble. We were due in
Providence. Is there a hotel in town?"

"Certainly," said Exetor, accepting payment for the
cigarettes and ringing up the sale. "The Blackthorn. Just

down the way. Right at the intersection. You walk left.
Big three-story building on the corner. Can't miss it.''

"I sure never expected to be staying *here* tonight."

"No problem getting a room at the Blackthorn. Not
many folks around anymore. Expect they'll be closing one
of these days. Like me. Just not enough business to keep
any of us going."

He nodded. "I can see that."

Exetor smiled thinly. "Sad. About this town, I mean.
So much history here. Have you heard of Roger Williams?"

"Can't say I have."

"Strong-minded man, he was. They banned him from
Massachusetts for religious nonconformity. But that didn't
stop him. He established the first settlement in Providence,
in 1636. Remarkable man." Exetor's voice grew more
intense. "Jonathan Doour was related to Williams. Had an
oil painting of him hanging on the wall of his office at the
mill. So this town's part of history, you see. All of it, tied
together—going back to 1636."

"Gives you something to hang on to, I guess." The old
guy was a real bore. Who gives a damn about some
religious nut from the 1600's? Maybe that's what the
Ceremony was all about—honoring his memory or some
such crap.

"Each year, more of us pass on," said Exetor. "Just
don't make it to the Holiday."

"You people seem to think a lot of Halloween."

"Oh, yes, indeed we *do*." Exetor nodded, the neck
vein pulsing. "It's very important to us here at the Mill.
We have our Ceremony at this time each year."

"So I've been told. I'm not much for ceremonies."

Exetor clucked his tongue against yellowed teeth. "It's
the only day I really look forward to anymore," he said,
his voice soft with regret. "My wife and I always attended
together. I'll be alone this year."

"Oh, yes—I heard about your wife. That's tough." He edged toward the door. This old geeze planned to talk all night.

"It's most difficult, getting on without Ettie."

He was almost to the door when a wall sign caught his eye.

HAPPY ALL HOLLOWS EVE

Again, misspelled. Should be All *Hallows*. Didn't anybody ever go to school in this burg?

He reached the door, opened it. The bell tinkled.

"You are invited to the Ceremony," said Exetor.

"No thanks." He started out—and heard Exetor say: "Attendance is not voluntary."

He left the drugstore. Now what the hell did *that* mean? He looked back through the cracked plate-glass window at the old guy. Exetor was standing there, staring out at him, not moving.

Weirdo. Him *and* that chick at the cafe. Both of them, weirdos.

It was still raining. He shifted the weight of his travel bag from right to left hand and began to walk in the direction of the Blackthorn. He was feeling kind of lousy. Stomach upset. Headache. Maybe it was the long bus ride and his missing the Sutter contract. He'd be fine once he'd moved up his total to fourteen.

Right now, he just needed a good night's sacktime. He checked his watch. Getting toward ten. Exetor and the cafe girl would be closing up, probably heading for their Ceremony. Fine. Just so they were quiet about it. No loud music or dancing. He grinned, thinking what ole Exetor would look like hopping around the floor. Exetor, the Dancing Skeleton!

He heard something behind him—the low-purring sound of a car's motor in the misting rain.

Cop's car. Sheriff. And with a deputy in the seat next to him. The car glided slowly alongside, stopped. Jeeze, he hated cops. *All* cops.

"Evening," said the sheriff.

"Evening," he said.

The lawman was gaunt and sharp-featured. So was his deputy. And both solemn. No smiles. But then, cops don't smile much.

"Just inta town, are you?"

They damn well *knew* he was—but they liked playing their cop games.

"I came in earlier with the bus. They're fixing it. We had a breakdown."

"Uh huh," said the sheriff. "Harley, over to the garage, he told me about the trouble."

A pause—as they stared at him from the car's shadowed interior. The motor throbbed softly, like a beating heart in the wet darkness.

Finally, the sheriff asked: "You staying at the hotel?"

"I plan to. Guess they've got plenty of room."

The sheriff chuckled wetly, a bubbling sound. "That they have, mister." Another pause. Then: "Mind if we look over your suitcase?"

He stiffened. The Mag .357! But unless they tore the travel bag to pieces, they wouldn't find it.

The sheriff remained behind the wheel as his deputy got out, knelt in the wet street to open the bag.

"Gonna ruin your pants, Dave," said the sheriff.

"They'll dry," said the deputy, sifting through the contents, patting down shirts, fingering coats.

He tried to look normal, but he was sweating. The hidden gun compartment was just under the deputy's right hand. If he . . .

"Thanks, mister," said the deputy, snapping the bag closed. "Never can tell what folks'll carry."

"Guess not."

The deputy got back in the car, leaned out from the rolled-down window. His voice was reedy. "Happy Holiday," he said.

And the car rolled forward, gradually losing definition in the misting darkness.

The hotel was no surprise. Meaning it looked crappy. Sagging. Falling apart. Paint-blistered. Wood missing from the upper porch steps.

Well, it's like my sweet mother used to say, beggars can't be choosers.

He walked up the steps, avoiding the broken areas, and entered the lobby through a loose-hinged, leaded-glass door. The lobby was bare, dusty, deserted.

A clerk dozed behind the wall counter. Another skinny character. Middle-aged scarecrow in a rumpled suit. His nose was long, thin, almost transparent.

"I'll need a room."

The clerk's head jerked up like a stringed puppet. He blinked, reached for a pair of thick-lensed glasses, put them on. Pale blue eyes swam behind the lenses. "Cost you five dollars."

"I think I can handle that."

"Sign here. Name and address." The clerk pushed a card across the grimed counter.

He signed it, using a phony name and address. Never tell anybody the truth about yourself. He'd learned that in Kansas City. And a lot of other places.

He gave the clerk a five-dollar bill. And got a key.

"Guess I'm not the first here tonight," he said.

"Don't get you, mister."

"There was an elderly couple on the bus with me, coming in. They must have registered earlier."

"Nope." The clerk shook his head. "You're our first in 'bout a week. Nobody else tonight."

Strange. Where would they *go*?

"Yours is on three. Use the elevator. Stairs are rotted out. Sidney will take you up. If he's sleepin', just give him a poke. Room 3-H."

He nodded, moved across the wide, vacant lobby with his travel bag to the elevator. It's metal-pleated door was open. Inside, draped over a high wooden stool like a discarded bundle of dirty clothes, was a stick-thin old man. His patchy hair was streaked gray-white over his long skull.

"You got a customer, Pop."

The deep-socket eyes opened slowly. He stared at the stranger out of large milky pupils. "What floor?"

"The top. Three."

He stepped into the cage and felt it give perceptibly under his weight. "This thing safe?"

"Weren't, I wouldn't be in it," said the old man.

The pitted grill-door slid closed and the old man pushed down a corroded wall lever. His wrist was ropy, spotted with sores. The ancient cage creaked rustily into upward motion.

The old man's odor was strong, almost fetid. "Staying the night, are you?"

"I'm not here for the floor show."

He was getting sick of dealing with these weirdos. Nothing to gain by continuing to answer their stupid questions. He *was* amused by the fact that a sleazy hotel like this actually employed an elevator operator. No wonder the old croak slept on the job; nothing the hell *else* to do.

"We were the first state to declare independence from the Mother Country. You know that?"

He grunted.

"May the 4th, 1776, it was. We declared *two* months ahead of all the other colonies! Little Rhody was first, yes sir. First to declare."

"Were you *there*, Pop?"

The old man chuckled like dry leaves scraping. "Not hardly. But I've been around a spell. Seen things happen. Seen a lotta people die. But I made it again this year. Made it to the Holiday."

Another Halloween freak.

They reached the top, and the black door folded back into itself like an iron spider.

He stepped out. The cage rattled downward as he walked toward 3-H. The hall reeked of mold and decay. Rug was damp, lumped. Ceiling was peeling away in thick, hanging folds, like strips of dead meat. He could hear the steady drip-drip-drip of rain coming in through holes in the roof. Jeez, what a pit!

He reached the hallway's end. The door on 3-H startled him. It was a lot fancier than the others, ornamented in an intricately carved rose design. The knob was scrolled brass. He keyed the door open and swore softly. They'd given him the bridal suite! Well, why not? Nobody was about to pick the Blackthorn in Doour's Mill for a honeymoon!

It wasn't a suite, actually. Just one big chamber, with a bathroom off to the side. The bed, centered in the room, was enormous. Talk about your antiques! The tall gilt headboard was decorated with plaster angels. The gold paint had dimmed, and most of the angels had cracked wings, but he had to admit that the effect was still damned impressive.

A big faded-pink dresser loomed against one wall. Two velve-black chairs, seedy but elegant, stood beside a huge cut-velvet couch fitted with rose-carved brass studs. A large mirror dominated the wall above them, framed in faded gold.

He walked over to it, looked at himself. Needed a shave. Coat and shirt wrinkled, damp from the rain. Looked like his old man. A bum.

The bathroom was full of badly chipped tile and rusted brass fittings. But at least there was a shower. He hadn't counted on one. Real bonus in a fleapit like this.

He opened his bag, took out the travel clock, set it for five-thirty. That would give him plenty of time to get dressed and down to the garage by six, when the bus was ready to leave. He'd be glad to shake this freak town. Gave him the creeps. After Doour's Mill, New York would be Paris in the spring!

Damn! No inside chain lock. Just the regular knob lock. Well, that was okay. He always slept with the .357 under his pillow. Best protection in the world.

He had expected that the hot shower would make him feel better, but it hadn't. He still felt lousy, really kind of hung over. Dog tired. And sickish. Had to be the food at Alma's. Those eggs were probably half-spoiled. And that rat-piss coffee—that stuff would kill Frankenstein!

He slid his loaded Magnum under the pillow and put on a pair of white silk pajamas. The bed was great. Deep and soft, not at all lumpy or damp. And the sheets were crisp, freshly ironed. Not so bad after all.

It wasn't much after ten. He'd get a full night's rest. God, but he was beat. He stretched out on the big mattress, closed his eyes—and was instantly asleep.

He awoke slowly. Not to the clock alarm. To a low murmur of voices. Here. *In* the room with him.

"It's wearing off." Man's voice. Old.

"He's coming round." Woman's. Also old.

His eyes opened. He blinked, trying to get a clear focus on the dim figures in the room. The only light came from the bathroom and the door was partially shut. Things were murky.

There were several of them, surrounding the bed in a rustling circle.

"Welcome to the Ceremony," said the bus driver.

It was him, all right, and no mistake. Before he could fully register the shock of this, another voice said: "Happy Holiday!"

Focus. On the source of this second voice. It was Harley, the garage owner. His greasy mechanic stood next to him.

Now, rapidly, he ran his gaze over all of them: the elderly couple from the bus . . . Exetor . . . Alma's daughter . . . the lobby clerk . . . the old elevator man . . . the two skinny teenagers . . . Even the sheriff and his bony-faced deputy were here. Everybody he'd seen in the whole damn town—all here, around his bed, smiling down at him. And all of them thin, gaunt, wasted-looking.

He counted. There must be . . . Oh, Christ, yes, there were *13* of them!

A long iced wave of absolute fear engulfed him, and he closed his eyes to shut out the horrific ring of skulled faces.

"As I pointed out earlier this evening," said Exetor, "your attendance at the Ceremony was not voluntary. It was *required*."

"Yes, indeedy," agreed the hotel clerk, peering down at him with swimming fish eyes. "You're our Guest of Honor."

He tried to speak but could not; the words were choked bile in his throat.

"Can't give our Ceremony without a Guest of Honor," said the elevator man.

The elderly couple were holding hands. The woman

spoke slowly, distinctly. "Henry and I weren't at all sure we'd last till the Hollow Day. Not at *all* sure."

"Each year at this time we gather to be replenished," said Exetor, "thanks to our Guest of Honor. Believe me, sir, we *appreciate* what you are giving us."

"I can have my baby now!" said the teenaged girl excitedly. The boy put his arm around her narrow waist. He kissed her gently on the cheek. Beside them, the garage owner's eyes shone with pride.

"Ain't many new babies born to Mill folk anymore," he said. "We cherish our young, we surely do. Laurie here—she'll have the strength to bear, thanks to you."

"That's right," the bus driver said. "I tell ya, buddy, we're *deeply* grateful!"

"I'm sure sorry that coffee I served you was so darn bitter," said Alma's daughter. "But the stuff I had to use in it tastes plain *awful*. Still, it's very restful. Keeps you from hurting when we're getting you ready."

He was fully awake now, and anger flushed through him. Under his pillow. The loaded .357 Magnum. He'd blow them away, every damned freakish one of them!

But he couldn't reach the gun. He suddenly became aware that his wrists were strapped to the sides of the bed, as were his ankles. And there was another wide leather strap across his chest, holding him down.

And . . . oh, God . . . there were the snakes!

Thirteen of them!

No, not snakes, they were . . . some kind of rubbery tubes. Coiling out from his body into the figures surrounding him, a tube for each of them, attached to his flesh and ending in *their* flesh—like obscene umbilical cords.

Jesus—they were *feeder* tubes!

"Ettie so wanted to be here," said Exetor sadly. "It would have meant more months of life for her. But she just couldn't last to the Ceremony."

The sheriff patted the old man's arm in sympathy. "Ettie was a mighty fine woman."

He strained desperately against the straps, but they held firm.

"No use pushin' like that," said the mechanic in the rotted dark coveralls. "You ain't goin' nowhere. Sheriff Morland fixed them straps personal. They're good and tight."

He felt himself weakening now. Moment by moment, his strength was being bled away—into them. As he grew weaker, they grew stronger. Their eyes were brighter; their cheeks began to acquire a glow.

The waitress tipped back her head, closed her eyes. "Ummmm, sure feels *good*!"

"Nothing will be wasted. I assure you," Exetor said. "We use *everything*. Even the marrow."

"Bone marrow's good for the teeth," said the teenaged boy. "And we need healthy teeth for our baby."

"Tell us your name and we'll call it after you," said the teenaged girl. "As a gesture, you might say."

"He won't tell," said the hotel clerk. "Gene Johnson was on the card, but I bet you ten dollars that name's a fake." He blinked downward. "*Will* you tell us your real name, mister?"

He gasped out the words: "You . . . can . . . all . . . go . . . to hell!"

They looked at one another. The bony deputy shook his head. "Well now, we sure hope the good Lord don't see fit to send us down *there*. We're all decent folk, here at the Mill. Always have been."

The figures in the rustling circle nodded agreement.

Things were dimming in the room. He blinked, feeling weak as a newborn cat. The anger was gone. The fear was gone. He was tired. Very, very tired. It was like being on the bus again, with the thrumming wheels making him drowsy. His eyelids were heavy. He wanted to close them. Did.

Darkness now.

And rest.

No more worry.

No more pain.

Everything was fine.

*The worst thing one can do is compare one
midnight with another. It's rather like comparing
roses—they're all beautiful, but they all have
thorns. Memories are like that as well.*

*Michael Bracken began writing with his own
fanzine, KNIGHTS, and when that finally passed,
he turned to fiction and has now published many
stories in publications ranging from TRUE CON-
FESSIONS to the SATURDAY EVENING POST.*

OF MEMORIES DYING

Michael Bracken

It was a small town on the northern California coast where
the teenagers still cruised Main Street, stopping at both the
stoplights on their trek from the A&W north to the bowling alley, then around and back again; a small town nes-
tled against the ocean where the Coast Ranges prevented

most radio and television signals from bringing in the latest fashions; a small town where progress rarely interfered and the A&W was still the only link to a world of fast food.

A full moon hung low in the evening sky, fragmented by naked branches and power lines. I stood in the shadows before the high school, staring at the faded spot on the wall where the capital *B* had fallen off, leaving only *aker High School* still intact. The school was much the same as it had been when I left, still a collection of single-story hallways intersecting to form inaccessible open courtyards.

I stood on a brown patch of grass, my knapsack at my feet. Faded green canvas, I'd bought it at an Army surplus store and carried it around the world with me, stuffing it with tiny objects I'd found in small villages and back-alley shops where tourists never went.

A breeze from the ocean blew up through town and sent a chill crawling through me. I pulled my jacket tighter around my gaunt frame, fumbling to tug the zipper upward with shaking fingers.

My clothes hung limply from my body, mismatched and out of style. The shirt, brown cotton gauze stained with sweat, I'd found in India. The jeans, now faded and frayed at the cuffs of the bell bottoms, were a pair of Levi's without the apostrophe I'd found in Hong Kong. The green jacket I'd received from an Army deserter in Cambodia after spending a five-day drunk with him, helping him through a bad case of the DT's and a good case of scotch. My shoes—a pair of low-top black tennis shoes—were new. I deserved that; I'd walked through the soles of so many others.

"Hey there!"

I was suddenly pinned against the school wall by a spotlight, silhouetted like a marionette with no strings.

"Hey there." The voice behind the spotlight called

again and I blinked my tired eyes against the light, squinting to see who was talking to me.

"What are you doing there?"

"I used to go to school here," I said. My voice was ragged, hesitant, because I could not see the other person.

The light snapped off and I blinked again, adjusting to the sudden darkness.

"Class of '80." The voice came from inside a police car. "You?"

"Class of '74," I said. It seemed like so many years had passed, like so many things had worn away at what I was, what I had dreamed of being, that I no longer had a sense of time.

"What brought you back?" he asked. He was broad-shouldered and serious, the type who had played football and been class president, gotten good grades and been liked by everyone.

I shook my head. There was nothing I could tell him.

He motioned me over to the patrol car and offered to buy me a cup of coffee. I gathered up my knapsack and climbed in the car beside him.

"Mike Morelli," he said as he stuck out a thick hand with strong fingers.

I grasped his hand firmly, shook it, and released it quickly. His touch burned in my memory, my palms sweaty and shaking. "Patrick Bates," I said.

Morelli slowly swung the patrol car out of the faculty parking lot and pointed it down the road toward the main part of town. Silence between us and the faint crackling and popping of the radio as he drove tickled at the razor-sharp edges of my nerves, rubbing the exposed ends like ground glass.

"Seventy-four," he said thoughtfully, his forehead wrinkled as if he strained to remember. "Wasn't that the year—"

"It was," I said, interrupting his question. I had wondered how long it would take him to remember.

Morelli grunted, silent again. He drove through town, down narrow streets between rows of houses washed pale by my memory of them, south to the A&W, pulling the patrol car to a halt in one of the stalls. He reached out his open window and pressed the button on the face of the speaker, ordering two coffees and a Papa Burger. He looked over at me, the details of my face lost in the shadows inside the car. "You want anything else?"

"No. Coffee's fine."

"That's it, sweatheart," he said to the teenaged voice in the speaker. Then he turned to me again. "They've all left, you know."

"I nodded. It wasn't hard to guess that my few remaining classmates would leave town just as I had left.

"Nobody else has ever come back," Morelli said. "Nobody I ever heard of."

I nodded. It wasn't hard to guess that my few remain- silent for a moment, watching as a Mustang careened into the parking lot, teenaged boys hanging from the open windows, yelling and waving. As soon as they saw the patrol car, they slowed and the driver very carefully pulled the rusting car into a stall at the far end of the row.

"Now them boys," Morelli said, pointing his finger at the Mustang, "they don't understand what this town does."

"They will," I said. "Give them time."

Before he could respond, our coffee and his hamburger arrived. He passed a steaming cup to me, then unwrapped his hamburger and took a bite. Catsup and mustard spewed out the other side of the bun. He wiped at his uniform with a napkin, the stain already evident and too late to wipe away.

"You surprise me," Morelli finally said.

"Yes?"

"You're not what I expected." He took another bite of the hamburger, more carefully this time. "You look late sixties," he said. "Like you forgot to leave an era behind."

"Here?" I questioned. "This town's always been an era behind."

Morelli didn't know whether to laugh or take me seriously. He considered a moment, then agreed with me. "This town moves slow. It always has."

A blonde waitress wiggled past, carrying a tray full of root beer mugs to the Mustang at the end of the aisle. Morelli's eyes followed her to the Mustang, then back into the restaurant.

"You must have a lot of bitter memories," Morelli said. "The whole class of '74 must have bitter memories."

I nodded. "It pushed them away. Kept them from coming back."

"It was a hell of an accident," he continued, oblivious to my comment. "Damn near the whole senior class." He shook his head as if to shake away the memories; then he said, "I lived three blocks away from the hotel. The explosion woke me up. My father and I watched the fire from down the street. I must have had nightmares for a month after that."

I knew what he meant. The nightmares would never end for me, had never stopped, and I didn't expect to free myself of them.

"Where were you when it happened?" Morelli asked.

"Outside," I said. "In the parking lot sneaking a drink from a bottle of Jack Daniels. My girl friend was inside."

"Jesus." Morelli finished his hamburger and crumpled up his napkin. "You were lucky."

"Maybe." I pulled aside my long, greasy black hair and showed him the purple splotches on the side of my face and the back of my neck. They extended far down my back and across my chest, a tattoo of burning tuxedo etched into my skin. "I went in after her. There was nothing I could do."

We sat together watching the boys in the Mustang as they piled out of the car and took their places on the hood. They laughed and swore at each other, pushed one another off the car, spilling root beer on the pavement. They were rough-and-tumble, as I had once been.

"Can I drop you somewhere?" Morelli asked as he started the car. "I have to make my rounds again."

I looked over at him in the darkness of the patrol car, seeing the hard lines already forming in his young face. "I want to go back to the school," I said.

"I could take you to a motel if you want."

"The school will be fine."

He shrugged and pulled from the parking lot. "They don't know how lucky they are," Morelli said as he motioned toward the boys. "In a few years they'll realize they can't escape from this town. Nobody does," he said. "They come back sooner or later."

I listened to him ramble, watching the town crawl slowly past the car window. In ten years, nothing much had changed. D'Grasso's Hardware Store had a new coat of white paint. Henderson's Floral Shop had become Johnson's Floral Gallery. The Hi-Ho Inn had expanded into the next building. And the remains of the old hotel had been swept away, replaced by a small park in the center of town. But the Standard station where I'd had my first part-time job still had full service and the weekly newspaper still posted the front page of the most recent edition in their front window. And the houses were still the same bland blend of clapboard and vinal siding.

"I came back," he said. "I had dreams. Big dreams. But I came back." He looked over at me. "Your class had dreams, too. But you're the first one to return."

"Most of us never had a chance to leave," I said.

"Hell of a tragedy, wasn't it? I mean, so many kids on their graduation night. They never really had a chance, did they?"

Morelli pulled the patrol car to a halt in the faculty parking lot and I climbed out with my knapsack firmly in hand.

"You sure you don't need a ride someplace else?" he asked. "I'd be happy to take you."

"No thanks," I told him. "I appreciate the offer, but I'll wait here a while."

I watched as the patrol car pulled away and I wondered if Morelli understood. Ten years is a long time for some of us.

I sat on the front porch of the school and waited, watched the moon and felt the breeze from the ocean sweep up from town to chill me. As chairman of the ten-year reunion committee, it was my responsibility to send out the invitations.

I began unpacking the knapsack; they would be arriving soon.

My classmates.

All of them.

When the world is too much with you, there are any number of escape routes—from books to television to just getting into the car and going for a drive. It is a quality of midnight that not even the simplest of things is really an escape.

Michael Bishop lives in Georgia and writes the way most of us wish we could, if only we were good enough.

A TAPESTRY OF LITTLE MURDERS

Michael Bishop

When Peter Mazarak left his house, it was two-thirty in the morning. Both pale and introspective, Mazarak was a young man, and he drove away from his house brooding on two separate but irrevocably yoked concerns.

His side ached with a malignancy of more than a month's tenure, and he had just killed his wife.

As he navigated the asphalt lane that skirted the country club, Mazarak looked out on the slumbering fairways and created monsters from their rolling flanks and moon-dappled surfaces. Shadows from the overarching pines played in the warp of his windshield. He thought the shadows were like ludicrously thin birds imprisoned in the glass, in the flat crystal heart of the windshield itself. But that was fancy, he kept telling himself, the confusion of his shredded sensibility. The shadows were only shadows: moonlight broken by the pine trees he was driving past. At two-goddamn-thirty in the morning.

Because you have to flee the pain you create, Mazarak thought, *as well as the pain within you*.

And he was fleeing from the gratuitous commission of pain he had effected, without even meaning to, against his own wife. The argument—the fatal argument—had resulted when he had come home long past a credible hour and then tried to shift the blame to Ruth's father. For that was Mazarak's position: In the indentured service of his own father-in-law he huckstered farm equipment, tried to sell monstrous yellow harvesting machines. Ordinarily the yellow machines sat on the company lot beneath an incandescent Georgia sun and grew as metallically scalding as electric hot plates. But just that afternoon, Mazarak told his wife, they had sold three such machines, and the Old Man had kept him there in the partitioned-off auditing room going over the papers, the contracts, the orders of delivery.

That was why he had been late.

As the daughter of a man who had made his fortune peddling farm equipment, Ruth had to understand the complexity of these transactions. (When he said this, Mazarak envisioned his wife's father sitting astride a yellow tractor, literally *pedaling*.) If she was angry, she could blame the Old Man. She could blame the tractors, cultivators, harvesters, threshing machines—all the things that provided the young Mazaraks such a respectable, gaudy livelihood. Or she could blame the paperwork.

Ultimately, however, they both knew the excuse was a ridiculous one. The Old Man, after all, worked on a strict priority basis. Customers had to present written orders for the machinery they required; all the company paperwork was handled well in advance. Besides, Mazarak had no particular skill in the area of clerical tasks.

The excuse didn't work. They both knew it.

To complicate things, Mazarak had been nursing the tension inside himself for well over a month, redirecting it outward as a kind of feeble static. An argument had been unavoidable, necessary, fated.

When it came, the violence of it momentarily quelled Mazarkak's vacillating tension, and he began to think about pain. Pain was like matter: It could be neither created nor destroyed. This incongruous excursion into metaphysics left Mazarak feeling as if he had discovered a universal maxim. He had felt that way even as he silenced Ruth's screaming amber eyes by fracturing her skull with a poker from the fireplace.

In fact, the pain that flared up in Ruth's eyes seemed almost to diminish the excruciating agony in his side. The one went a small way toward canceling the other. But only a small way. As he swung the blackened iron over her head, he cursed Ruth's helplessness. He cursed the Old Man. He cursed the pain that had driven him out of his customary introspection into so brutal and heinous an act.

And finally he cursed the sleek-skulled little man who had been the cause of his tardiness that evening.

For even though it was now two-thirty, only a few short hours ago that same little man, wrapped in the graceful white wings of his medical smock, had confirmed Mazarak's malignancy. With exasperating compassion. His only suggestion had been that Mazarak resign himself to the disease while actively seeking a cure.

Now Mazarak was fleeing that inescapable pain as the shadow of a crystal-thin bird struggled inside his windshield.

It seemed to him that he had been driving along the peripheries of the country club forever. When would he reach the main highway? How long would it take him to pass into the teemingly dense woods of Alabama? The route was westward, necessarily westward, but Mazarak began to believe he would never find an exit from the labyrinth of Oleander Springs, his own rural-suburban neighborhood. He began to think he would never see the chiseled granite faces of the mountains toward which necessity was driving him. The house where his wife lay dead was only fifteen minutes distant.

Then his automobile headlamps delineated the bulk of some small living thing on the asphalt.

Pain caressed Mazarak's hip, his side.

Whatever the living thing was, it presented a form of surprising plasticity under the headlamps. Advancing from the left-hand shoulder, it moved by a series of filliping jerks until it was in the center of the roadway.

Mazarak ran over it.

With a nearly inaudible *pop* the thing exploded against the automobile's heavy chassis.

Two more of the things appeared on the roadway. They were cream-colored excrescences in the yellow light, mere distortions on the asphalt. In a very brief moment, however, they had become amorphous lumps juggling one another without the aid of a magician. Mazarak ran over these things, too, and they made hollow popping sounds beneath the tires. Brittle implosions. Like the lungs of a diver at too great a depth.

Then, for as far as Mazarak could see by the shimmering wash of his headlights, the roadway accommodated endless swarms of these filliping things. Shapeless lumps of moving, migrating matter. The night was heavy with their pilgrimage.

"Toads," Mazarak said. "The road is full of toads."

It was. In the early morning dampness the toads had come out to let cool moisture seep lubricatingly into their grainy hides. Now they were migrating from the lawns of Mazarak's neighbors, across the asphalt, to the fetid ditch water on the perimeters of the golf course. Over this mad exodus fireflies winked like lanterns at sea, and Mazarak ran over toad after toad, toad after toad. Under his tires he felt the vital amphibian plasma spill in life-quenching gouts, drain away with each revolution, each thumping revolution. But as he grimaced at each dull thump, he forgot the agony that plagued him. That agony subsided. It diminished. In its place came a numb awareness that permitted him to recall, with something like disinterest, Ruth's preoccupation with a specific toad that had lived in their backyard.

Just two evenings ago—how was it that Ruth was dead? —they had walked together along the patio wall. Simply to be walking. Detecting a movement under her foot, Ruth had made a small inward gasp and clutched at Mazarak's arm.

"What is it?" he asked her.

"A toad. A toad pretending to be a lump of dirt."

"He's not much of a pretender if he doesn't know to keep still."

"He knows he doesn't have to be a pretender."

"Very analytical of the toad. How does he know?"

"Because he knows that I know him," Ruth said. "He lives under the cinder block by the water faucet, and he knows that nobody here is going to evict him."

"Oh, good."

"And he eats insects."

"Tough for the insects."

"But good for the flowers," Ruth said.

Then she had faced away, to lean against the wall. Mazarak watched the toad move lumpily through the flower bed and disappear under the cinder block.

"When I was a little girl," Ruth had said musingly, "Daddy went to a sales conference in eastern Colorado and brought me home a horned toad. From the prairie."

"Well, your father always had a knack for giving you just what you wanted."

"Do you know what happened to it?"

"It died," Mazarak said. "All your fond memories about pets have tragic endings."

He had not attempted levity in a long time. Ruth turned from the wall and stuck her tongue out at him. He reciprocated. Then she threw her head back and laughed indelicately, a hard, dry laugh that altered the contours of her face.

"Smart aleck. Do you know *why* it died?"

"No."

"Well, when I first saw it, I thought it was suffering from a skin disorder of some kind. Dishpan body, I suppose. All the bumps and spines on its back, you know."

"A horny toad. I know."

"So I covered its back with a thick layer of hand lotion. To smooth away the blemishes and render the helpless creature attractive to his girlfriends."

"Commendable."

"I covered it with hand lotion every day for three days, and it died. It died in spite of my intentions."

"How about that," Mazarak said. "How tragic."

Ruth had looked at him then with those thinly shrouded amber eyes, eyes seemingly hidden behind a nictitating film. She touched the collar of Mazarak's shirt and spoke reflectively.

"The colored man who worked for us when I was

little—he once ran over a toad with our power mower. Did you know that?''

"No. It's been a long time since your daddy's regaled his salesmen with an amusing anecdote about the help.''

"Do you know what happened?''

"Ruth!'' he had shouted. "For God's sake!''

"The blades chewed up that toad and spat him out in a hundred horrible gray and white pieces.''

Mazarak had tried to silence her; he had tried to rebuke her for her self-defeating morbidity. But before he could speak, she was weeping painfully and leaning into his arms.

"It hurt, Pete. It hurt me to watch that happen. The blades made a thumping sound and . . ."

And the toads died under his automobile. Unperturbedly they continued to hop across the roadway, perishing with scarcely audible thumps. But with the windows down Mazarak could hear their resilient bodies on every impact—bursting, imploding.

The asphalt behind him was strewn with their flattened carcasses, and he knew himself to be very much like the Negro lawnman of Ruth's childhood. Very much like him. The similarities, in fact, went beyond a simple inadvertent participation in slaughter. But although his side now hurt almost not at all, Mazarak did not try to enumerate these similarities. Instead, he waited. The toads' *danse macabre* finally came to an end, and he accelerated.

In the ripening darkness he found the highway that would carry him toward the mountains.

Small towns, inviolate hamlets, flashed by and then swept away like pasteboard tickets on the wind: Cuthbert, Eufaula, Comer, Three Notch.

Going through the darkened town squares, Mazarak stared out on the empedestaled heroes of the Confederate dead. The roughly hewn, piebald faces of the statues stared back, but their empty eyes haunted Mazarak, and the pain in his side reasserted itself so strongly that he cursed all heroes, living and dead alike. At last the statues disappeared in the lacework wisteria of the night, however, and he saw ahead of him the harsh floodlit glare of a truckstop.

They can't be after me yet, he thought. *It could be another ten hours before they find her. Maybe more.*

He pulled in. While an attendant filled his car with gas, Mazarak ate a half-melted Hershey bar and watched the hard brown beetles that were rattling against the floodlights. Western music buzzed from a jukebox behind the cafe's screen door. Among the trucks and truckers, he felt helplessly out of place.

A strange incident heightened his sense of alienation.

Just before he got back in his car, Mazarak saw a trucker come out of the cafe, stop by a gasoline pump, and crush between his hard fingers the shells of two or three peanuts. The man threw the shells down as if they were somehow contemptible and then found himself staring, over the pumps and oil display racks, into Mazarak's eyes. Immediately the trucker's expression took on a cast distinctly hostile, and Mazarak looked down.

He looks like Ruth's father, he thought. *But Ruth's father made taut and glassy-eyed by long hours in the lofty cab of a diesel truck.*

When he looked up again, the man was mounting to the mustard-colored cab and preparing to back out of the trucker's station. But before he could leave, Mazarak paid the attendant, started his own vehicle, and fled.

For miles the pungent, heavily warm odors of a paper mill followed him. So intense was his resurging pain, however, that he didn't care.

He drove all that morning and into the first light of a colorless dawn. He encountered no traffic on the highway, and the road's warm surfacing seemed to melt into the consistency of licorice, impending motion.

The world slowed down.

Suddenly Mazarak began to have hallucinatory flashes in which he saw—of all illogical things—his own backyard. The further westward he traveled, the more frequently came the flashes.

It was Christmas day. The afternoon was bright, blue, wispy, as in Indian summer, and he and Ruth were standing beside the soot-blackened incinerator behind the patio wall. The two of them had built the incinerator shortly after their marriage. A pile of stones—loosely cemented stones. It was the only "improvement" on their property that they had even attempted to make, an improvement which doubled, with its mortared chimney and removable steel grating, as a barbecue grill. But on that Christmas day (Mazarak could not remember how many Christmases had intervened) they had gone into the backyard not to sear a pair of steaks into charcoaled anonymity but to finish an argument. Mazarak remembered that he had been angry. There had been no sinister animal gnawing at his flank on that day, no nameless organic hurt to conceal, but he had suffered an emotional pain that compensated utterly for these lacks.

Ruth stood a little away from him, in the shadow of a tall blue conifer. He was occupied, however, and made no pretense of listening to what she said.

"Pete, this doesn't make sense."

He didn't answer. He was feeding the contents of a huge manila envelope onto the broken coals beneath the incinerator's grate. Policies. Bonds. Premiums. Sheet after sheet of ornately stenciled paper. Christmas presents. Each sheet grew crimson along its edges, curled, and then crumpled upon itself like a delicate, otherworld flower. When Mazarak had distributed these items, he tossed the manila envelope on the coals. This act had something of a dramatic finality about it, and Ruth spoke bitterly.

"I suppose you think you've reclaimed your manhood."

"Instant psychoanalysis," Mazarak said. "Too damn easy."

"Well, it doesn't make sense. Tossing everything on the fire."

"It makes sense to me," Mazarak said. "The Old Man can take his twenty-year harvest of insurance policies and half-ripe bonds and lug them back to the deposit box. Who does he think he is, sending us this patronizing crap?"

"He thinks he's my father."

Mazarak raged at this reply and told Ruth that her understanding of the relationship was too shallow. The Old Man was not so much her father as she was his earnestly cleaving daughter, forevermore under his wing. But in the shadow of the blue pine Ruth behaved not at all like a child. Her arguments made him step away from the incinerator, out of the vapory heat, and reconsider his tactics.

Nothing more than a fine, but insane, gesture. That was what she called his burning of the documents. It proved nothing—except perhaps that he indulged in purblind self-deception.

"You know he keeps copies of everything," Ruth said. "You know you've had it both ways this afternoon."

"Maybe I have," he responded. "But at least it's a gesture; it's better than nothing."

Then they had stood together and watched the updraft from the incinerator carry the charred remains of her father's papers into the sky. Through the blue openings fringed with pine needles. Up into the dappled afternoon. When Ruth finally spoke to him again, she said only a few anguished syllables.

"The ashes. They look like dying birds."

As Mazarak remembered this, the brutality of the outside world shattered his reverie. Something struck his windshield—with a dull, frightening thud. It was a bird. Even though he had been dreaming of another time, he knew immediately it was a bird. It had penetrated his farsightedness, appeared at sudden close range (as if bursting through the membranes of another continuum), and smacked against the glass. The bird then ricocheted off the windshield into oblivion.

And Mazarak, at once awake, sat up behind the steering wheel and experienced a fierce recrudescence of pain.

The corridor of vacancy above the roadway had filled with wings. Never had he seen so many floating scraps of plumage, like ashes drifting on the sky. All the wings belonged to mockingbirds. Mobile abstractions, the mockingbirds glided out of the tar-smeared conifers on each side of the highway and inscribed huge interlocking circles of descent.

Alabama, Mazarak thought, *I'm still in Alabama*.

But it was a gentle paperweight snowstorm of feathers that had engulfed him. With one violent exception: An occasional thud against Mazarak's windshield killed for him the illusion of gentleness.

Three, four, five, six—perhaps seven mockingbirds struck the windshield. Oriental in their delicate hovering beauty, they immolated themselves with all the ruthlessness of miniature kamikaze intelligences. Mazarak watched, unbelieving. Unbelieving, he tried to keep track. One bird undulated over the highway in chiaroscuro suspension and then rushed forward to die against the glass. Mazarak, horrified, saw that the creature was immune to fear—just before it struck, one of the bird's opalescent eyes reflected back at him, in blood-red microcosm, his own uncontrollable fear. Then the thud.

And still Mazarak had in his nostrils the oppressive

odors from the paper mill. They had followed him all night, growing stronger rather than weaker.

How many birds ultimately died escaping that stimulus, he had no idea. But at last it seemed to him that the entire species had participated in ritualistic suicide. There were russet smears on the windshield, and Mazarak automatically turned on the wiper blades.

He discovered his mistake at once.

Fluid grime swept back and forth in incomplete semicircles, altering the landscape. Soon he was looking not through the glass but at it, for caught beneath the wiper blade was a single mockingbird's quill that hypnotized Mazarak with its fluttering *klihk-klihk, klihk-klihk*. Like a metronome. As always, the end result was numb imprisonment inside his own mind.

His automobile rocked and slewed. It bounced forward like a guttered bowling ball. Then the tires caught the shoulder and churned through the gravel there. Savagely, Mazarak slammed the brake pedal. In a moment he was sitting inside his quivering automobile at a dead stop, half on the road, half off. He held his head in his hands and looked disconsolately at the knob of the cigarette lighter.

Where does all the pain go? he asked the cigarette lighter.

The cigarette lighter did not respond.

But that was just as well. For even though Mazarak had no pain at all in his thoroughly punished flank, he knew fear. A terribly palpable fear.

That night Mazarak found a motel and holed up in it like a reptile seeking shelter under a rock. *Holed up.* Those words, as melodramatic and luridly western as they sounded, were the only ones that adequately summarized his predicament. Because the pain in his side had begun very subtly to reestablish its presence, causing him to picture himself as that small reptilian beast secreting itself away from man's inquisitive eye.

But the next morning he left that motel and drove for an entire day. Without incident. Blessedly without incident. The evening found him quartered in another nondescript motel, and then, once again, he resumed driving westward. He spent his time on the road, however, thinking about the strange occurrences of his first day's travel.

Killing the mockingbirds seemed to Mazarak the antithesis of running over the toads. It was a crime more reprehensible, more poignant to take part in. After all, a toad was a creature unfeelingly cold-blooded, a thing so removed from man's rational spectrum that he couldn't seriously regret murdering one.

But the mockingbirds.

They presented a completely different case. In their choreographed aerial beauty, Mazarak thought, they were very nearly specimens of a higher life-form. That they could cause him to be the instrument of their dying offended Mazarak; it made him dimly aware of his own crassly motivated flight. It made his mind touch on, and then immediately relinquish, the circumstance from which he was fleeing. And pain coursed through him.

But if he could reach the mountains—or even the shadows of the mountains—he would be all right. His pursuers might not follow him into that hard masculine country where the tall grain and arroyo-gutted prairies provided a natural sanctuary. But there were no sanctuaries, really. Mazarak understood that some things did not admit of a simple, unretributive escape; some things required merciless retribution, and there were always people who could be counted on to carry it out.

No. You had to be afraid of the grain fields and the prairies. It was impossible to rely on them.

Mazarak was afraid of roadblocks. He was afraid his

pursuers would capture him in the open wasteland, before he had a chance to abandon his automobile and clamber into the sharp, concealing crevices of the Sangre de Cristo foothills. He had several imprecise ideas about how life would be after he had eluded the men carrying his retribution.

Therefore, he drove until it was dark. And kept driving even after the stars had appeared in the beaten silver night overhead. The thought of *holing up* again, of crawling into a three-dollar-a-throw roadhouse, had no allure. It was best to keep moving. Always toward the mountains. In the darkness the prairie surrounded him on all sides, like an ocean beneath which something insidious moved.

Then it happened again.

Mazarak had no time to adjust to the change.

Creatures were moving in the prairie grasses. They were tiny creatures, the sort a man could take between his thumb and forefinger and squeeze until the brittle skull made a crumpling sound of capitulation.

Kangaroo rats.

Mazarak had never seen one before, but he knew what they were as soon as he saw them leaping fragilely through the alkaline grasses. At once they came up on the highway in a disorganized parade of singles: delicate little animals with palsied forelegs and eyes that burned amber in his headlights. Each kangaroo rat tested the asphalt with a series of diminutive hops and then confonted his automobile. The headlights hypnotized them, froze them upright.

Not again, Mazarak said to himself. *Dear God, not again.*

Then he was counting, involuntarily recording the number of deaths. It was not an easy process. The kangaroo rats made so little noise when the undergirding of his automobile drove their bodies to the ground or wrenched their heads aside. And there were so many of them. How could he keep count? Nevertheless, he made the effort, for he had the building suspicion now that each rat's death was a black mark in the register of his own precariously salvable life. Already, he knew, a more telling IOU weighted the register against him. He had to keep count—just to determine his place in purgatory.

Seven, eight, nine.

Congregations of little bodies, all tentatively leaping. Mazarak could not help but see how much they resembled naked little men, with undeveloped arms and frozen eyes. Each death pained him, pained him deeply—even though the successive collisions brought him closer to the painless state of a straw-stuffed dummy. He could do nothing with his automobile; it rushed forward, as if free of rational control.

Twenty? Twenty-one? He wasn't sure. Numbers eluded him, but the kangaroo rats did not.

A dimly luminous mist crossed the highway, blotting out both moon and stars. Mazarak could still see the rats dancing onto the highway and then halting in blind petrifaction—but he was like a man looking through surgical gauze. The mist accomplished that much against him.

Finally, he couldn't see.

All he could do was ride out the intransigence of his car and listen to the rats going under. The car fishtailed, swerved, and scattered wisps of fog. Then he knew that it had carried him off the road.

The sound of shattering glass echoed inside his head even after unconsciousness had overtaken him.

After a long time Mazarak awoke and struggled free of the wreckage. It was morning. At a distant remove he could see the precisely carven mountains toward which he had been directing himself for nearly three days.

He stood in the ditch beside his crumpled automobile

and tried to orient his faculties. But nothing worked, nothing fell into place.

Besides the highway there was an open field, part of the prairie, but it didn't fit Mazarak's conception of the country he had been traveling through the night before. Something was very different. Grain grew on the prairie, tall, rippling stands of wheat so brilliant in the sunlight that he had to stare. Each separate stalk was a miracle, for Mazarak felt certain that no field of grain had bordered the roadside when his accident took place.

Briefly he feared that his pursuers had caught up with him and done something to alter his perception of the world. But this fear flickered out.

Mazarak saw something that made him forget his pursuers. Deep in the wheat field a woman was beckoning to him with the elegant winglike sleeve of her dressing gown. A hood covered her face, a royal-blue hood. He could see her between the stalks, and she was definitely signaling him to follow her into the rhythmically swaying grain.

He wanted to comply.

But so empty of feeling was he that even the simple act of lifting his foot proved difficult. The ground had almost no resiliency under him—no texture, no firmness. Only by willing the movement inside his head, willing himself to action, was he able to follow the beckoning arm. He approached the woman through the grain. And, as he knew she would, the woman retreated two steps for each numb step forward that he was able to manage. At last her blue garment disappeared in a far stand of wheat and he was left facing the mountains.

He shouted a name. The name echoed away.

Because of this shout, Mazarak almost failed to see the harvesting machine that bore down on him out of the stalks. It made no sound, no noise whatsoever, and the dark figure astride the machine very nearly succeeded in overtaking Mazarak on his blind side. But he turned in time and looked up into the grinning countenance of the driver and simultaneously saw the brutal, silently humming blades. How tall the machine was. This thought comforted Mazarak. He turned again, to face the blades head on.

"All right," he said aloud.

Somehow he knew that there would be no pain, even when the inevitable shredding began. For he was emptied of pain, cured of his malignancy, and it was sweet to die. He noticed with satisfaction that the harvesting machine was yellow, like the voluptuous sun.

One of the obligations a true fantasist has is to examine, in one way or another, the foundations of civilization—as we know it and as it might very well be, a distinction important enough to place it just before the last stroke of twelve.

R. Bretnor's stories have appeared in, among other major publications, ESQUIRE and ELLERY QUEEN'S MYSTERY MAGAZINE, not to mention just about all anthologies and periodicals devoted exclusively to the genres of science fiction and fantasy.

NO OTHER GODS

R. Bretnor

Never, in his fourteen years as rector of St. Luke's, had the Reverend E. Baxter Craddock questioned the nature of God or the ultimate purpose of His designs. Mr. Craddock was no theologian (though the devout Baxter aunt who had put him through divinity school had died hoping he would become one) and indeed he had left all such troublesome speculations behind him on his graduation. He was, of course, aware of God, as any minister or priest must be, but it was rather as a director, evoking Hamlet on the stage, is aware of Shakespeare. He had never formulated the idea specifically, but he was satisfied that God, in His goodness and wisdom, approved of St. Luke's, its congregation, and its pastor.

St. Luke's certainly was a church of which anyone could be proud. The building, and the land on which it stood, had been the gift of a Dr. Branfield, now several years dead. Shortly before the Great War, he had brought Bernard Maybeck down from Berkeley to design it, and the result had been an edifice all of gentle redwood, with a magnificent rose window and the balance of its stained glass in art nouveau, a vaulted ceiling which made up in the grandeur of its concept whatever it may have lacked in size, an austere altar, and a treasure of a baroque organ which the doctor had purchased out of Lichtenstein. The rectory, in a similar subdued style, was separated from the church by a rose garden, by trellises of climbing roses and honeysuckle, which Mr. Craddock had adopted as his own and where he spent many happy hours.

When St. Luke's was built, Dr. Branfield's Victorian mansion had loomed over it serenely and at a decent distance, but shortly after the crash of '29, his heirs were forced to sell, presumably to save on taxes and to make way for some humbler edifice which, after a year or two, still had not been put up. So church and rectory stood almost alone, their nearest neighbors two or three hundred feet away, and behind them a still-wild canyon which, despite the fact that they were only a short walk from

Cabrillo Bridge and Balboa Park, still cut off the street they stood on. In Dr. Branfield's remote youth, the district had been San Diego's finest, and its gradual deterioration— grand old residences turned into boarding houses or demolished or simply allowed to wear the scars of a new poverty— had had little or no effect on the nature of the congregation. There were still enough of the old families surviving to maintain its exclusive character, and indeed quite a number who had made the more fashionable move to Mission Hills continued their attendance every Sunday. The few intruders—those who too obviously did not belong—were gently and courteously, but very firmly, discouraged, and almost all of them took the hint, transferring their devotions elsewhere.

One who did not was Eunice Gammon, and in her case the hint was neither as firm nor as persistently repeated as it usually was. She had returned to San Diego after many years of absence, wrapped in a shabby aura of half-forgotten gossip, but everybody knew that she was related to the Jonathan McKays—a poor relation, but kin nonetheless— and they, though they now spent almost all their time in La Jolla, were still among the most generous benefactors of St. Luke's. As the months went by, she became more and more a thorn in Mr. Craddock's flesh.

Baxter Craddock was not a big man, but he had presence. His aureole of graying hair gave him an almost medievally clerical appearance, and everything he wore—his beautifully tailored gray suits, his Roman collars, his vestments— spoke of elegance. Anything his sermons and his services may have lacked in passion, he made up for, as far as his congregation was concerned, in studied artistry. His homilies distressed no one, sent chills down no sinners' spines, and if no one, of a Sunday, left St. Luke's exalted, almost invariably everyone left a little happier, a little easier in their own minds, than they had been on entering. It was what they wanted, comparable perhaps to the spiritual ambience created by many a hard-drinking, hail-fellow-well-met hunting parson in eighteenth-century England, though of course less boisterous.

Mr. Craddock applied the same principle when called upon to counsel or comfort his parishioners, and so did his wife Dorothy, as gracious and graceful in her role as he in his. Both of them had taken graduate courses in psychology, which gave them convenient generalizations to rely on when otherwise religion might have wielded too harsh a rod.

None of this helped where Eunice Gammon was concerned. The congregation of St. Luke's did its best to reflect the elegance and precision of its pastor, even those few who, having fallen on hard times, could not afford to be properly fashionable. She did not. St. Luke's would have sympathized with a genteel shabbiness, but she was definitely messy. Her gray hair straggled out here and there under the bent rim of her mistreated purple hat; her nondescript clothing always showed spots and stains. She attended every service, every open church function, always sitting by herself in a back pew, sometimes snuffling, sometimes muttering audibly, hovering around the edges, anxious to be a part of the congregation but not daring to. There was something at once feral and frightened about her small, black, nervous eyes and her ghost-pale, thin face. She never asked for or received Communion, and when Dorothy Craddock once mentioned it to her, she simply backed away, wringing her hands and shaking her head desperately.

She lived, on a pittance from the Jonathan McKays, in a boarding house run by a German couple at the corner of First and Laurel, a few blocks from the church, and she took long, lonely walks at night, always passing St. Luke's at least once. Sometimes she seemed to be talking either to herself or to imaginary companions, and once or twice people had seen her suddenly break into a run—only to stop after fifty or so feet, gasping and looking back furtively over her shoulder. Gossip whispered that Gammon had died, or that he'd left her, that she had been a nun or almost a nun, or had she been in prison? or in a mental hospital? Once Dorothy Craddock had, very tactfully and obliquely, tried to question Mrs. Jonathan McKay, and the old lady had made it very clear that Eunice's past was done with and her own affair—and that line of enquiry had ended there.

From the moment of her return, before she had so much as said a dozen words to him, Eunice Gammon had troubled Baxter Craddock, and time after time, when he and Dorothy were alone, he had complained about her. "She simply doesn't *belong* here," he'd say. "She—she's a discord, like a dog howling during a *Te Deum*, like a sudden stink in our rose garden." And Dorothy would reprove him mildly, saying she understood, but they should still be charitable, now shouldn't they? Poor Eunice—when she said it, Mr. Craddock always sighed—was just a cross she supposed they'd have to bear.

Considering himself a realist, Mr. Craddock had always envied Dorothy's ability to seal the tight compartments of her mind against anything that threatened the serenity of her neat universe. Eunice Gammon was a cross he did not *want* to bear, but he did not argue, and when his wife suggested that perhaps they should be nicer to the poor thing, he made himself agree that it would be the Christian thing to do. So Dorothy had invited her to tea, with Mrs. Berryman, the verger's wife, and they had spent a tortured hour trying to bridge the gap between their own down-to-earth sanity and that other uncanny world in which her mind seemed to wander. Her laugh was small, shrill, reedy, and she laughed when the conversation demanded anything but laughter—as though, Mrs. Craddock thought with a little shiver, she was in pain. She spoke only when they addressed themselves directly to her. Oh, yes, she liked St. Luke's. She always had liked churches. Maybe it was because there was a holiness inside them. She laughed. At least inside some of them. Did Mrs. Craddock think all churches had holiness inside them? And so the hour dragged by. They asked her no questions about herself, and when they spoke to her about places and people and motion picture shows and happenings, her responses more often than not bore no relation to the subject. When Daisy Berryman asked her whether she had ever been abroad, she answered that she had never weighed much more than she did now, and for just a moment Dorothy Craddock had suspected her of having a sense of humor, then saw that she was quite unaware of any double meaning in the words.

She thanked them when she left, and they could hear her laughing and mumbling to herself as she picked her way through the rose garden.

Mrs. Craddock told her husband all about it. "I'm sorry we didn't really accomplish anything, Edwin," she declared. "But I do feel better about having tried. After all, it was our *duty,* wasn't it?"

He agreed, secretly glad that no rapprochement had been achieved. "I'm sure you did your very best," he said. "It's no fault of yours that she's unreachable."

Three days later, on Sunday, he found out that they had both been wrong. After the morning service, when everybody had dispersed, he had gone back into the church alone and found Eunice Gammon there, waiting uneasily near the door. When she saw him, she laughed apprehen-

sively, coughed a little, and whispered, "F-Father Craddock—"

He flinched. While he was more or less High Church—
though never uncomfortably so—it always embarrassed
him when parishioners, especially those to whom he wasn't
close, addressed him as *Father*, though Dorothy always did
refer to him as Father Craddock when she spoke of him.
He managed a small smile, and said, "Yes, Mrs. Gammon?
I trust that all is well with you?"

"I— It's a question I want to ask you, Father—just a
question. Mrs. Craddock was so nice to me, I thought
maybe I could—" Her laughter shrilled.

Dear God! he thought, forcing the smile to appear again.
"Why, of course," he answered. "I'll answer it if I can."

She darted a look over her shoulder. Her voice dropped
until it was practically inaudible. "Father," she said, *"what
does God look like?"*

He recoiled before the sudden intensity of her voice.
"What does God *look* like?"

"Yes, yes, yes! Father, I want to *know!*"

Good Lord! he thought. I wish she'd at least sit down.
In his mind's eye, he saw the form of the Creator as
Michelangelo had painted him. He groped for words. "How
can we know?" he said at last. "The Bible tells us that
'God created Man in his own image,' so there's good
reason to believe that He is at least anthropomorphic—"
Instantly, he regretted his choice of words. "That is, his
form is human, but of course gloriously human, unimagin-
ably noble, far beyond our comprehension."

She backed a step or two. "Do you think so? Father, do
you really *think* so?" Her head shook. "I—I wish I could
believe it."

It came to him with a shock that he himself—though he
had given the matter very little thought—did not believe in

an anthropomorphic God. But he assured her again that she could believe it. "We have it on Biblical authority," he stated firmly, "and on the authority of the Church."

She shook her head again, muttered her thanks, darted to one side, and hurried out. She vanished down the path, her head nodding like a thin pecking bird's.

He sat down in the nearest pew, trying to think the situation out. Obviously, Dorothy's tea party had borne fruit—like the Mad Hatter's, he thought a bit hysterically. He sat there, wondering whether there were to be more such questions in the future, wondering what went on in Eunice Gammon's obviously troubled mind—and, in spite of himself, wondering what God would indeed look like were he to manifest himself directly to mortal eyes. He remembered old Urquhart, his professor of comparative religion, a typical Scottish dominee and probably a predestinationist, a gaunt crag of a man with wild eyes and the determination to throw the fear of God into his pupils, far more taken with preaching than with teaching. Urquhart would have thundered his answer out of the Old Testament, out of its most terrifying passages—

Mr. Craddock thrust away these thoughts, forcing himself to concentrate on the daily duties of his pastorate. As he too left the church, he decided not to tell Dorothy about the incident; he hoped Eunice Gammon might never speak to him again.

The hope was vain. Only a few days later she came to him, finding him in the rose garden, hesitating as she came down the path, waiting until she saw him put down his shears and take off one of his gardening gloves. Even then she advanced as timidly as a wild animal fearful of a trap.

He sighed and gestured to her to approach.

"Can I help you, Mrs. Gammon?" he said, trying not to let his voice betray unpastoral annoyance.

"I—I didn't want to interrupt," she answered. Again

her voice, barely audible, was small and shrill, apprehensive and yet curiously assertive. "But, Father—Father Craddock, there's something else I'd like to ask you— something I have to know." She broke off to look over her shoulder.

"Yes?" he said, he hoped encouragingly.

"Father"—the words burst from her—*"why is God so holy?"*

For an instant only, Mr. Craddock closed his eyes, found himself confronting a mental image of old Urquhart, then opened them again. "Mrs. Gammon," he replied, "God is holy because he *is* God. *He* is eternal. *He* is the Author of the Universe and of our being."

"You— You mean he's holier than *other* gods?"

Mr. Craddock drew his glove back on, trusting she'd take the hint. "There *are* no other gods," he told her, making no attempt to hide his irritation. "May I suggest, Mrs. Gammon, that you read your Bible? That will make it clear. And pray to God for guidance."

"N-no other gods?" she echoed, starting to back down the path.

"None."

She backed a few short steps, head shaking, then whirled abruptly and almost ran, down past the church, back into the street.

And her pastor stood there for a moment, staring at his roses and not seeing them, remembering how old Urquhart, in one of his aggressive moods, had quoted the Commandment, *Thou shalt have no other Gods but me,* and pointed out that it did not say specifically that there *were* no other gods, and then had assigned it as an essay topic—an essay on which Baxter Craddock had scored only a C+.

He gave up gardening for the afternoon and went back into the rectory to telephone Max Danforth, an army captain retired on disability from the Tientsin station, who was scoutmaster of the church's troop. Danforth was a friend and fishing companion, an anchor of sanity to whom he could unburden himself.

"Why don't you run over here, Max?" he said. "McKay's sent me some Johnny Walker—just about the first in the country since repeal. It's late enough so we can broach one of them, and anyhow, I'd like to talk to you."

Danforth arrived promptly, parking his Hudson touring car in front, still a straight and powerful figure despite his militarily disabling limp.

Craddock was waiting for him, and they shook hands. "Sounds like you have troubles, Padre." Danforth grinned. "You didn't tell me, but your voice did."

They went into the rectory, into Mr. Craddock's study. There they opened the scotch ceremoniously, toasted each other, drank. Dorothy was away for the afternoon, and Mr. Craddock, under the influence of good liquor and companionship, began to relax. He told Danforth the whole story.

When he had finished, the captain rubbed his close-cropped reddish hair. "Well," he said, "her being related to the McKays doesn't make things any easier. But look at it this way. The old girl's a looney—it's that simple. She needs help, but as I see it, she needs a doctor—you know, a psychiatrist or something—more than she needs anything you can do for her. Anyway, could you talk her into trying it?"

Mr. Craddock said he doubted it; she had no money, and he knew the McKays would turn a deaf ear if he suggested it

"Well,"—Danforth held his glass out for a refill—"then it looks like you'll just have to ride it out. As long as she doesn't start bothering the rest of the congregation, you ought to be okay. Just don't take her too seriously."

"Max, believe me, I *do* feel sorry for her. So does Dorothy. But what can we *do?*"

"Don't do anything unless you think of something foolproof. Pat her on the head. Say you'll pray for her. But I wouldn't go much beyond that if I was you."

As the weeks passed and spring turned into summer, Eunice Gammon's questions became more and more frequent. After almost every service, she lingered on the fringes, hoping to catch Mr. Craddock by himself, and she made a practice of walking down the street during those hours when he was most likely to be in the garden. Finally—and always when Dorothy wasn't home—she started coming to the rectory door, ringing the bell. She could tell he was alone because Dorothy always left the garage doors open when she drove off in their green Franklin sedan.

Her questions were repetitive, about God's holiness, about His nature and probable appearance, and about other gods, like those the people off in India and places believed in, and did Mr. Craddock believe He might destroy you if you sinned? and if He did, how would He do it?

Mr. Craddock was as brief with her as possible; his answers all were stereotypes, either directly from the Bible or out of his courses in counseling and psychology. But he could not bring himself to turn her away completely; he could see that, insane or not, she was suffering. Then, suddenly, her questions ceased to be merely questions and became importunities. Would he pray for her, he himself, in the holiness of the church? Would he? She had sinned, terribly, terribly. If he would pray for her, perhaps God—*her* God was the way she put it—wouldn't be so angry with her or maybe wouldn't want to punish her. She didn't tell her pastor how she'd sinned. When he hinted gently that perhaps it might be good for her to talk of it, she simply backed away, shaking her head jerkily.

Baxter Craddock forced himself to suffer her in patience. Late in August, he told himself—now not very far away—he and Dorothy would drive north to San Francisco, where they would join his classmate and old friend Joel Jamieson, now a suffragan bishop, who had a cabin in the mountains near Lake Tahoe. For three weeks they would be free of Mrs. Gammon and her madnesses. He and Joel could go fishing. Dorothy and Joel's wife, Candida, could make up a bridge foursome from among the Jamiesons' acquaintances. Just the prospect of it, he told Max Danforth, made it easier for him to bear up.

Then, scarcely a week before they were scheduled to depart, she found her way somehow to the door of his study, rapped on it with her sharp knuckles, and when he opened the door, she thrust two wrinkled dollar bills into his hand.

"Father—oh, Father Craddock! You're leaving us, going away! Who—Who's going to *pray* for me?"

He looked down at the money. "Mrs. Gammon, Reverend Schorer—you remember him? he's retired—he's going to take my place while I'm gone. He'll pray for you, I'm sure."

"It won't be the *same!*" She almost screamed the words. "Oh, Father Craddock, can't you keep on praying for me while you're away? Father Schorer doesn't know me, and I don't know how much holiness he has. Please, please, *please!* Otherwise something dreadful's going to happen. I know it, I *know* it!"

Baxter Craddock was shaken. He pushed the money back at her. "Of course I'll pray for you, Mrs. Gammon. I'll pray every day, and I'll ask the bishop to pray for you, too."

Tears were streaming down her emaciated, roughly rouged cheeks, and she was trembling.

It came to Baxter Craddock that the situation demanded more of him than mere passivity, that he should do what he had carefully avoided doing—make some effort to see into her mind. "Mrs. Gammon," he said, speaking very gently but very firmly, "I am your pastor. I know you're frightened, desperately. Isn't it time you really confided in me? If I don't know exactly what it is that frightens you, I can't very well contend with it. You certainly don't need to pay me for my prayers. Here, take back your money and come in. We can sit down, and I'll give you a glass of port to steady you, and you can tell me everything."

He stepped back from the door, gestured at an armchair near his desk.

For a moment she stood there uncertainly, her mouth working. Then, still unsure, she edged past him and suddenly darted for the chair, as though to take refuge there.

He closed the door. He went to the cabinet behind his desk where he kept a bottle of good California port, mostly to comfort an occasional overwrought elderly parishioner. With a not too steady hand, he poured two glasses, passed one to her. He seated himself, smiled at her, sipped—and saw that she had emptied her glass at a gulp. He rose and refilled it.

"And now—" he said, sitting down again.

She swallowed, put her glass down, leaned forward. Her voice, as always, was small and shrill and strained. Her small black eyes flicked from side to side, trapped fugitives. "F-Father Craddock," she said, "I can't protect myself. I have no holiness, not anymore. That's why I need your prayers, to protect me from—from the vengeance."

She paused, breathing spasmodically, and Mr. Craddock broke in on her. "My dear Mrs. Gammon," he said softly, "you must rely on God. Remember the Twenty-Third Psalm, 'The Lord is my Shepherd, I shall not want . . .' Repeat it to yourself. Believe in it—"

Shaking her head violently, she interrupted him. "No, *no!*" she cried. "Father, you don't *understand!* Your God's not mine! Your God is gentle and kind and merciful.

Mine—'' She sobbed, controlled herself. "My God is cruel and angry. I— I've seen him in my dreams. He's huge. His eyes burn in the darkness. And he has claws and fangs, great terrible fangs! Oh, Father, *I know he's real!* I've seen him in my dreams, and he will come for me. Unless I'm protected, I *know* he will!''

Mr. Craddock cringed within himself. Delusions of this magnitude were beyond his practical experience. He held up a hand to stem her spate of fear.

She broke off, gasping.

"There is only *one* God,'' he told her, his voice by no means as Urquhartian as he might have wished. "All others are false gods, contrived by men. There is no need to fear them, nor to fear demons—no, not even Satan. All you need is faith—faith in the one true God and in His Son.''

Again, her head shook absolute negation. "No, no, *no!* It's not at all like that! People like me, who've sinned and sinned, we get the sort of God that we deserve. Don't you understand? That's how we're punished, before we even die!''

Mr. Craddock had never questioned God's intentions toward himself, but now, secretly, in his appalled mind, he thought, Lord, why have you visited this upon me? Have I not served you? Have I not— My God, how did I get myself into this mess? There was no use arguing with the woman. There was no use trying to cure her of her mad belief. All he could do was give her what she wanted, the assurance of his prayers, to get her out of here as speedily as possible.

He promised her he'd pray. He promised her that Dorothy and Bishop Jamieson would pray each day for her protection against her ravening god. Making his promises, he poured each of them another glass of port. It wouldn't matter if he was away, he told her, for God—his God—

would hear him anywhere. But she too must pray, in
church, in the odor of sanctity. And Reverend Schorer
would pray too, and—

"No, no!" she cried again. "Don't tell *them*. I can't
trust any of them. I don't want anybody to know but you!
They'd only think I'm crazy!"

"They don't have to know. They'll simply pray God to
protect you, that is all. And their prayers will help, I
promise you—"

She had begun to weep. Now, as he reiterated his
promises, she wiped her eyes on her dingy, worn gray
sleeve. She emptied her glass, fussed with her handbag,
tried to adjust her musty purple hat.

She stood, and he moved around his desk to let her out.

At the door, she turned once. "Oh, thank you, thank
you, *thank you*, Father Craddock!"

Then she fled.

He forced himself to close the door quietly. He went
back to his chair. Sitting there, he was struck abruptly by
the thought that her belief in her false savage god was as
strong—or perhaps even stronger—than his own faith in
the Almighty. The idea troubled him. So did the sudden
memory of old Urquhart thundering, "How can you dare
think that you know God? How can you presume to ex-
pound His mystery?"

He frowned. what else was it Urquhart had said? Oh,
yes: "Remember Micah 6:8, *What doth the Lord require
of thee, but to do justly, and to love mercy, and to walk
humbly with thy God?*"

Immediately, he felt better. While he had had a good
deal to say about the Lord in his sermons over the years,
he didn't think anyone could accuse him of failing where
justice and mercy and humility were concerned.

Sipping his port, he thought of his soon-to-start vacation,

and presently he was able to file old Urquhart safely away in a bottom drawer of his mind. Then he tried to push the interview with Eunice Gammon in after it, but it wouldn't quite fit.

Driving north, Baxter Craddock finally told Dorothy something of his troubles, first the minor annoyances, then their increasing frequency, and finally that last interview, making it sound less traumatic than it had been. She listened patiently, and then reacted exactly as he had known she would. "Edwin," she told him, "I simply can't understand why you let these insane ideas of hers bother you. All you have to do is remember she isn't normal. Promise me that when we get back, you'll make it clear you have no time for that sort of nonsense. Be *firm* with her."

He could almost hear the compartment click shut as she changed the subject, and it wasn't until he and Joel Jamieson were together on the lake, their lines in the water, that he brought it up again.

Jamieson, a long, lean, learned-looking man, listened more attentively, and the questions he asked were intelligent and always to the point. "It's a pity," he said, when Craddock had finished, "that you couldn't find out just where she spent her life and what her alleged sins were. If it's true she was a nun, we might have half our answer right there. Rome's enforced celibacy can sometimes be the last straw where unstable personalities are concerned. During the Church's witch-hunting days, nuns did appear to be especially vulnerable to intense hysteria, delusions of demoniac possession, and similar psychotic episodes. Very well, this Eunice Gammon is psychotic, and her psychosis has turned her, very plainly, into a pagan. Apparently, she still believes in God, else she wouldn't pester you to pray to Him, but she also has become a polytheist, though who knows whether she thinks her imaginary were-tiger-god is a separate entity or something God himself is going to send to chastise her. . . . What would *I* do in your shoes? I'd do my best to get her into a mental institution, of course, or at least into therapy. I know—you've told me about the Jonathan McKays and how they've made any such rational course almost impossible. However, what if Candida and I come down and stay a few days with you, say in October? You could introduce us, and maybe I could talk to them without it bouncing back at you at all. I've found that people who won't listen to their clergyman will often listen to a bishop—even a suffragan bishop." He laughed. "They probably think we're closer to having the keys to the Kingdom."

Mr. Craddock accepted the suggestion gratefully, not only because he recognized its merit, but also because he was genuinely fond of his old friend. The fishing was good, the trout fighters and fun to catch; on a table set before the cabin fireplace, they went excellently with the Gray Riesling now once more available. The Craddocks enjoyed themselves, renewed old friendships, made some new ones. Only when they were actually about to drive away did anyone speak again of Eunice Gammon, and that was when Joel Jamieson renewed his promise to come down to San Diego and see what he could do to help. "We'll take the *Yale* or *Harvard*," he said. "Candida'll love the sea trip there and back, and you can run me round while I'm there."

The drive south was uneventful. Their Franklin, only three years old, ran like a charm; the road, especially around San Luis Obispo, had been improved. They stopped overnight at a huge old frame hotel at Paso Robles; they stopped again at Santa Barbara, enjoying a wonderful seafood dinner on the pier. They reached San Diego late in the afternoon, coming in on India Street and turning left up the hill at Laurel. The sky had clouded over; there was a slight, warm drizzle; they were happy to be home again. Mr. Craddock felt more optimistic than he had for many a week.

They were four or five blocks from the church when they saw the boy walking and recognized him.

"Isn't that one of our scouts, the Sampson kid?" said Mr. Craddock. "What's his name? Calvin?"

"Yes," Dorothy replied, "and he's limping a little bit. Hadn't we better offer him a ride? Even if we take him home, it'll only be a minute or two out of our way."

"Sure enough." He slowed the car, pulled over to the curb.

"Calvin!" Dorothy called. "Calvin Sampson, have you hurt yourself?"

The boy, a sturdy eleven-year-old, turned around. He grinned cheerfully. "Hey, Mrs. Craddock, you're back! My leg? Aw, I just twisted it in track; it'll be all right."

"Well, we'll give you a ride home if you want."

"Hey, that'd be great!" He opened the back door, climbed in. "I hope I don't get your car dirty—my shoes are sort of muddy."

"Don't worry about it." Mr. Craddock smiled, and let his clutch out.

The boy leaned forward, hands on the robe rail. "Did ya have a good time, Mr. Craddock? Catch a lotta fish?"

Both the Craddocks assured him that they'd enjoyed themselves immensely.

"Well, I guess you don't know what happened here, huh?" There was sudden excitement in his voice. "To Crazy Eunie?"

"Crazy Eunie?" Dorothy momentarily was puzzled. "Who—" Then she understood. *"Mrs. Gammon,"* she said severely. "Calvin, you shouldn't talk about anybody that way."

"Gee, I'm sorry, Mrs. Craddock. That was what all the kids called her."

"What *did* happen to her?" demanded Mr. Craddock, feeling a little guilty at his quickly suppressed hope that perhaps a psychotic episode even the McKays couldn't ignore had necessitated her confinement in a mental hospital or nursing home.

"She was kilt!"

"*Killed?*" Dorothy exclaimed. "How, for goodness' sake?"

"Was it an accident?" asked her husband, with a twinge of apprehension.

"Uh-*uh!*" Calvin shook his head vigorously. "It gives me shivers just to think about it. The cops said she'd been *murdered!*"

"*Good Lord!*"

"It was only about a week after you went away. The people in her boarding house said she'd gone out Friday night and next morning hadn't come back, so they called the cops, and the cops found somebody who'd seen her heading up towards the canyon, so the cops called Mr. Danforth and he phoned all us kids to help 'em search down there. It was Timmy Maher found her, and boy, was he shook up." Calvin dramatized his story by shuddering appropriately. "He threw his breakfast up right there. Boy, was she a mess! Mr. Danforth wouldn't let the rest of us go look. He said it was just as if a great big lion had gotten at her, from the zoo!"

Baxter Craddock's foot jerked on the accelerator and the Franklin hesitated, coughed, lurched on.

"How horrible!" remarked Dorothy, looking at him out of the corner of her eye. "Calvin, maybe you'd better not tell us any more about it right now, please. We'll call Captain Danforth the minute we get home and find out everything."

Calvin, clearly disappointed, let go of the robe rail and sat back. During the rest of the short run to his house, the conversation was stiff and artificial—how was he doing at school? and had his sister Millie recovered from the measles? and, yes, Mr. Craddock had caught some great big trout—that sort of thing.

As they started off after dropping him, Dorothy—in her most authoritative voice—said, "Undoubtedly, it was a tramp who murdered her. Or maybe, in that canyon, a mountain lion."

Her husband wiped his suddenly sweating palms on his trouser legs. "Undoubtedly," he said, a little shakily, thinking, My God, I hope so! I hope that's what it was! "I'll call Max. Also that police lieutenant, Muller. They'll know. If it was some creature from the zoo, they probably wouldn't admit it publicly for fear of scaring visitors, but I think they'll tell me."

He scraped a fender slightly when he ran the car into the garage, and neither of them said anything as they carried their luggage in. Then: "Dorothy," he said, "what a horrible thing to happen! I think we could both do with a drink before we phone anybody. Let's pour them and take them in the study. We can call from there."

Dorothy looked at him a little disapprovingly, but she accepted a small glass of port and said nothing when he poured himself a double scotch and water.

He needed it. His world had always been safely predictable. The natural was taken care of by science; the supernatural by doctrine and by ritual. Minutes before, he had been confident that come October Joel Jamieson, with his undoubted persuasive talents, would help him solve the problem of Eunice Gammon. Now, though she was dead, that problem rode his shoulders far, far more heavily than it had ever done, and into his world, for the first time, the first chill tendrils of the fog of uncertainty and doubt had entered, and not doubt and uncertainty alone, but also the threat of an awareness so appalling he dared not confront it.

He finished his drink and phoned Reverend Schorer. "John," he said, "what's all this I hear about poor Eunice Gammon? Why didn't anybody get in touch with me?"

"Well, I'll tell you," Schorer answered, "when it happened, everybody was pretty much in shock. I got in touch with the McKays as her next of kin, and asked them if they wanted you informed. They said it would just spoil your vacation, which you two certainly had earned, and it wouldn't help her in any way. So I officiated—a small private service with only the McKays and two or three people from her boarding house."

Baxter Craddock thanked him; it had been very considerate of them all. And had they caught whoever did it?

Schorer waited long seconds before replying. "No—" he said finally, in a low, uncertain voice. "No—neither man nor beast."

Baxter Craddock told his wife about it while he poured himself one more drink. Then he called, first, Max Danforth, who was unable to add much to what Calvin had already told him, then Lieutenant Muller, who had just come on duty for the swing shift. He told him who he was and where he'd been, and how much of a shock the news had been to him and to his wife.

"Damn right," Muller rumbled. "Reverend, I seen some pretty nasty ones in my time, but she was just about the worst. She was tore up something awful, and half her bones were broken. We couldn't find a clue. No tracks or anything. At first, we thought some critter might've sneaked out of the zoo, but they were all present and accounted for."

"Could it— Could it have been a tramp, or—or possibly a mountain lion?"

"Not unless you find a tramp or mountain lion with teeth six inches long!" growled Muller. "I'm sorry, Reverend, but in this game you get these cases you just have to write off. They got no answer. Just like all those people who simply disappear. It happens all the time."

Mr. Craddock hung up. To Dorothy, he repeated what Muller told him.

"I don't believe it," she replied. "Those police are just downright lazy, and poor Eunice Gammon wasn't important enough to count. Some tramp did it, or maybe an escaped lunatic, probably with some awful kind of dagger."

Her tone told her husband that, once again, she had shut the compartment up tight, and he did not argue with her.

The Craddocks went downtown to a restaurant for dinner, and Dorothy made all the conversation: about plans for the parish, and catching up with the people in the congregation, and what Schorer might have scheduled for Mr. Craddock— baptisms, weddings, and whatever.

She talked, while he picked at his food and answered her in monosyllables. She talked as they drove back. She turned on the radio to listen to the news after they were in the house. Then: "I'm awfully tired, Edwin," she declared. "I think I'll go to bed. Are you going to look over your schedule before you come too?"

"Yes," he said, "yes, I think I will. In the study. I'll come to bed after a while. I'll not wake you up."

She said good night, and he went into his study and closed the door. He sat down at his desk, staring at the bookshelves along the panelled wall. Tonight he found no comfort in the warm, glowing redwood. He sat there, and dark thoughts flooded him. He felt very small and fragile and very, very much alone.

What if there *were* not only God, but gods? What if Crazy Eunie, with her talk of each sinner getting the god he or she deserved, had indeed been right? And could it be that God Himself could evoke such godlings as His instruments? His mind flicked him scenes out of his life, recollections of small unkindnesses, little betrayals, sins of commission and omission, of pride and envy. In the acid of Eunice Gammon's death all his certainties had been dissolved. He closed his eyes, repeated the Lord's Prayer silently, repeated the Twenty-Third Psalm. He opened them and saw, on a middle shelf, a copy of old Urquhart's *God in the Bible: An Exegesis,* given to him on his ordination and unopened since. Again he closed them, and remembered Isaish's words: "And he shall stretch out upon it the line of confusion and the stones of emptiness."

His eyes opened. He stood. He walked around his desk and took down Urquhart's book. He opened it. On the title page, the old man had written:

To the now-Reverend Edwin Baxter Craddock,
My boy, never forget Hebrews 10:31,
With my sincere good wishes and my prayers,
                    Alexander Urquhart

Baxter Craddock frowned. He had indeed forgotten the citation. Walking quietly, he left his study and the house, and went into the church. He knelt before the altar and did his best to pray, but Urquhart's words would not depart from him. He walked over to his pulpit, turned on the light over the lectern. The Bible there was a thing of beauty—Bruce Rogers' great Lectern Bible, another gift from Dr. Branfield.

Hebrews 10:31. He turned the noble pages. Then he read the words aloud: *"It is a fearful thing to fall into the hands of the living God."*

He looked up. He realized that he was cold, with a coldness that penetrated his entire being. There was no warmth in St. Luke's redwood now, no comfort, no source of strength. The church too was cold, cold, cold. And suddenly he knew, with a terrible certainty, that it was not merely empty.

It was deserted.

BESTSELLING BOOKS FROM TOR

MORE BESTSELLERS FROM TOR